TASTY DISH

DISH

A That's Entertainment Novel

By Christine Harvey

That's Entertainment Series
Take Two
In Concert
Tasty Dish
Rising Stars: a Prequel Novella

TASTY DISH

A That's Entertainment Novel

Christine Harvey

Published in the United States by Meadow View Press

Copyright © 2016 by Christine Harvey

Second Edition 2020

This is a work of fiction. Names, characters, places and incidents are products of the author's imagination or are used fictitiously and are not to be construed as real. Any resemblance to actual events, locales, organizations, or persons, living or dead, is entirely coincidental.

ISBN: 978-0-9963152-5-8

Meadow View Press
www.meadowviewpress.com

DEDICATION

For Tammy Kaehler, Cary Sparks, and Tracy Tandy
For all the usual reasons, and then some
I heart you three

CHAPTER ONE

In case Teresa Steplowski's plan to stand up to her parents fell through, she brought along her pregnant, unmarried, liberal friend to Sunday family dinner.

Teresa took a deep breath and shoved her micro braids behind her ears. She'd thought of shaving her hair back to a simple afro, but figured the braids, purple cowboy boots, a red floral handkerchief dress, and denim jacket should make enough of a rebellious outward statement.

She raised her hand to ring the bell, then paused. She knew she should walk right in, but old habits held her back.

"It's your family home, T," Kristen said, correctly reading her thoughts.

"It's not proper."

Kristen squeezed her free hand. "They're just people."

"Ultra-conservative people," Teresa replied. "Repressed, uptight, follow the rules..."

"You made a brave decision to face conflict with daring and strength, and the Universe is going to challenge you now," Kristen said. "Stick with it and you'll be rewarded with great personal growth. But take whatever time you need." She rested her hands on her belly. "We'll be right here."

Teresa took a deep breath, reminding herself that she couldn't— wouldn't—tolerate her family's criticism anymore. She'd spent too many years not defending herself against their accusations that there was something wrong with her because she didn't fit the white-collar mold they wanted for her. They thought she didn't have a "real" job, normal friends, or respectable boyfriends. Okay, so she did get caught having sex on reality TV with her last one, but still.

Her phone buzzed and she pulled it from her bag with more enthusiasm than a text usually warranted. She peeked at it and sighed.

C yr mail nu sng

Cort. The ex-boyfriend she'd gotten caught having sex with on reality TV. And who couldn't take the time to spell out "your." She should have left the phone in her purse.

Kristen glanced over Teresa's shoulder. "Is that 'new song'? He wrote you another one?"

"This is the third or fourth one." Cort was in a country western band called Tyler Landry. His best friend Luke was engaged to Teresa's best friend Victoria, who was also Kristen's sister. It had been quite a family affair there for awhile.

"Do you think I should give us a second chance? Or a third, really..."

She'd broken up with Cort about six months ago. Then the lyrics, "Baby, I'm a better man because of you," in his first song, got him back in the house and her bedroom. And three weeks later, she'd had to initiate another breakup to prove to both of them that she meant it. His songwriting had been extremely prolific since then.

"How do *you* feel?" Kristen asked, rubbing a hand across her belly. "Just because he thinks you're the perfect one for him doesn't mean he's perfect for you."

"I don't know..." Queen of Indecision, that was her; so much easier to avoid conflict that way. "Victoria told me you knew early on that she and Luke were meant to be together."

"Oh, I just knew she needed some sex. And Luke Tyler has 'I give good sex' written all over him."

Depressed, Teresa rang the doorbell. But Kristen wasn't finished.

"Victoria already knew he was the one. She wouldn't let herself see past her own denial."

"So how do I know if that's my problem, too?"

"Oh, honey." Kristen put an arm around her, her firm belly pressing against Teresa's side. "If you have to question it so much, maybe that's your answer."

The door opened right as Kristen gave her a loud smack on the cheek.

After a significant pause, Teresa's mother adjusted her pearls against the neckline of her black sheath and said in her formal tone, "Hello, darling,"

Good manners kept Beverly Steplowski from outwardly criticizing either woman's outfit but she did raise her eyebrows at Teresa's, and gave Kristen's orange leggings and skintight paisley t-shirt a quick review as she ushered them both inside. Kristen's normally voluptuous breasts threatened to pop right out of the v-neck and her belly button had become a semi-permanent outie.

Teresa thought she looked gorgeous. And brave.

As her mother clasped her shoulders and gave her an air kiss, Teresa was reduced to her seven-year-old self, saddled with braces, glasses, and frizzy hair. And a mother who never understood her.

"How are you? And Kristen, how are you feeling? You must be close to term."

They passed the front sitting room and walked though a long hallway to the living room. Teresa's older siblings Olivia, Anna, Patricia, Robert and Michael, and their respective spouses and children, had already arrived. She didn't see her youngest sister Julia, who at seventeen was the last child at home. About ten years separated them, and while they'd never been close, Teresa hadn't been able to persuade Julia that her own reality TV experiences were not high glamour. She didn't want Julia to follow in her footsteps, but feared her little sister would refuse to be dissuaded.

"I'm thirty-eight weeks, Mrs. Steplowski," said Kristen. "Only a couple weeks away, and your daughter is going to be the best birth coach ever." Teresa appreciated the kudos, but her mom believed only fathers, AKA a husband, should be in the delivery room. And single Kristen refused to name the father.

Teresa's mom nodded, but her nostrils pinched together at Kristen's next words. "And this was supposed to happen earlier in my pregnancy, but I'm also incredibly horny." She looked down at herself. "And my boobs are uncontrollable. Thanks for asking! Oh, there's Patricia." She waved to Teresa's sister, pregnant with her third child. "I want to ask her something about breastfeeding."

Kristen began to wind her way through the crowded living room and Teresa's mother whispered, "She kissed you. She hasn't gone lesbian, has she?"

Horrified, Teresa could only gape at her mother, but Kristen paused long enough to say, "Oh, Mrs. S, I like men and penises too much. But it's also all about finding the right person, isn't it?" Then she joined Patricia on the couch, completely oblivious to the stares of everyone within earshot who heard the "p" word, which, as far as Teresa knew, had never been spoken in the elder Steplowskis' household.

Teresa's mom waited until Kristen was out of earshot before muttering, "Why must she be so crass?"

"Kristen's just honest, Mom." She took a deep breath and added, "I wish everyone around me could be so open and understanding." Unnerved at her own bravado, she said, "I'm going to say hi to Mama Step."

She waved to her siblings, and rushed across the room to the far corner where Mama Step, her paternal grandmother, sat in her red recliner near the sliding glass door, with a view of the back patio, rose garden, and swimming pool.

Mama Step saw her coming and scooted to one side, patting the worn leather by her hip. "You come sit here with me," she ordered, as if Teresa would do anything else.

Teresa snuggled close to her grandmother's tiny frame, gave her a long hug, then took one of her soft-skinned hands in her own. The best thing about Sunday dinners, and the only reason Teresa continued to show up, was Mama Step.

She'd married Jakub Steplowski, a white man, in the '50s and they'd fled racism in Virginia to raise their three children in California and open a Polish deli. She'd been verbally abused, spit on and beaten, and her husband left her a widow at thirty-two, but when Teresa looked at Mama Step's barely lined face, the colorful scarf wrapped around her head and the carefully applied eyebrow pencil, all she saw was serenity.

"How's my best girl?" Mama Step asked.

She asked this at every dinner and Teresa always launched into a few cheerful details of her life. Today, however, she choked up at the simple question. She wanted to burrow under one of her grandmother's hand-sewn quilts, like when she was seven and they made *chruściki*. While Mama Step fried the ribbons of dough and Teresa covered them in powdered sugar, she talked about the mean girls at school who ridiculed her dark skin and crazy hair. Then the two of them would curl up together, devour the pastries known as "angel wings," and Mama Step shared the stories her beloved Jakub had told her about his homeland.

Mama Step always knew how to make it better. And the sweet, fried dough didn't hurt.

But now, Teresa's problems felt both substantial and frivolous at the same time. Her boss belittled her and her job didn't fulfill her, but at least she had one in a field she loved. A talented, handsome man desired her, but his pursuit smothered her. Her roommate had the biggest heart of anyone she knew, but was about to become a mom, and Teresa worried it would change their relationship. And her best friend Victoria, loyal, smart and generous, currently lived in Nashville with the love of her life.

Teresa had been teased a few times for the color of her skin, but never beaten for it, like Mama Step, never refused service anywhere or treated like an animal. How could she complain about anything in her life when her issues seemed so trivial, especially compared to Mama Step's experiences?

But still.

She shook her head, tears pricking her eyes.

Mama Step nudged her with one knee. "Not nothing, sweetheart," she said in response to Teresa's head shake. "Sometimes saying it makes a body feel better."

Teresa looked at Mama Step's beautiful face, the light in her eyes, then down at the gold cross her husband had given her the night before he died. She never took it off.

Teresa's chest tightened at the thought of the love her grandparent's shared, Mama Step's unwavering belief that they'd be together in the next world, and wondered if she'd ever know such clear conviction herself. "I don't like my life right now," she whispered.

Nearby, her brothers and sisters drank their cocktails and talked about their successful careers, while their well-behaved children played quietly.

"Maybe it's time for a change."

"But I don't know what to do," Teresa admitted.

"Go with your instincts, baby. Spent my life doing that, and it never steered me wrong." She touched the cross at her neck. "Maybe something interesting will happen at that kitchen convention you're going to next week in Daly City."

Maybe. Except Teresa believed her boss was making her go to the trade show as a form of punishment, simply because he didn't like her. And the event was in town, so Teresa couldn't even pretend to get a vacation out of it.

As for change, in the last six months, Teresa had gone from being a reality TV production assistant, to having an on-screen romance, to working as a caterer. In between, Kristen came to live with her and Victoria, then Victoria hit the road with Luke and his band. Teresa split up with Cort twice, and she was now babysitting Luke's cat, who usually sat on the back of the couch and glared at her. Wouldn't some stability be better? She thought about that for a second.

No. That sounded so dull.

Maybe she was an excitement junkie in heavy denial.

"Maybe," she agreed out loud. But was she agreeing to Mama Step suggesting a change or to herself being an excitement junkie? Before she could further explore that idea, her mother called them to the dining room.

As everyone sat in their usual places, Teresa's youngest sister Julia finally made an appearance, striding to her spot in high heels, dark lipstick, and a skintight beige dress, the bodice of which seemed to be made of fishnet. Teresa could clearly see her sister's beige bra, and possibly a nipple.

Julia took hold of the back of a chair to pull it out, and everyone else in the room froze. Their oldest sister Olivia started to say, "Julia, good heavens, what—" when their mother interrupted. Her voice had never thundered, but it came close now when she pointed to the door and commanded, "Change out of that indecent outfit this instant."

Julia set down her cell phone and tugged at one shoulder of the dress, as if she'd remove it right then.

"Julia Anne Steplowski," came the next command. "You are smart enough to understand my meaning without an explanation or a flagrant display of disrespect. Change. Now. None of us will eat until you return. And if you return in jeans and a t-shirt, like a child, you will sit at the children's table."

Julia gave Teresa a knowing smile and flounced out of the room. Mama Step, already seated next to Kristen, stage-whispered to her, "And here I thought you were going to be the entertainment, honey."

Mrs. Steplowski glared at Teresa, as if Julia's behavior and Mama

Step's comment were her fault. Few situations were, but as the rebel afraid of conflict, Teresa took the blame. Her mother called and lectured her for half an hour about being a bad influence after she caught Julia watching episodes of *In Concert*, the infamous show Teresa had been on. Teresa didn't think of herself that way, but had no defense against her behavior. Not only had she seduced Cort on a lounge chair, the stairs, and his couch—in one night—but she'd had plenty to drink before, during and after. Countless women her age had engaged in similar exploits, only they didn't get caught on camera.

She and Julia could have bonded as the family rebels, but the difference between them was that Julia *wanted* to be a reality TV star. And Teresa didn't want her baby sister to repeat her mistakes. So, even though the show had ended months ago, Teresa regularly left voicemail messages and "just checking in" texts with hints that the reality TV life didn't deserve Julia's adoration. The majority went unanswered. Teresa didn't see how she could be blamed for Julia dressing like Kim Kardashian.

As they all shuffled in their seats and placed napkins in their laps, her father's stomach growled. He had a pained look on his face, but who knew the source: Julia, Teresa, his own wife, or hunger. While Mama Step shared her life stories with Teresa, her father never discussed his experiences as a bi-racial person. He barely talked about himself at all; he quietly ran his accounting firm and let his wife take charge of everything else.

Julia returned in a dress with a high neckline and hem down to her ankles. Because of the angle of the doorway to the table, Teresa thought she was the only one to see that Julia's dress was backless, held from slipping off completely by a thin string at her neck. She sat at the high-backed chair and smirked, covering her cell phone in her lap with her napkin.

Teresa whispered to her, "What are you up to?"

Julia shook her head, and passed the potatoes without a word.

Teresa automatically surveyed the other dishes: pork roast, sauerkraut, and *Sałatka wiosenna,* a spring salad with a variety of vegetables in a mayonnaise dressing. She gave an internal sigh. Time to face another challenge.

"Mom, remember Kristen's a vegan? I reminded you when I called and said she would be my guest."

"There's salad, darling," her mother said with a tight smile.

"Potatoes, sauerkraut."

Yes, Teresa thought, lots of hearty Polish food, despite the fact that her father would rather have a good burger and a beer. He'd once admitted he didn't think of himself as Polish, and since his father had died young, he hadn't passed along many traditions. But Mama Step still owned the deli, so Teresa's mother occasionally got their Sunday dinner from there.

"Mayonnaise, Mom. Eggs."

"No worries, Mrs. S.," Kristen said. She plunked her huge orange macramé bag onto her empty plate and rummaged through it. "I always come prepared." Teresa caught a glimpse of the infamous smiley face condoms Kristen carried around and thought her statement could have more than one meaning. She ducked her head to hide a smile.

"Whoa," said Julia, peering across the table at the variety of items Kristen shuffled around in her bag. "Were those—"

"Found it!" Kristen said, pulling out a glass container with a bagel inside. "Soy cream cheese." She gave Mama Step a grin. "I would say it's the best, but I'm sitting with two excellent chefs who might disagree." She dropped her bag back down to the floor with a clunk, and the others unfroze and started passing the dishes again.

They paused for her father to say grace, then everyone dug in. While her family members talked high finance, white collar clients and spreadsheets, Teresa tried to entice Julia into a conversation. But her youngest sister only shrugged or checked the phone on her lap between tiny bites of food.

"How is your job going, Teresa?" her father asked. It was the one question he asked her every time they saw each other. He and her mother couldn't understand why she hadn't followed the family trend of law, accounting, high finance, or insurance. Or why she'd attended Berkeley instead of Stanford, like everyone else in the family.

"Fine, Dad," she said automatically. She took a big bite of food, chewing conspicuously to ward off further questions. Maybe this wasn't the dinner to conquer all of her family issues. This rebellious thing was harder than it looked.

Julia chose this moment to lift her head and say, "You texted me that it sucked and you wanted to quit."

The room stilled again and Teresa thought her mother gasped. Steplowskis did not quit, they sucked it up and stuck it out, but

Teresa had left multiple jobs in her life. Of course, her other family members would have chosen stellar jobs to begin with.

She hadn't used the word "sucked" in her text, but her job had definitely lost its sparkle recently. Not only had she been demoted to children's parties, which paid less for more work, but she had to attend the kitchen trade show next week. Worst of all, her boss Reginald had stolen Teresa's recipe for her lemon bars and claimed it as his own.

She took a deep breath, remembering her determination and Mama Step's words: *maybe it's time for a change,* and *go with your instincts.* "I don't like my job," she admitted.

"I think you should've stayed at the TV studio," Julia said. "You were practically *famous.*"

She said the word "famous" with such reverence that Teresa shuddered. Did shame, regret and a hangover equate fame these days? She supposed they did, in reality TV, and in her sister's world. She opened her mouth to tell Julia fame had a price.

Teresa's mother stiffened. "Disgracing your family doesn't make you famous."

"Mom, that's kind of harsh," said Olivia. "Everyone makes mistakes." She smiled at Teresa, as if her last comment demonstrated support, but it only reinforced their mother's statement.

"Yeah," Anna added. "We all know Teresa's a free spirit. Sometimes free spirits fall."

Kiss-ass, Teresa thought bitterly. Anna agreed with Olivia on everything. Over ten years older than Teresa, they had considered her a little interloper when she arrived in the family; they'd finally agreed to tolerate her if they could make her their personal slave. The bitter truth was that it had worked, and Teresa hated that she'd accepted the situation as normal until they left for college, and joined the family accounting firm. Teresa was left with two older brothers more interested in video games than her.

"Free spirits only fall when someone tries to crush their spirit," Kristen said, going tough-mama and giving everyone the stink-eye, even Teresa's mother. "Most of the time, they're too busy flying." She winked at Teresa from across the table, and Teresa could have hugged her.

"Well, I don't want to fly," Julia said. "I want to soar into the stratosphere." She pouted at Teresa like only a seventeen-year-old could, filled with righteous indignation and a belief that the world centered around her. "You promised me a job at the TV studio." She crossed her arms over her chest.

"What?!" her mother cried.

"Now, Beverly," her father said.

"I didn't promise you that," Teresa said. "I only said you could visit the set."

Mrs. Steplowski stood up.

Olivia's youngest son Darren walked into the dining room. "Are we getting dessert soon?"

Olivia gave him a stern look and pointed toward the door. He let out an aggrieved sigh and shuffled back to the kids' table in the adjoining room. Teresa hoped the interruption would lower her mother's blood pressure, but it only fanned the flames.

"You were going to involve my impressionable baby child—"

"I'm not a baby," Julia protested.

"—in that sinful business?"

"Mom, it's not—"

"After what this family already suffered—the gossip, the snide comments at church, the suggestion that I had not raised my child right—I cannot believe you would do this to us, Teresa Marie. Have you no shame? No pride? The entire world saw you with that country bumpkin, that loud, strutting...in that chair, doing...having..."

"Sex," Julia supplied, with too much glee in her voice. "And she got *paid* for it."

The table erupted, everyone talking at once, and Teresa couldn't believe she heard the word "prostitute" from one of her brothers-in-law. Her father stood, and she thought he might say something to defend her and defuse the situation, but instead he went to her mother at the other end of the table and put an arm around her shoulders.

He pointed at Teresa. "You've made your mother cry for the last time, young lady."

Teresa gaped at him, her determination flying out the window. She was used to her mother's ire, but her father's reaction completely deflated her.

From the corner of her eye, Teresa saw Kristen tip a glass of water across the table and shoot up from her chair. "My water broke!" she yelled. "T, we have to go!"

CHAPTER TWO

Gabe De Luca strolled through the Bay City Convention Center surrounded by mouth-watering aromas, luscious models touting the latest kitchen gadgets, and celebrity chefs signing their newest cookbooks—and felt bored out of his mind.

He brushed back his hair, shoved a small bag of sample toothpicks in his pocket, passed by the water purifier systems, and headed straight for the elevators. He'd covered the weekend-long exposition for CuisineTV's magazine the past two years, and this year's hadn't changed. The unveiling of the latest potato peeler would proceed whether he observed it or not.

He judged it close enough to beer-thirty for a quick break, then he'd dive into some fiction writing. His bestselling first novel, *Sonder*, earned him a movie deal, but his publisher dropped him after the second, *Ennui*, tanked. They'd insisted on the name, and hell, with a title like that, it deserved to rot in obscurity. In response to his rapid success and failure, he'd made a dumbass decision or two, including dropping out of the Culinary Institute of America because of the restaurant industry's "corporate" slant. But his experience and his friendship with the marketing head of CuisineTV had landed him this gig. He didn't miss the irony.

His agent Ondrea believed in him and the potential of his third book, talking them both up at every opportunity, and a couple of big publishers had expressed interest in it. If he could finish the damn thing, he might not have to return to the trade show next year. He was ready to leave behind this gig along with a few other unpalatable situations in his recent past.

A stunning woman waited next to the elevator, the UP button already lit. She wore a long blue crinkly skirt, white sleeveless top, and purple cowboy boots. Her skin was the color of sautéed butterscotch and her black hair, braided into a lot of tiny unbound plaits, fell past her shoulders. She faced him as he got closer and he caught sight of high cheekbones, a wide mouth and uptilted cat's eyes before her gaze shifted back to the elevator.

He stopped short, pushing a hand against his sternum until his breathing returned to a normal rhythm. The convention wasn't looking so bad now.

He leaned around to push the UP button and caught the scent of nutmeg, which aroused him more than any perfume ever had.

"I think we're genetically predisposed to push the button even if it's already lit up," he said, standing next to her and dutifully watching the elevator doors.

She glanced at him with a smile. "I always do that with the crosswalk signal."

He smiled back and she looked at her feet while he studied her until the elevator dinged and the doors slid open. They waited for the people inside to depart and he gestured her ahead of him. She pushed the button for four, the rooftop restaurant, and said, "What floor?"

"Three," he replied, watching her long slim fingers press the round button. Rows of narrow silver and turquoise bracelets adorned her left wrist, one in the middle with a wider band of orange stones. No wedding ring.

They stood in opposite corners, angled toward each other to avoid disrespect, but not so much to force unwanted conversation. He would have liked to talk, but she seemed preoccupied, and how much could really come up in three floors? He entertained himself instead with thoughts of adding a woman like her to his novel. Exotic, mysterious, and chic. Would she be loud and outrageous or serene and wise? The best friend? A love interest?

Her eyes cut to him so quickly he wondered if he'd spoken aloud. He sometimes found himself the center of attention in the midst of friends at a bar or in a business meeting, everyone gone silent and staring at him because he'd plotted out loud.

He smiled at her and she offered a beautiful, generous smile back. She didn't look offended, so he must not have spoken aloud.

"I—" he began, not even sure what to say, when the elevator jolted to a stop, snapping his jaw shut and throwing the woman off balance. When she stumbled forward, he automatically braced his legs and gripped her waist to steady her. She clutched his upper arms at the same time.

"Are you all right?" he asked.

She nodded. "What happened?"

He shook his head, and they released each other to look around. The indicator lights blinked out, and the overhead fluorescents flickered, but stayed lit.

"I thought stuck elevators only happened in movies."

She crossed her arms over her chest and looked up and around the small beige space. "No cameras," she murmured. "Maybe Mama Step was right."

"Mama Step knew the elevator would get stuck?"

She laughed, a rich sound. "No. She said something 'interesting' would happen at the trade show." She looked at him with unnerving stillness before turning her head away. "And I should trust my instincts."

"Ah." He nodded as if that made sense, but hoped she'd elaborate. "That's not bad advice—"

A small round speaker set high to the left of the door let out a crackle and a tinny voice announced, "Anyone in Elevator 10, please remain calm. The convention center's maintenance staff has everything under control and we will have the elevators operational momentarily."

A click, then silence.

Both Gabe and the woman stared up at the speaker as if expecting more.

"Well," she finally said, glancing at him and then away. "How much time do you think we have?"

Gabe thought that an odd question, but didn't say so. They were two strangers stuck in a small box; maybe she was nervous. "Five, maybe ten minutes."

"Oh." She stared down at her boots. He could swear she sounded disappointed.

The speaker crackled again, and they both jumped. "Passengers of Elevator 10, please remain calm," it repeated. "Having the elevator operational may take longer than we initially anticipated. We will keep you informed."

The woman brushed a section of braids from her face, still looking down, and Gabe thought he saw her smile.

"If we're going to be stuck here together, I might as well introduce myself." He held out a hand.

"Please don't," she said, leaning back.

The expression on her face seemed to combine sad, desperate and excited together. He lowered his hand to his side. "I'm sorry?"

She licked her lips, then said just above a whisper, "It's better if we don't know each others' names."

He wasn't about to argue with a woman he didn't know, especially one showing signs of claustrophobia. He rested against the narrow railing that ran along the elevator's three walls, and crossed his arms over his chest.

"It's better that way," she continued, looking less freaked out.

"Why's that?"

"Because I want you to have sex with me, and I don't want to complicate it with names." Before he could reply, or even begin to comprehend her words, she rummaged through her bag, pulled out a condom, and held it up. "I'm prepared."

Gabe straightened as the full impact of her suggestion hit him.

He was definitely no longer bored.

Things like this didn't happen in real life, and no reader would believe it if he wrote this scenario. But he had to admit his gut and groin tightened at the suggestion.

Gathering his thoughts, he said, "How about a date first? Find out I'm not a psycho? If I love dogs? What kind of music I like?"

Her eyes narrowed, turning them more feline than before, and she lowered the hand holding the condom. "What kind of music *do* you like?"

"Classic rock." He kept his tone casual, but her intent gaze indicated she was carefully weighing his response. "Zeppelin, AC/DC, Creedence. Most current music is crap."

She took a step closer, her eyes never leaving his face. "Do you love dogs?"

Was she serious? Did she really want to have sex with him in the elevator? He cleared his throat. "I loved *my* dog. But he died a couple years ago and my job's kept me too busy for another one."

She sighed. "I'm sorry to hear that." She took a couple steps back, again staring at her boots. "Maybe this isn't a good idea."

Gabe held up a hand. "Wait. What about a date?" Jesus, what was wrong with him, turning down sex from a beautiful woman.

"Not exciting enough." She glanced at her watch. The band consisted of multicolored stones strung together like a bracelet. "Besides, time's running out." She shrugged and her blouse shifted to one side, revealing more of her slim neck and the sharp V of her collarbone.

Before the idea fully formed, he knew he wanted to part that white material at her throat, expose the dark creamy skin, and press his lips there.

"You're not psycho, are you?" he asked.

When she shook her head, he closed the gap between them in one step and ducked his head to that dip at her throat, licking as if a dollop of whipped cream sat there.

She gasped, her head falling back, and gripped his shoulders. She tasted better than he'd imagined, warm and sweet. He slid his thumbs along her jaw and cupped the back of her neck as he sampled the flavors of her sharp chin, rounded cheek, and tender earlobe.

Her hands relaxed on his shoulders, smoothing his shirt along his upper arms, but her body stayed rigid. Even though it was a rookie move, he wanted to murmur, "Relax," but as she'd said, they didn't have much time. Still, no one could accuse Gabe De Luca of not doing right by a woman, even one he was having sex with in an elevator.

He spread his hand along the flat of her back, easing her closer and trailed kisses down the exquisite inside of her arm. She shivered against him and he straightened, watching her face until she met his eyes.

"Tell me to stop at any time, and I stop."

"I won't," she whispered.

"I mean it," he insisted, determined to wait for a response, despite the fuck-me-now look in her eyes.

Her voice throaty, she said, "Okay."

He nodded, smiling, and when she smiled back, her shoulders lowering, he dipped his head and tasted one of his favorite delicacies: warm, smooth lips. When they parted and she touched her tongue to his, he groaned, wrapped both arms around her and pulled her up tight. Her back felt long and lean, her breasts lush against his chest.

As he deepened the kiss, brushing his tongue along hers, over her lips, then deeper into her mouth, her hands roamed his body. Along his sides, across his back, up toward his shoulders, then down to his waist.

Her exploratory touches fueled his desire as her warm fingertips pressed the material of his shirt against his tense muscles. The cloth stretched across his back, constricting and rough on his skin. His erection strained against his jeans and he wanted to press it naked to her belly, to feel her bare skin brush the length of his body.

She tugged the hem of his shirt from his pants, then her long, warm fingers played along his spine and a jolt and shiver ran from his neck to his butt.

Her kisses still firing him up, he reached between them to undo the tiny buttons on her blouse. His urgency was so great he wanted to rip it open with his teeth, and it only intensified when he finally parted the material and cupped the warm weight of her breasts in his hands.

He brushed his thumbs over the rose-colored fabric covering them and the nipples peaked against the thin material. She moaned, arching back, and he bent to take a nipple in his mouth, swirling his tongue on the fabric to create more friction. She gasped and shuddered, pulling him closer, his thigh between hers as they backed into the corner.

Sucking her nipple deeper into his mouth made her cry out, but he wanted more. He pushed the fabric aside and pressed his cheek to her warm skin; his eyes closed, and his lashes brushed the upper curve of her breast. Up close, honey and cinnamon combined with her scent of nutmeg. Her heart beat strong and fast, and his own echoed it.

She swept her hands along his sides and he shuddered, tightening his hold on her. Her fingers moved between them, undoing his buttons, and he could have helped by giving her space, but he wanted to stay close, and fully surrender to this feeling.

She spread his shirt to bare his chest, and pressed her palms flat on his abs. Her bracelets chilled his skin, and when she brushed her fingertips over his nipples, he jolted forward, galvanized by her touch. He caressed her face, ran a thumb over her lips, and kissed her hard and well, like he'd known her for years, but still couldn't get enough of her.

And he couldn't. He stroked her temples, and under her eyes, the edge of her nose, rubbed her braids between his fingers, caressed her arms.

Then he was tugging her skirt up and she grabbed it from him, tucked it over one arm and reached for his belt buckle.

He plucked the condom from her fingers before she pushed his pants and boxers down, then hissed in a breath as her hand caressed the length of him, warm, firm, as if she had known *him*, and the best way to arouse him, for years.

Resting his hand lightly over hers, he whispered in her ear, "No time." He wouldn't have minded her continuing to stroke him, but the damn elevator could start up at any minute. He kissed the side of her neck, said, "Maybe later," then pressed his lips to hers again before she could protest.

He let go of her only long enough to roll on the condom, then wrapped one arm around her waist and slid the other along her thigh, easing her leg up and around his hip.

He pressed against her, planning to take it slow despite the immediate danger of discovery, to tease and torment her with pleasure, but she shifted her hips and he was inside her, gasping as she enveloped his full length. He let her take the lead, moving with her until they found a rhythm together, arms and legs tangled in an upright dance.

He fell into her heat, her breath, the sheen of sweat on her collarbone, her panting and shuddering as he reached between them. Time fell away, the location, everything. Nothing mattered but the two of them, their rhythm, her crying out, clenching around him with a series of shudders, then collapsing even as his own pleasure burst through, so strong he thought he couldn't stand it. Then it peaked, and he cried out, his mouth against hers through the release. They rocked together to prolong the pleasure, then slowed and clung to each other, panting.

"Thank you," she finally said into his chest, then turned her face away and pulled back from him.

She'd been backed into a corner, so he reluctantly left her and turned his body to dispose of the condom in the sample bag, shoving it in his jeans pocket, and let her rearrange her clothes. He wanted to face her, gently do up her buttons, straighten her skirt, smooth the thin braids back from her face, then kiss her softly, hold her close, and tumble into bed to do it all again. Properly. But he couldn't do that. Because they were strangers. Sex in an elevator wasn't off limits, but tenderly dressing each other would be too intimate. So he stood away from her, tucking, buttoning, zipping and fastening while she did the same.

"I'm decent," she finally whispered.

He wasn't. He stayed facing the other direction, discomfited. And changed.

He turned to ask her name, to remove the intimacy barrier, when the elevator jolted again, throwing him off balance. It shuddered down, heading back to the convention room floor.

"Shit," he said, and looked over at her.

She'd returned everything to its place and still stood in the corner, her purse clutched at her chest, her face composed as she watched the numbers changing, not looking at him.

"Are you all right?" he asked.

She nodded, her eyes still raised.

"Can I—?"

Ding!

The elevator doors slid open to reveal a mass of people: trade show guests filming with cell phones, technicians, and EMTs. Everyone started to talk at once, and the EMTs got her out, separating her from Gabe. By the time he'd convinced everyone he was not having a heart attack like someone in another elevator, and searched for the woman whose scent still suffused his body, she'd disappeared.

And he still didn't know her name.

CHAPTER THREE

Teresa slunk into her flat and paused in the doorway. Kristen lay on her back on the coffee table, facing the door—arms, legs and head dangling, curly hair pooled on the floor. Frog, Luke's tiny cat, slept on the floor at her feet. A short person of indefinite gender who looked like an ancient witch doctor, hovered over Kristen, chanting and tossing something like roasted sesame seeds on her exposed belly. A copy of *The Hippie Mama's Guide to Childbirth* lay spine up on the carpet.

"Uh."

Kristen's eyes opened and she gave Teresa a serene upside down smile. "Hey, T, how was your conference?" She caught Teresa's glance at the witch doctor. "Oh, don't mind Mooshree. Total concentration. Something to aspire to. Hey." She gestured at the book. "Did you know the mucus plug can be greenish in color?"

"Guh." Teresa cleared her throat. "I forgot something at the convention," she blurted and backed out. Slamming the door behind her and hoping it didn't disturb Mothra or whoever, she ran down the stairs, wondering if she should laugh or feel ill.

She really didn't need to hear about mucus plugs after screwing a stranger in an elevator. A *gorgeous* stranger, she amended. But, really, what did she need after sex with a gorgeous stranger in an elevator? "Maybe talking to him for more than two minutes before falling onto his penis," she muttered to herself.

She sighed, shifted her bag on her shoulder, and trudged up the steep hill, arms crossed against the chill of the drifting fog. Best stranger sex ever. Well. Her only stranger sex. He'd wanted her to know he wasn't psycho, but maybe *she* was the psycho one. She hadn't planned to, but who propositioned someone in a situation like that? Who went *through* with it?

At the top of the hill, she took a deep breath of cool San Francisco air, and peeked through the fog at the bay below. What the gorgeous stranger didn't know was that she'd noticed him earlier in the day, watching his press pass sway as he leaned into his interview subjects or when he helped an older woman move a heavy table.

His unconscious grace, easy smile, and the casual way he ran a hand through his long, dark blonde hair so it feathered back into place left her speechless. He was an attractive man kept from being too pretty by a strong mouth, straight nose, and crinkles at the corners of his eyes.

"What were you thinking, Teresa?" she said out loud as she crossed the street toward the small grocery on the corner.

She was thinking he'd been beautiful and she needed to shake up her life, and there they were, trapped together in an elevator. Why not?

And then her mortification when she thought he was going to say no. Or try to psychoanalyze her. She'd been preparing to act like she propositioned men all the time and didn't care if he said no.

Then he'd kissed her collarbone, his lips warm, the tip of his tongue a teasing caress, and her world focused razor-sharp on the two of them together.

She stopped in front of the grocery, tingling at the memory of her body's intense response, to a degree she hadn't experienced before, not even with Cort. Cort was an experienced lover, but with a primal focus, his technique one of pillaging and plundering rather than finessing and seducing. He'd kept at her until she orgasmed.

She'd liked the pirate approach, craved it actually, that intense maleness focused on her. It was heady and disarming and she'd thought she couldn't get enough.

But she'd been wrong. The entire time they'd been together, she'd wondered when Cort's wandering ways would take over, and he'd go looking for his next conquest. Instead, he'd gotten serious, saying he'd changed and all he wanted was her. Toward the end of their relationship, all that maleness smothered instead of aroused her.

Her Elevator Man had that masculinity, too, softened with refinement. Yet that's all she knew about him. He could be some emotional pillager and plunderer.

But she'd never see him again, so it didn't matter, right?

She sighed. Right. He was a blip on the radar of the rest of her life, a naughty little moment of wildness to recollect once the shame passed.

"Hey, T," said a small woman sitting against the building, a blanket draped over her and a battered, overflowing shopping cart nearby.

"Oh, hey, Cleo," Teresa said, shaken from her obsessive thoughts. She took this walk a lot for exercise and to clear her head, and had gotten in the habit of handing work leftovers to Cleo. Teresa loved feeding people, and what better recipient than someone like Cleo? She pulled her bag forward and unzipped it. "I'm sorry. No catering fare today. How about a protein bar?" In her search, she shoved aside a strip of condoms, now missing one.

"That'll do, but I sure liked them lemon things you brought last week."

Teresa handed over the bar and smiled. "Those are my favorites, too. I'll see what I can do next time." She waved and continued up the hill, berating herself for fussing over trivial matters like persistent ex-boyfriends when someone like Cleo had no place to call home on a cold, overcast day.

Still restless, she zipped her bag and hiked the steep steps to the local park, ignoring the boats bobbing far below in the bay and the seagulls calling overhead.

Ten minutes of sex in an elevator didn't change your life. She was still frustrated with her job, freaked out about the horrible episode at her parents' house, and unsure of her future. Oh, and she lived with a cat that didn't like her and a pregnant woman who brought gender neutral shamans into the house to bless her baby.

Puffing from the climb, she stepped onto a small patch of grass, dug out her phone and dialed her best friend. *Enough*, she thought. *No more craziness*. She'd only topped crazy with crazy by seducing Elevator Man. She needed some sanity instead.

Teresa didn't know where Victoria might be at the moment—in the recording studio, at her apartment in Nashville, or traveling—but had full confidence that V would answer her phone.

"T!" Victoria cried with pleasure. "I was just about to call you. It's like—"

"Please don't say kismet," Teresa interrupted.

Victoria laughed. "Kristen getting to you?"

Teresa paced as they talked, kicking her purple boots through the dark damp grass, her mood already improved. "Honey, you know I love her, but she's getting pretty wacky with the baby stuff. Today she brought in a...a..."

"I know," Victoria said. "I just talked to her. She brought Mooshree in because she thought you'd be at the trade show all day. And why aren't you at the trade show?"

"Oh. Um." Teresa froze with one foot kicked up. She set it solidly back on the ground before answering. "You know, same old, same old with these things."

"So you snuck away to play a little hooky?"

Or a little nookie, Teresa thought and choked back a laugh. "Something like that." She finally looked around at the long green benches, gray-blue water, and Alcatraz Island in the distance. "I'm at our favorite park, and it's cold and foggy."

Victoria sighed. "I miss the city."

"So where are you?" Teresa asked, suddenly nervous about telling Victoria of her recent exploit. She'd fess up at some point, but right now she wanted a distraction.

"Macon, Georgia," Victoria replied. "Luke's still debating getting in touch with his parents. But Cort's here, too, to visit with his mom. And Luke wants to see her."

Luke had had a falling out with his alcoholic parents a few months ago, and Cort's mom lived next door to them. Teresa wanted things to work out for Luke, but she needed to avoid any discussion of Cort right now. "Oh. Wedding things. How's that going?"

"We finally agreed on a date. That's why I was going to call you. You know how we thought it would be in Nashville?"

"Yes?" Teresa asked, wary. She settled on one of the benches, pulled her knees up and tucked her skirt around her feet, waiting for the big reveal.

"We moved the location and date," Victoria continued. "Two weeks."

"You moved the wedding up two weeks?" That didn't sound so bad; they'd been talking about getting married in the fall.

"No, we're getting married in two weeks."

"Oh my God. Are you pregnant, too?"

Victoria laughed. "No, I'll leave the baby-making to Kristen. Although if Luke had his way...well, that's another conversation. But Kristen has something to do with the change. She can't travel now, and Tyler Landry officially got asked to open for Jason Aldean, so everything has to get pushed up. And we didn't want to wait."

Teresa heard an unfamiliar tone in her friend's voice: tenderness. It caused a surge of wistfulness in her, along with joy for her friend, who had experienced great pain on the way to this place.

"We've moved it to San Francisco, two weeks from tomorrow," Victoria continued.

There was a pause and Teresa realized that was her cue to jump in with enthusiastic words. "Wow, that's great," sounded lame even to her, but Victoria's excitement ruled her life right now and she missed Teresa's weak response.

"It's going to be at the Flood Mansion," Victoria said. "They had a cancellation, so it worked out perfectly. Very simple, but with everyone we love there. My dad's coming out with Margaret. Kristen will be there, of course, you and the boys—oh, damn. I did it again, didn't I?"

Teresa nodded, knowing Victoria couldn't see her. Victoria had a way of shooting first and asking questions later. The "boys" referred to the band members: Marty, who would bring his new bride Miranda, and probably their baby boy. Parker, and of course...

"We all knew ages ago that Cort would be best man," Teresa said.

"We also thought there'd be more time between your breakup and the wedding."

Teresa nodded again. Time to be a grown-up about Cort, too.

"T, Cort is still—"

"It'll be fine, V. It's your day. Yours and Luke's."

"Are we crazy? Having the wedding so soon?"

"Yes."

Victoria laughed again. "You're right. I'm finishing some things up here and flying out in a couple days. In the meantime, I'll need some help coordinating the caterer and baker. Do you have anything to write with?"

Teresa rooted through her bag for a pen and pulled out one of the many flyers she'd been handed at the trade show. She glanced at the title—*Want Your Own Restaurant? Enter CuisineTV's New Contest!*—before flipping it over and resting it on her knees. She'd been Victoria's assistant at the television studio, and she went into auto-mode now. As she rapidly noted the details Victoria tossed at her, the breeze kept reminding her of warm breath caressing her skin, and she shivered even as the fog shifted and the sun broke through.

CHAPTER FOUR

Gabe typed THE END, saved the document, and shot a fist into the air with a triumphant shout.

After turning in his trade show piece to CuisineTV, he'd spent the last two weeks, head down, writing in his Brooklyn studio. He lived on takeout, caffeine, and the sublimated lust that shot through him like adrenaline every time he thought of his beautiful stranger.

He'd spent the rest of the trade show completely distracted, describing her to other trade show attendees in an attempt to find her, or learn her name. Many of them acknowledged seeing or talking to her, but even the ones who'd heard her name couldn't remember it. He'd finagled a list of the registrants, but without accompanying pictures, it did him no good.

He closed the laptop and pushed away from his desk, turning around to lean against the back of the chair. To his right was the tiny kitchen, a few oak cabinets, stainless appliances; across from him, a sofa sleeper and chair; and to his left a combo Murphy bed/shelving unit. Not fancy digs, but he didn't care. One of the few sensible decisions he'd made in the last five years was to buy the building; it provided income and a home base. He stood staring at the colorful rag rug his sister Ellen had made. His dog, Moody, had lain there on warm days. Other times, he'd wedge himself under the desk and Gabe would massage the Basenji's belly with his bare feet, laughing at Moody's groans of pleasure.

He hadn't thought of Moody in quite awhile, but, like everything else these days, the reason for that circled back to Mystery Woman. When she'd asked if Gabe loved dogs, he could've said "yes" and left it at that. Instead, he'd told her about Moody dying, how he'd loved him, but his job had kept him too busy to get another. That was true, to a degree. But he'd actually pursued more out-of-town assignments to distract him after Moody was gone.

The real reason he hadn't gotten another dog was because Moody's death had broken his heart.

After getting his balls handed to him in a trifecta of book bomb, divorce and the death of a good friend, he'd been grateful for his Brooklyn studio. Its size had been a comfort when his grief threatened to consume him. Instead of the walls closing in on him, they kept him in one piece, and when even this space felt too big, he'd pull out his bed, curl up in a fetal position with a blanket over his head, and hide from everything. Only Moody could pull him out of it, and he owed that dog his life.

Even as he'd been pulling himself hand-over-hand out of that hole, the studio worked for him, kept him calm. After Moody died, he wanted to move, but he'd learned by then to sit with his heartache and let it happen, to honor the dead with his grief.

He bent forward, rested his hands on his thighs and let out a deep breath. He needed to get a grip. Detach from Mystery Woman. Let go of Moody. Get rid of that old rug. Maybe go back to culinary school in case his third book tanked as hard as the second.

But first he needed to get the hell out of here. He stuffed his phone and keys in his pockets, and swept his jacket from the couch right as the doorbell rang.

"We heard your shout," a cheerful voice said. "You have finished?"

He tossed his jacket to the side, threw open his door, and gently swept up his 75-year-old neighbor and twirled her around. She threw her arms around his neck while her beau, Raul clapped. Gabe set Natalia on her feet, her long colorful skirt still swirling, and kissed both her cheeks.

"Yes," he said, unable to hold back a grin. "I've finished."

Natalia clasped her hands in front of her heart then reached for Raul's hand. "We are so proud," she said in her heavy Slavic accent. "We have been quiet with the sex so as to help you with the concentration."

Raul nodded solemnly.

As their next door neighbor for the past few years, Gabe understood and appreciated this sacrifice. Despite their age, and thirty year relationship, they had regular, vocal, and what seemed to be excessively satisfying sex.

Gabe clapped Raul on the shoulder. "Thank you both."

"This will call for a celebration," Natalia said with an impish smile. "Dinner?"

"The usual?" Gabe asked, knowing what was coming.

Natalia gestured between herself and Raul. "We will be purchasing the supplies." She reached way up to pat Gabe's jaw. "You will be cooking everyone's favorite."

An hour later, after emailing the manuscript to his agent, freshly showered and euphoric, Gabe stood in Natalia and Raul's kitchen mincing parsley for spaghetti and meatballs. His friends argued amiably in Czech and Spanish nearby, and he couldn't stop smiling. Not much satisfied him like finishing a novel and cooking for his loved ones.

He tried to avoid the obvious addendum, which was that sex with his mystery woman had satisfied him more than anything had in years. "Damn it," he muttered, and chopped faster.

Natalia and Raul's argument broke off and Natalia asked, "The knife is sharp enough?"

"The knife is fine," he reassured her. "Just thinking out loud again."

Natalia stood in a rustle of multicolored clothing, including scarves, jewelry and tall green boots with pointy toes. He loved her and thoughtful Raul unreservedly, and hoped he could be half as fascinating and energetic at their age.

"You are troubled by the book?" she asked, topping off his wine glass.

"A little worried, yeah." He gave the pot of water a quick check. Not boiling yet.

"You can tell us the synopsis now that it is complete?"

They respected his superstition of reticence while writing, but it still didn't stop them from buying large quantities of food and standing outside his door with sad tales about it going to waste, and could he help them prepare and eat it? They knew he missed spreading out to cook large meals, and they didn't let any opportunity pass to ask if he needed "talking time" about his novel. He usually managed to change the subject, but with the book now finished, he didn't mind sharing a summary.

"It's a coming-of-age tale," he told them. Raul adjusted his tie and nodded encouragement. "About a young man searching for his birth parents," Gabe continued. "He goes on a cross-country trek to find them and meets a variety of people along the way." He noticed the sauce starting to bubble and lowered the temperature to let it simmer. He wasn't quite ready to share that in a scene he eventually cut, a beautiful stranger propositions his protagonist in an elevator. It had somehow worked beautifully in life, and was crap on the page. His literary creation came across as brazen and slutty; his own beautiful stranger had been neither. He assumed this was because he was too close to the source material.

Raul nodded again, but Gabe could tell by the satisfied expression on his face that he approved of the storyline. Natalia patted Gabe's shoulder and when his phone buzzed, he said, "Sorry, I need to check that in case it's Ondrea."

His agent lived and breathed her job, and contacted him at all hours. If she had questions about the manuscript, he wanted to answer them right away. Natalia took over sauce stirring duties while Gabe glanced at his phone. Not Onnie, but his friend Lionel at CuisineTV.

In an email, Lionel wrote that the higher ups liked his work at the trade show, which made Gabe laugh out loud. "So did I, my friend," he muttered. "So did I."

They were offering him a regular gig, writing for a new cooking show on CuisineTV. For a nice chunk of change.

The studios were in Manhattan, so no major travel involved. He'd interview the contestants during the six weeks of filming, produce articles for a companion magazine, and discuss highlights of each show. He'd summarize events on the blog and profile two contestants a week.

He hit Reply, said he was very interested, and would like to meet to discuss terms. Unless there was some hidden downside, the job was a no-brainer. Great pay, writing about food, and interviewing people. The perfect recipe for ditching his obsession over a woman he'd never see again.

CHAPTER FIVE

Teresa hid behind a white column in the ornate Flood Mansion reception room, watching the happy couple in their first dance.

Victoria glowed in her satin and tulle wedding dress, the skirt's scalloped lace hem flowing around her high heels as she swayed. Luke, his eyes never leaving his bride's, was her perfect counterpart, dashingly handsome in his tux.

Teresa didn't know if the most current champagne glass in her hand was her third or fourth; she kept grabbing them from the roaming waiters' trays to distract herself, drinking their contents to avoid eye contact with anyone. Since the column she stood near stuck out from the wall, she used it to shield herself from Cort, who had been tracking her movements all evening. She'd last seen him chatting with one of the waitresses, though, and her shoulders lowered as she observed the other guests.

Kristen, despite being a week past her due date, fluttered around the circle of watchers in her pale pink Grecian-style gown, chatting, flirting, and letting people rub her belly. Teresa wondered if Kristen shared any of her own melancholic feelings as they watched two people express and share their deep love in front of two hundred people. If she were pregnant, with no baby's father in sight, she didn't think she could appear as carefree.

Kristen and Victoria's father, Joe, visiting from Illinois, escorted his own new wife, Margaret, over to chat with Kristen, who threw her arms around both of them and beamed.

Two members of the band, Marty and Pierce, stood to Teresa's left, chatting with Marty's wife, Miranda, who held their sleeping two month old son. While Teresa watched, Miranda shifted the baby into Marty's arms, and everyone around them leaned closer to peer at the little one.

Maybe Teresa was the only melancholy one.

Reflecting her own thoughts, a voice asked in her ear, "They look real happy, don't they?"

Startled out of her reverie, Teresa straightened and took a small step away from Cort Landry, who cleaned up really well, damn him. In his own tux, his dark blonde hair growing out from its buzz cut and his blue eyes sparkling, he sorely tempted her to be a cliché: the maid of honor who goes home with the best man.

Since her movement edged her up against the column, and both he and her slutty thoughts made her nervous, she took a sip of champagne before answering. "The bride and groom or the new family?" She gestured toward Marty, Miranda and baby Alex.

"All of 'em." Cort closed the small amount of space between them. "But I meant Luke and Victoria."

"Yes." Teresa let out an inadvertent sigh, her gaze shifting. Cort's mom, Glory, standing in for mother-of-the-groom, joined the newlyweds on the dance floor, soon followed by Victoria's father and step-mother.

Cort held out his arm. "Ready for our maid of honor, best man dance?"

"Oh, I…" She held up her champagne glass. "Should finish this first, and then…" She shrugged, the fabric flowers of her purple one-shoulder dress brushing against her neck. She wanted to dance, but even though Victoria hadn't required her wedding party to participate, tradition had won out, and everyone but Teresa and Cort was on the floor. Even Kristen and her escort Parker were doing little Grateful Dead-style pirouettes around each other.

But with her brawny ex-boyfriend so close she could smell the warmth of his skin, and see his eyes dilate with desire, Teresa hesitated. How could she touch a man she'd once told in a fit of anger, "You will never see my orgasm face again"? A girl couldn't take something like that back. She'd barely touched his arm when he escorted her down the aisle for the ceremony, and even then his yearning expression remained through the vows and all afternoon at the reception. Cort wasn't the yearning type. Seeing him like this broke down her defenses.

Either that or all the love in the room overwhelmed her. It certainly couldn't be the excess of champagne she'd consumed.

A waiter walked by, and Cort plucked the glass from her hand and set it on a tray.

"Now you're done," he said with his familiar grin.

She shook her head, but a return smile slipped through. Tucking her hand in his arm, feeling his biceps flex in response, she commanded, "No funny business."

Cort slipped one arm around her, and took her free hand, turning her slowly in time to Blake Shelton's "Sure Be Cool if you Did."

"Wouldn't think of it," he said.

"Yes, you would." She lifted his hand up from her rear end and repositioned it at her waist.

Undaunted, he spread his fingers wide, keeping her close. "Well, now, darlin', you didn't let me finish. I wouldn't think of any funny business without your permission."

Cort's persistence remained the insurmountable issue in their relationship. He held the reins and they both knew it, although he was gentleman enough to let her believe otherwise. After she'd flirted shamelessly and gotten his interest, he amiably dictated the what, where, and when. And she'd enjoyed it so much, damn him. At least at first. It had worn off quickly, but by then it was too late to shift the power.

"So how's the album going?" she asked, hoping to distract both of them.

"You look real beautiful," he whispered, his mouth at her ear. His breath fluttered the chiffon roses that made up the strap of her gown and a shimmy drifted down her spine.

"Oh, Cort," she said. "Don't…"

He straightened, his smile impish. "What? I can't give you a compliment?"

"Of course you can," she said, trying for a light tone. She shut her mouth at the hope in his eyes. "I just don't…let's not get serious, okay?"

"Sure thing." He nodded at her. "Sleeping together doesn't have to be serious."

"Cort…"

His expression sobered. He rested their clasped hands on his chest and pulled her so close his thigh drifted between hers. "You do look beautiful, Tessa," he said, and she winced inside at his nickname for her. "I haven't stopped thinking about you since that night you broke my heart."

Which time? she thought, cringing at the memory of sleeping with him after their first breakup. One mistake of many with him.

She pulled back, pushing his thigh away with one knee, and he eased his hold, but didn't let go or stop watching her. She looked away, but happy couples holding each other close and swaying to the music surrounded them.

She remembered her determination to face her parents, and the resulting shitstorm. To Teresa's surprise, Kristen called it a success. "You stood up for yourself. You took a huge step. The next will be easier, and the one after that." Teresa hadn't realized at the time those "steps" involved more than her family. She had plenty of steps she needed to take elsewhere. No more Queen of Indecision, and no more fear of conflict.

So she turned back to Cort to close the door on her past with him. "I'm sorry," she said. "I didn't want to hurt you."

"And when we first got together, I didn't think you could."

She held his gaze. He was right, but that had been her fault for not standing up to hm. "You know we weren't right for each other. Not in the long term."

He shook his head. "You turned my world sideways, Tessa."

"Don't..."

"And it was all for the good." He leaned close enough to kiss her. "I'm going to do what it takes to get you back."

Filled with dismay, Teresa stopped moving. Cort tightened his grip, expression hopeful but determined.

Well, she could be determined, too. "I mean it, Cort."

"So do I, darlin'."

Close to tears now, but refusing to let him see that, Teresa glared at him.

"Mind if I cut in?" Luke Tyler eased himself between their bodies as soon as Teresa dropped her hand from Cort's shoulder.

"Now, Luke, Tessa and I were having an important conversation here."

Luke took Teresa's now cold hand in his and turned her away from Cort, saying over his shoulder, "And my wife would really like a

31

dance with the best man."

Once Cort had made his way through the crowd to Victoria, Luke turned Teresa very gently in time to the music. "Are you all right?" he asked.

"Did Victoria send you over here?"

"I came of my own accord," he said, straightening. She waited, her eyes never leaving his, and he let out a sigh. "She did," he admitted with a nod.

"You know we're not right for each other, right?" It was so much easier to say it to Luke than to Cort.

He lifted his head and looked around, and her conscience stung her for accosting him on his wedding day, but Cort's resolute attitude left her rattled. How much of his determination to get her back related to his feelings and how much was stubborn pride?

Luke gave another sigh. "He might not know that."

"I don't want him back." Again, so much easier to say to Luke. "But I don't want to hurt him, either."

"Your split hit him hard, darlin', no denying that. But he'll bounce back fine, I'll make sure. You just take care of yourself. Now how's that fancy catering job of yours?"

"Oh..." Eight months earlier, Teresa had quit her position as Victoria's assistant to attend culinary school, only to drop out and beg for her job back. Then she quit again to work for a caterer. The pattern made her squirm. "We don't want to talk about work right now. The wedding was beautiful. I love the western theme."

They both peered at his cowboy boots, and Luke grinned. "Almost didn't get to wear 'em. We compromised on no Stetsons." He glanced around the room, and Teresa saw his eye fall on diminutive Victoria, laughing at something Cort said. Teresa sighed at Luke's obvious love for his bride. "Never thought I'd be so glad to have cameras around," Luke continued. He leaned closer and confided, "I was so nervous, I don't remember half of it. How'd I do?"

She reassured him he'd done fine, he spun her around, and the rest of the evening went by in a blur. Later, she remembered Kristen catching the bouquet, waving the happy couple off to a getaway in Monterey before a week in Hawaii, and sneaking out at the end of the reception to avoid Cort. But she needed a better plan than avoidance to truly convince him they were over.

When she got home, she leaned on her desk to pull off one spiked heel, and saw the flyer for the CuisineTV contest—*Own Your Own Restaurant!* —on one corner. She'd written her notes about the wedding on it from Victoria, and the event had come and gone so fast, she'd forgotten to throw it out. Her own restaurant. Being her own boss. No one stealing her lemon bar recipe. Taking charge of her life and escaping the madness that seemed to surround her. She examined the flyer more closely: the deadline was tomorrow. She glanced at the clock. Make that today, 12:00 p.m. Eastern time.

Before she could stop to think about it, she turned on her computer. Still in her party dress, both shoes tossed in the corner, she spent the next few hours filling out the application and creating a video audition, channeling her frustration over Cort, her family and her job into something positive. She passionately explained her love for feeding people and how owning a restaurant would be life-altering, both for herself and for a local homeless shelter because she would include a gleaned food donation program. Ironically, thanks to her unintentional stint on *In Concert*, one of her strengths besides cooking was comfort in front of a camera. She searched in vain for a suitable head shot, but before she could second-guess herself, pasted an older picture with a short 'fro, then didn't look at it again. She finished at 3:15 a.m., hit Send before reason could set in, and sat contemplating a hot bath and bed.

Then at 3:20 a.m., Teresa's door was flung open and Kristen stood panting in the hallway, clutching her belly. This time Teresa knew Kristen hadn't spilled a glass of water down her front as a diversion.

CHAPTER SIX

In the excitement leading up to Daisy Anna Clausen's arrival in the world, and her introduction to her new home, Teresa completely forgot about the application for the CuisineTV show.

Victoria and Luke postponed their Hawaiian honeymoon and spent a lot of time at the Russian Hill flat, Victoria in awe of and often keeping her distance from the baby, and Luke holding her like she was his own. Since they'd already been in town for the wedding, Joe and Margaret extended their stay and showed up early each morning with coffee, food, baby supplies, and—at least in Margaret's case—child-rearing advice.

Teresa liked Kristen and Victoria's straightforward step-mother, but thought she might scream if she had to hear, "Watch her little neck, hold up her head," one more time.

Watching Kristen on the couch with Daisy, bookended by family members, everyone focused on this tiny person, made Teresa ache. The ache didn't come from her maternal instincts suddenly switching on, but because they were all so in love with each other, so happy and satisfied with their lives. Although she'd been in touch with Mama Step, Teresa hadn't talked to her own parents since the disastrous dinner a few weeks earlier.

Along with the newly wed Tylers and their friends came a parade of Kristen's friends, representing the full spectrum of San Francisco residents: gay, straight, married, single, yuppie, hippie, homeless, white, Asian, Hispanic, and African American, and every combination thereof.

At first the variety of people who came to see Daisy and bring gifts fascinated Teresa. She thought Daisy might be the only baby with not one, but two transgender godparents. Mooshree even showed up for a Blessing of a New Soul, but when they started talking about placenta soup, Teresa shot out of the flat and up the hill to give Cleo some freshly made lemon bars. Eventually she tired of the constant stream of visitors, especially Cort, who continued his suit. To avoid him, Teresa either slid between two guests and made desperate conversation about anything from the weather to football scores, or left the house altogether. When she realized that going to work felt like a getaway, even though her boss put her on dishwashing duty, she sank further into depression.

She tried using fantasies of Elevator Man to escape, but the more time passed, the less real the entire incident seemed, and her daydreams lost their escapist power. She couldn't go past a certain point in her reveries without knowing his name.

When Daisy was three weeks old, Joe and Margaret went back to their lives in Illinois, and Victoria and the band returned to Nashville. She and Luke would take a belated honeymoon in a couple of months. Other than a few of Kristen's close friends, the stream of guests subsided. Teresa thought life might get back to normal after that, but she didn't take into account that with all the well-wishers gone, it was only herself and Kristen with a new baby. And little Daisy was as vocal—and sleepless—as her mother.

Unable to sleep through the colicky screams, Teresa often found herself face to face with Frog, still glaring from the back of the couch, and offering various food and drink to Kristen— including shots of whisky—to help calm everyone down.

One night around 3:00 a.m., she shuffled into the living room to find Kristen holding Daisy to one shoulder, both of them sobbing quietly.

Teresa shot to Kristen's side. "Honey, what is it?"

Patting Daisy's back and joggling her at the same time, Kristen blubbered something that sounded like, "Bu-bu-bu...mmm, muh-muh-muh," then shook her head and cried harder, which only caused Daisy to follow suit. Kristen finally spit out, *Bad mother,* and covered her face with one hand.

"No, you're not, you're amazing." Teresa held out her hands, wanting to hug or pat or make some other consoling gesture, but they all seemed so inadequate. Teresa had only held Daisy a couple of times, but Kristen's sobbing and joggling only increased the baby's distress, so Teresa pressed a hand to Kristen's shoulder and said, "Let me take Daisy."

Kristen poured the baby bundle into Teresa's hands and she tightened the blanket around Daisy's flailing legs, remembering Margaret's information that new babies liked to be well-wrapped; it reminded them of the comfort of the womb. She cuddled Daisy close, her boneless weight a surprise, considering she barely weighed more than the cat. Teresa swayed gently back and forth with Daisy in the crook of one arm, and patted her friend with her free hand, watching the baby's scrunched red face transform to smooth pink and relaxed in seconds. She let out a breath and looked at Kristen whose own face remained pink and tear-stained. Kristen glanced between Teresa and her now sleeping daughter and burst into noisy tears again.

"See? Bad mom!" she declared.

Daisy startled, her arms and legs kicking out in their wrapping, but soon settled back to sleep, her mouth pursed into a nursing motion.

"No. You're amazing," Teresa repeated. "I saw you give birth without drugs, that has to count for something."

"Biology," Kristen snuffled, wiping her nose on a clean diaper. She pulled her legs up on the couch and curled against Teresa, staring down at her daughter. "You do it because you have to. The rest, though? The rest is all choices, and I don't know if I'm making any right ones."

Other than her statement relating to motherhood, Teresa completely understood her sentiment.

"I'm already starting her off without a dad," Kristen continued. "And I know what it's like to grow up without a parent." Kristen and Victoria's mother had died when they were young, and their dad hadn't remarried until recently.

Teresa stilled. Ever since Kristen announced her pregnancy, she'd refused to talk about the baby's father. Was she now going to reveal his identity?

"But then, is an imp from hell as a dad better than no dad at all?" Kristen said, then yawned so hard her jaw cracked. "I never thought I could get this tired. I don't *do* tired."

This was true; Teresa had never witnessed Kristen sleep. But the "imp from hell" statement, the first real clue Kristen had ever revealed about Daisy's father, shocked any response out of her. Who was this guy, and what had he done?

"I don't mind keeping *her* from *him*. He doesn't deserve her," Kristen added, and Teresa could hear the tired slur in Kristen's voice as she tucked closer. "But is it fair to keep *him* from *her*? There are too many choices," she repeated, "and I don't know if I'm making the right ones."

"I don't know," Teresa ventured, staring down at Daisy's peaceful face, the tired weight of her friend against her side. "Maybe none of them are right, and you just do the best you can."

Kristen rested her head on Teresa's shoulder and warmth washed through Teresa. Despite her elevator man experience shifting into a surreal dream, she suddenly, almost desperately, wanted to talk about it. "I might've made a bad choice recently," she ventured. "Maybe even two," she added, thinking about the cooking show contest. Considering the potential anguish, why in the world would she want to go on another reality TV show? "I'll start with the man, though."

Because didn't it always start with a man?

She paused to let that sink in, knowing how much Kristen loved men and talking about them, but all she heard was an exhausted mother and daughter snoring softly.

As HE RODE UP to the CuisineTV offices on the 20th floor, Gabe knew he wouldn't miraculously run into Mystery Woman in a Manhattan elevator, but he couldn't help a quick scan around the small space. Two suits, a bike messenger, and a beautiful Asian woman with bangs that brushed her eyelashes, a skin-tight catsuit and closed expression. She caught Gabe looking at her, peered at him from under those crazy bangs, gave him a quick up-and-down, then turned away.

Exotic, Gabe thought. Beautiful, but not as captivating as his mystery woman. The dread-locked messenger got off first, then the suits together, and he and Cat Woman stood face forward, heads tilted up and watching the numbers change. Gabe made no attempt at any witty elevator repartee with this woman. He looked at the panel and noticed the only button still lit up was number 20.

CuisineTV's marketing staff was on that floor, but it also housed administrative offices and their legal department. She could belong to any of those places—or none.

She didn't look at him again as the doors slid open and she marched out in super-high black boots. She tossed a brief nod at the receptionist, then as if she knew Gabe watched, peered at him over her shoulder, flipped her hair out of the way so it rippled down her back, and produced what he'd best describe as a brief, saucy smile. She turned the corner, her heels clicking authoritatively down the hall.

He smiled at the receptionist, an overly made up blonde, her hair sleeked back in a ponytail that curled around the front of one shoulder. She moved her gaze from the Asian woman and focused on Gabe. Her big brown eyes widened, her lips shifted from pursed to smiling, and her appearance lost the sour look.

"Gabe De Luca," he said. "Here to see Lionel Schemmerling."

He wanted to ask who Cat Woman was, but he'd noted the receptionist's expression when she'd walked by; referencing her now would only return the sour look.

"Of course, Mr. De Luca." She pressed a button on her phone, murmured into her headset, then addressed him again. "This way, please."

Gabe appreciated the receptionist's nice, round ass in its tight gray skirt as he followed her down the same hall as Cat Woman. The sway in her walk reminded him how he liked a woman in high heels, especially after seeing so much practical footwear in northern California last month. The receptionist led him down a corridor lined with framed posters of CuisineTV's celebrity chefs. At the end, she knocked on one of the many maple doors, announced Gabe, then smiled brightly before backing out and closing the door behind her.

Five people sat at a large oval conference table. Gabe nodded to Lionel Schemmerling, new head of PR and the friend who'd initially offered him the job. Lionel shook Gabe's hand and introduced him to the others. Unusual for him, Gabe completely forgot three of the four people's names. The only one he remembered was Lily Wen, CEO of CuisineTV.

Cat Woman.

Curious, he observed Lily Wen's reaction during their introduction and his intentional businesslike handshake. Her friendly but distant expression revealed nothing, but she squeezed Gabe's fingers before letting go. *Good*, he thought. He liked a challenge.

Gabe handed out his CV and writing samples from *Epicurean Times*, *Gourmet*, and *Rolling Stone*, while Lionel filled him in on the show and the job. They'd talked earlier in the week and Gabe knew his speech was for the other suits.

"*Tasty Dish* is a competition show. A six-week film schedule, with twelve contestants in two to three challenges a week. The winner will get his or her own restaurant, one hundred grand to cover start-up costs, and CuisineTV will follow them for the next six months for a spin-off show.

"The filming itself will sometimes take twelve or more hours a day, but you won't be required at every shoot. We'll have a corresponding website with contestant bios, show recaps, small giveaways, and sequences not shown on that week's episode, but want a more personal touch, too. That's where you come in. You'll follow the contestants each week, write a daily blog entry—without revealing too many details, since the show won't air for another few months—and conduct contestant interviews. You'll also be writing pieces for our CuisineTV companion magazine."

Gabe nodded. The gig would take a lot of hours, but he needed a damn distraction. And he liked replenishing his savings account. And eating.

"We will also have celebrity and guest judges," Lionel continued, "rotating through the episodes. Our regular judging panel will consist of three people from the CuisineTV staff. They will be celebrity chef Darren Michaels, star of *Light My Fire*; Joel Klein, executive director of *Tasty Dish*; and our own Lily Wen." He gestured toward Cat Woman, who gave a small nod, her face still impassive.

Gabe smiled at Lily, who tilted her head to the side, closed her eyes in a long blink, then turned her attention back to Lionel, a hint of a smile on her lips.

Good enough, Gabe thought. This was going to be a fun gig.

CHAPTER SEVEN

Teresa's heart skipped a beat, then hammered hard when she saw the fat CuisineTV envelope on the coffee table stained with something like baby spit or breast milk. She'd already gotten both the congratulatory phone call and email letting her know she was a finalist, but this envelope reinforced their reality. It contained the contract she needed to sign and return so they could set up a Skype interview next week.

That was, if she really wanted to go through with this. Which she did. And didn't. The entire situation scared the hell out of her. Back out, and what was she going to do next with her life? Or go on with it, and...open up endless prospects.

She picked up the envelope by a clean corner and sat in a chair, pulling a BPA-free rubber ducky out from beneath her thigh.

She stared at the CuisineTV return address, considering all of the possibilities, then ripped the envelope open and pulled out a thick sheaf of papers. She scanned the cover letter: congratulations again, one of thirty finalists, further interviews and eliminations, six weeks of filming, and she could be the grand prize winner with her own restaurant.

Heart still pounding hard, she leaned back in the chair, the papers clutched to her chest. Such a big risk, entering this contest, flying to New York, for possibly nothing. Or everything. She could get kicked off in the first week. Or win the whole thing. All while exposing herself on camera to the world. Well, she'd done that already, quite recently, revealing more than just her life, and she'd survived it. But she hadn't intentionally signed up to be on TV then. Was she willing to make this decision and accept all the potential consequences, including her past TV exploits used against her? Or was this just another impulsive decision where she jumped in without looking? Did she trust her instinct on this one?

As she considered the answers, a key turned in the lock and Kristen glided in with a hemp diaper bag on one shoulder and Daisy tucked into a sling against her chest. A thatch of strawberry blond hair matching Kristen's stuck straight up from the baby's head.

"Hey, T," Kristen said, dropping the bag on the floor and her keys in a tray on a side table. "I just ran a session of Naked Yoga for Seniors, and it was *amazing*. Truly inspiring." She sat on the couch end nearest Teresa's chair and beamed at her. "Some days I can't wait to get older. How was your day?"

Teresa closed her gaping mouth as unobtrusively as possible and said, "Oh, it was—"

"Oh, I forgot!" Kristen said, easing herself up with one hand while cradling Daisy with the other. "I picked up the mail yesterday and forgot to give it to you." She looked at Teresa over her shoulder. "A package from Cort. It's in my bag."

"Don't," Teresa said, as Daisy stirred and made little mewing sounds. "You sit, don't disturb the baby. I can get it."

She set the CuisineTV papers on the table and strode across the room, crouching down to dig into Kristen's diaper bag. She moved aside miniature socks, witch hazel, coconut oil, what was probably a vibrator, and a container of dried fruit, eventually pulling out a padded envelope with Cort's blocky handwriting. The label read: *Tessa's Song*.

"Oh," she said, tilting back and sitting hard on her butt. Teresa hadn't heard from Cort since he went back to Nashville with the rest of Tyler Landry to finish their album, and she'd hoped he'd finally gotten the message,

"Another song?" Kristen asked, sympathy in her tone.

Teresa brushed her braids over her shoulder and held up the CD case with a nod. "'Tessa's Song'."

On a sigh, Kristen said, "Like John Denver's 'Annie's Song.' Are you going to listen to this one?"

"I don't want to encourage him." Teresa headed across the room to the long table Kristen had painted turquoise, hoping to use it as a dinner table for the two of them and Victoria, when she lived there, too. But falling in love with Luke distracted Victoria, Teresa often worked odd hours, and Kristen was starting up her yoga teaching. The table had, instead, become a repository for mail, handbags, iPods, clean cotton diapers, plants that needed tending—and now Cort's CDs.

As a closet romantic, Teresa loved the idea of a suitor sending notes and writing songs for her, of someone wanting her so much he'd go to great lengths to show it. But she didn't want Cort as that suitor.

"He still loves you," Kristen said, "but he doesn't get it, does he?"

Teresa set the CD on top of the small stack and turned around in time to see Kristen offer a breast to a wriggling Daisy, who settled down as soon as she began to nurse.

Teresa rested against the table before remembering Victoria once confessed she and Luke had had sex on it. She missed sex. And at that thought, she remembered Elevator Man holding her thigh up before sliding into her. With a sigh, she sat down. "What do you mean, he doesn't get it?"

Kristen brushed her fingers over the baby's pale ear. "Pushing so hard like this upsets the universe. We all know it's better to go with the flow than to force something. He needs a more subtle approach, or he'll keep driving you away."

"But I don't want him back." But she still wanted *something* in her life, a rewarding job, a well-balanced relationship. Victoria had that. Kristen had Daisy. Teresa had turbulence.

"I know," Kristen said, "but he hasn't figured that out yet. And he thinks if he lets up at all, he'll lose any ground he's gained with you."

Something ached in Teresa's chest at that, and her eyes drifted down to Daisy's delicate strawberry blonde curls. She forced her gaze back to the papers on the coffee table. "Did he tell you that?"

"No. It's just a feeling. Have you talked to your mom yet?" As a fiercely protective new mom with doubts about her parenting abilities, Kristen was intensely focused on mother-daughter relationships.

"No. Julia won't talk to me because she's basically grounded for life. Mama Step said mom's spending a lot of time at the office. My dad finally called back and said she 'regretted her words,' but he hedged when I asked if she was going to call me or ever talk to me again." Teresa rested her feet against the edge of the coffee table and moved the papers around with the side of one boot. "My family's pretty good at hedging stuff."

Kristen reached out and squeezed Teresa's knee. "I'm sorry. Your mom's really repressed, but don't give up. What did you get in the mail?"

Teresa started at the change in topic and Kristen's unsettling perceptiveness. "What? Oh, it's nothing. I…entered a contest."

"Did you win?"

Teresa picked up the paperwork and set it in her lap. "No, I…I made it to the first round."

By a small margin, her fear of revealing the reality TV part edged out her guilt at not telling Kristen and Victoria before now. During the filming of *In Concert*, Victoria herself had been fired when the studio executives discovered her relationship with Luke, which was considered a breach of contract. This had left Teresa's footage at the mercy of the editors and new producer.

She'd watched a couple episodes, holding tight to Kristen's hand as her mistakes, missteps and undressings were shown to the world. She cried in equal parts over the humiliation and the realization that she needed to end her relationship with Cort. To re-live the beginning of the end had been incredibly painful, so she stopped viewing episodes.

As different as *Tasty Dish* seemed to be from *In Concert*, she couldn't predict how her friends would react to the idea of her going on another reality TV show. She decided to start by emphasizing the good side. "I could win a restaurant. With start up costs."

Kristen's face brightened. "Really? That sounds amazing." She pulled a clean diaper from a stack on the coffee table and flipped it over her shoulder, then propped Daisy up and patted her back. "How does it work?" she asked, tucking her shirt over her exposed breast.

"Well, there's a series of contests and it's over a six week period and—"

Daisy let out a resounding belch, made a noise that sounded like "neh!" and started to cry. "Goodness," Kristen said, standing up and patting the baby. "That usually puts her right to sleep, doesn't make her cry." She peeked down the back of Daisy's diaper, and shook her head. "All clear there."

Daisy's face flushed pink and she added screams to her sobs. Kristen stepped around the table and reached for the diaper bag. "I'm going to put her back in the sling and see if walking helps," she said, her voice raised over the baby's cries. "I'm sorry, T, we can talk later. I'm really glad for you about the contest."

Daisy's screams faded as Kristen headed out and down the street, and Teresa fell back in the chair, letting out a long breath, her ears still ringing. She wondered if it made a difference if the baby was yours when it screamed like that.

She reached for the papers again and looked down at them. Was she ready for this? She thought about her life as it was at the moment—unfulfilling job; distant family; no man, except the wrong one; good friends currently occupied with their own lives—and decided that yes, she was ready for all of it. She *needed* it.

"Come and get me," she said.

CHAPTER EIGHT

G abe handed out the beers, and as soon as the guys settled around the campfire, they toasted him.

"To the new gig." Adam raised his beer in salute.

"To loads of dough and great exposure," Nick added.

"To Cat Woman," Stephan tossed in with a wink.

Gabe clinked his bottle against each of theirs, took a long swig, then lounged against the log they'd pulled up to the fire. Ushering out winter with a trip to Cranberry Lake in the Adirondacks had become a tradition, and they spent the time fishing, hiking, and swimming. The general R&R and shooting the shit didn't hurt either. Besides Gabe's new gig, Stephan was raising his four-year-old daughter Kaily alone, and had recently passed his Realtor's exam; Adam was on spring break as a professor from NYU; and Nick never needed an excuse to go on vacation, but admitted recently to antacid abuse over his Wall Street mergers and acquisitions job.

"So an elevator, huh?" Stephan said, setting his beer down with a thump. He rubbed a palm over the scruff along his jaw. "Nice."

Gabe's chest constricted and he choked on his beer. He hadn't told a soul about Mystery Woman, he was sure of it, not even in any of his unconscious mutterings.

Nick, the biggest talker of the four, jumped in before Gabe had to think of a reply.

"Imagine meeting Cat Woman on an elevator, of all places." Nick shook his head. "A damn elevator. Only you, Gabe," he added, pointing with his beer, "would meet a woman in an elevator."

Gabe shook his head, laughing in relief. Of course. He'd told the guys all about Lily Wen in her tight outfit, the two of them in an elevator on their way to the same meeting. He liked the woman, and planned a pursuit, but didn't miss his thoughts arrowing straight to Mystery Woman in connection to an elevator reference, instead of Lily Wen.

"Not much of an introduction," Gabe said with a shrug. "A quick glance in the elevator."

He'd assumed Lily Wen's up-and-down glances, extended blinks and little cat smiles were her way of flirting. And he meant to test his assumption. Normally he'd be talking that up with the guys, not downplaying it like he'd just done, but it seemed disrespectful to his mystery woman. And that was nuts. Damn, but he needed to let her go.

Later, he sat on a boulder watching the sun set and skipping small pebbles across the flat surface of the lake.

"You'll scare away the fish," said a voice behind him, and Gabe smiled. Stephan, Gabe's best friend since second grade, when he rescued Gabe from a fourth grade bully threatening to break his glasses. Gabe shared his PB&J with Stephan at lunch, Steph handed over half his Oreos, and they'd been sidekicks ever since, at each other's houses every day after school, on the same sports teams, part of the prom queen's court. At each other's sides for all of it.

At least up until Gabe's first book hit the New York Times Bestseller list and was optioned into a film and he went on a global celebratory bender. And became a world-class asshole. Nick helped crush the attitude out of him, and he worked on atonement every day, but guilt still sucker-punched him when he thought of Stephan and Kaily's situation and how his alcohol- and drug-induced haze had kept him away when Steph needed him most.

"The fish'll be back in time for us to snag a few in the morning," Gabe said, as Stephan climbed up and settled on the rock next to him.

Stephan slipped a pebble from Gabe's collected pile and skipped it eight times across the lake's surface, more skips than Gabe had managed so far. Stephan excelled at whatever he tried: sports and academics, a scholarship to Columbia, and the most beautiful girl at school who became his bride. He'd made buckets of money as a Wall Street analyst, same as Nick.

Then his wife Hannah died from eclampsia almost five years ago, his daughter Kaily got sick when she was a baby, and he lost his job. Gabe thought life sucked the big one sometimes.

"Bet I'll catch more than you," Stephan said, looking across at the far shore.

"Bet you don't."

Stephan held out his hand. "Five bucks?"

"Ten."

They shook, grinning at each other. Stephan sobered first, looking into the distance again. He'd always been quiet, but the last few years had drained a lot of joy from him.

"How's Kaily?" Gabe asked. One of the negative results of his out-of-town jobs was time away from his friends, and his goddaughter, Kaily.

"A firecracker," Stephan said. "Getting more energy every day. She can't wait to go to Disney World."

Gabe tossed a pebble between his palms. "Nothing like some Disney magic to…" His voice trailed off. They'd all learned in the past few years that magic had nothing to do with it. And yet, conversely, it had every damn thing to do with it. He chucked the rock into the water; it hit with a dull "*plonk!*"

"Sorry, man," he said.

"No," Stephan replied, his voice thick. "Don't be. You can stop being sorry, Gabe." He gave Gabe a crooked smile, but his eyes still looked tight. "We talked about it, remember, and we're putting it in the past. None of it was your fault."

"If I'd been there…" He hadn't. He'd been partying it up in another country.

Stephan gripped his upper arm, hard. "It wouldn't've changed *anything.*"

Steph was right. Being there wouldn't have kept Hannah alive. But it could have changed everything about his friendship with Stephan.

Stephan shook him. "You're my best friend, Gabe. You fucked up, but you came back, too. And you're still here. That's the most important thing." He let go and skipped another stone.

Gabe stared at the widening ripples. "Maybe I need a little Disney magic myself."

"Yeah. Kaily's convinced Mickey will make it all better and she'll stay in remission. That the cancer won't ever come back." Stephan's voice hitched and he cleared his throat. "And goddamn it if I'm not

47

right there with her."

Gabe blinked fast in the sharp light of the setting sun. It had been hard, in the beginning, to hold off on the platitudes, like, "*It'll be okay,*" and "*don't worry,*" and let Stephan have his feelings, especially since the supposedly comforting words didn't work. Gabe had gotten better at shutting up, but the situation itself still sucked.

He squeezed Stephan's shoulder back, his hard grip expressing his feelings the way words never could, then let go. "Another ten bucks says Nick falls in the water before 8:00 a.m.," Gabe said.

Stephan grinned at him. "Deal."

THE DAY TERESA got a call from a producer and learned she had a spot on *Tasty Dish*, she knew she had to face reality. She finally confessed to her best friends, first in person to Kristen and then via Skype to Victoria in Nashville.

At 6:30 the next morning, Victoria showed up at the flat and said they needed to celebrate.

She hugged Teresa, then Kristen, who carried a sleeping Daisy in a sling against her chest.

Teresa, bleary and still in her flannel PJs covered in large-eyed owls, asked, "What are you doing here?"

"Celebrating," Victoria repeated. She rolled her overnight bag to one corner, and strode to the middle of the living room in her usual super high heels, her curvy figure dressed in dark grey trousers and a pink sweater. "You," she added, pointing at Teresa.

"Oh, fun." Kristen clapped her hands quietly so as not to wake Daisy. "When do we start?"

Victoria glanced at her phone. "Any time now. I ordered breakfast to be delivered from Kalina's Kitchen. Eggs, toast, bacon, waffles, bagels, juice, coffee—"

Teresa plopped onto the couch. "Oh, thank God there'll be coffee."

"And for my sister," Victoria added, squeezing Kristen's arm, "soy cream cheese, tofu omelets, granola and additional vegan selections."

Kristen bent to kiss her much shorter sister on the cheek, then lowered herself to the couch, an arm around Daisy. "I love it when we celebrate with food."

Teresa remembered a few months earlier when Victoria asked

them up to their favorite park around the corner and brought along an amazing array of lunch foods. She'd wanted to celebrate, but also affirm their friendships after losing her job and herself in Luke.

"I'm glad you're here," Teresa said around a yawn; she really had missed Victoria. "And I'm super glad there's going to be coffee, but I don't understand what would bring you out from Nashville to celebrate."

"Actually, while the celebration is primary, my secondary reason was to apologize to you."

"What for? You haven't done anything wrong." Teresa stared at her friend in astonishment; Victoria rarely apologized.

Victoria perched on the couch arm. "My husband gently pointed out to me that our wedding would not have gone so smoothly with such a rushed schedule without your help."

"I was happy to help, you know that."

"I do know, because you're amazing, and you're always there for me." She crossed her legs and flexed one foot so the sole of her shoe slipped off and on. "But I treated you like an assistant, instead of my best friend. And I was wrong." She slipped an arm around Teresa's shoulders and hugged her. "So consider this an apology breakfast, along with a celebration." She stood and straightened her sweater. "I'm still nervous about you going on this show, though. Are you sure about it?"

"Hell, no," Teresa admitted, warmth washing through her at Victoria's apology and support. "But I feel like I have to do it."

The doorbell rang then and Victoria ushered in the delivery boy, directing him to set the huge array of dishes and drinks out on their oversized coffee table. She tipped him on his way out, then kicked off her shoes and plunked down across from Teresa and Kristen with a big smile on her face.

"Is it the food or the frequent hot sex?" Kristen asked.

"Is what those two things?"

"Why you're so warm and fuzzy," Teresa said, reaching for one of the containers. She opened it and inhaled warm yeasty goodness, syrup, powdered sugar and cinnamon. She fell back against the couch and closed her eyes. "Oh, God, French toast." Wanting to savor the moment, and wake up a little more, she drank more coffee before diving into the toast.

"Well, we know what makes T happy." Kristen handed her a fork.

"At least we're in the same boat of having to use food as a sex substitute. It's been forever for both of us, but—"

She stopped when Teresa coughed and straightened up. Victoria eyed her over a forkful of eggs and Kristen shifted on the couch to face her, easing Daisy's legs off to one side.

"Or maybe it's only been forever for *me*. The rest of this trio seems to be getting some on the regular."

"No," Teresa sputtered, setting down her coffee. "No." She looked from one to the other and saw matching looks on the sisters' faces: avid interest combined with love, and a touch of disappointment that she hadn't revealed her amour to them. But how could she? She didn't even know his *name*.

"Not...regular," she told them.

Victoria gasped. "Did you have a one-night stand?"

"Did you get back together with Cort?" Kristen added.

Teresa answered Kristen's easier question first. "No. That's truly over." She glanced at Victoria and then at the big bite of French toast calling to her. "And...not at night," she whispered.

Oh God, how she wanted to talk about her elevator man, but it was so mortifying.

"You had a one-*day* stand?" Victoria asked.

"More like a ten-minute stand," Teresa responded without thinking.

Kristen laid a warm hand on Teresa's arm. "Oh, honey, that's disappointing."

"No, that's just it." Teresa set the container on the table, her breakfast forgotten as the memories from that day flooded back. "I think it was the best sex I've ever had."

"In ten minutes?" Victoria asked.

"Poor Cort." Kristen sighed. "I always figured he'd be good, you know, that primal thing he has going on that sort of consumes you. And he's so brawny, and I know that doesn't translate to a big—"

Victoria snapped her fingers. "Focus." She turned to Teresa. "Did you want to talk about it?"

"Yes!" Teresa announced, then put a hand over her mouth when Daisy gave a sleepy yip. "Sorry."

Kristen rubbed circles on Daisy's back, then scooted closer to Teresa on the couch. "She's fine. Spill."

"You remember the trade show I went to about three months

ago?" At their nods, Teresa reviewed her time at the convention, her extreme boredom, and belief her boss had sent her there because he didn't like her. She'd been considering ditching when the cute guy she'd seen earlier got on the elevator with her. She glanced from Victoria to Kristen before staring at the coffee cup on the table in front of her. "And then the elevator stalled."

Kristen pressed her fingertips to her lips and let out a long breath. "Ohh...my goodness."

Victoria stared at Teresa. "You didn't."

"We did," Teresa admitted with a thrill, at both the memory and saying 'we.'"

"Holy..." Victoria shook her head, then shoved her long auburn hair behind her ears. "In an elevator?"

"With a perfect stranger?" Kristen asked. Daisy had started to squirm, so she unbuttoned the top of her shirt to feed her.

Kristen's question reminded Teresa what a dumb thing she'd done. With a perfect stranger. Humiliation rushed through her.

"He loves his dog," she said lamely. She grabbed her coffee for something to do, and clutched it to her chest. "Yes," she admitted. "A perfect stranger." She flashed back to her hands sliding up his back, and around to his abs—his very firm, ripped abs. The way he'd lapped at her collarbone, and made her come so hard she thought she'd break into a million pieces. "And he really was perfect," she added on a sigh.

Victoria reached a hand out to her across the table and Teresa slipped down to the floor and grasped her friend's fingers.

"T," Victoria said, her expression serious. "Please tell me you were safe."

Teresa glanced at Kristen, unsure how to word her response considering the nursing baby in their presence. "I took your sister's advice and started keeping condoms in my bag."

Kristen patted Daisy's chubby thigh. "It's still good advice, and I took my own." She shrugged. "Some things are meant to be."

This time, Teresa reached her hand out and squeezed Kristen's fingers.

"So tell us more about Mr. Perfect One-Afternoon Stand," Kristen said.

"And eat," Victoria encouraged. "Daisy shouldn't be the only one."

Teresa ate that big tempting bite of French toast, savoring the sweet, chewy goodness before reaching for a container of eggs and bacon. Where to start? "He's beautiful," she finally said. "Tall and lean, finely muscled, but broad in the chest so you feel you could lean on him and be comforted. Or picked up and tossed over his shoulder."

"Yum," Kristen said.

"Dark brown eyes, and this crazy long blonde hair that..." She didn't know how to explain it.

"Long like 'I'm too lazy to take care of myself' or long like Chris Hemsworth in *Thor*?" Victoria asked.

"Long like male model long. He did this thing where he tilted his head to one side and a section fell over his face. But with a little flick, it fell away, feathering back in place. But it was completely subconscious, not any kind of 'move.' He didn't seem to realize how gorgeous he is."

Victoria and Kristen sighed.

"So what's his name?"

Teresa's face heated up. To avoid answering right away, she scooted up on the couch and pressed herself into the back corner. That didn't buy her enough time to come up with a good answer, so she shoved a bite of omelet in her mouth.

Unfortunately, her friends were both curious and perceptive, and didn't fall for her tactic.

Victoria tilted her head and said, "T," in her commanding producer voice.

Kristen said, "The universe is finding this very humorous right now. Revel in that. So you don't know his name."

Mouth still full, Teresa shook her head.

"Does he know yours?" Victoria asked.

Teresa swallowed and shook her head again.

"This is so hot," Kristen said, squirming. "True stranger sex. It's making me kinda horny."

"Are you ready to tell us about Daisy's father?" Victoria demanded of her sister.

Teresa didn't mind the change of subject, but the conflict between the sisters made her want to hide farther back in the corner of the couch.

"Whiplash," Kristen replied cheerfully to Victoria. "From the conversational change. But, no, he's pretty much dead to me, hopefully gone back to the depths of hell from whence he came. Let's call him Asmodeus and be done with it."

Victoria let out a sigh, a combination of aggrieved and concerned. "Asmodeus?"

"The demon of lust," Kristen said with distaste. "Now, I have no problem with lust, but—"

Victoria spoke over her. "I hope you can tell us the story someday. In the meantime, can you focus on Teresa and away from your own horniness?"

With a smile in her voice, Kristen replied, "So says the woman getting regular sex from one of the hottest guys on the planet."

Victoria stopped simmering. "I can't deny that." She turned to Teresa. "So how did sex in the elevator with the perfect stranger happen? Did you want to tell us about that?"

Teresa recognized Victoria's softer producer tone, the one used to coax stories from her show subjects for use on film. But even though she was mostly mortified, the worst was out. And she really did want to talk about it. She wasn't ready to provide the details of the sex itself, but while they ate the rest of their delectable breakfast, she walked them through the encounter. From both bored and crazed by her life, to seeing this attractive guy on the showroom floor, and her spontaneous suggestion when the elevator stopped, to racing away when the doors opened, she told the rest of the story.

"In some ways I wish I could put a name to his face." She shrugged and reached for a piece of toast. "I guess it doesn't matter, though, since I'll never see him again."

CHAPTER NINE

The soundtrack to *Honeymoon in Vegas* was playing when Gabe and Adam walked into the gym. Adam snorted as "Devil in Disguise" started up; not only was it their friend Nick's self-described anthem, but it suited the irony of the place. Simply called "The Ring," the gym was heavy on all forms of ring fighting and light on Zumba. So light, most of the patrons might think Zumba was a cocktail instead of a form of exercise. Its owner, Benny Burtuth, also had a sense of humor, and often played music no one in their right mind would match with boxers and cage fighters.

Gabe had first walked into the place as a cocky twenty-year-old Brooklyn transplant. And walked out with a split lip, ringing ears and a limp that lingered for days. But he'd also returned, eventually earning the respect of Benny and the other guys, if for nothing else than dumbass determination. The workouts kept him fit, the fighters kept his perspective in check, and sometimes he could talk his friends into joining him. This month, Adam, a professor of archaeology at NYU, agreed he needed more than a jog around Washington Square Park.

They nodded at a few of the guys, stowed their gym bags, and sat on a long bench in front of the lockers to wrap their hands. Gabe flexed the fingers of his right hand and slipped the loop at one end of the wrap over his thumb.

Doing the same, Adam asked, "How's the cooking show gig?"

"Hasn't started filming yet, so it's all prep." He straightened a wrinkle between his thumb and forefinger in the wrap, then tilted his head toward the lockers. "I just got the contestants' bios and was going to review them after this. You good for coffee?"

Adam nodded, frowning at his hand. "I never get this shit right."

Gabe clapped him on the back. "Too cerebral, my friend."

"Pot, kettle, black," Adam replied, undoing the wrap and starting over.

"Yeah, but I stay away from scholarly journals on archaeobotany of the Old World and the effects of cultivation on seed germination."

"You're ruining my rakish rep here. Indiana Jones never had to defend scientific journals." He gave Gabe a light shove.

"Too busy fighting off snakes." Gabe shoved back and went to work on his other hand.

He and Adam had known each other since they were kids, but their friendship took awhile to develop. Adam's family lived around the corner from Gabe's, and their moms had attended the same quilting group, gotten pregnant at the same time, and assumed their little darlings would be lifelong best friends from day one. Instead, in Gabe's version of the story, Adam cried when set in the crib with Gabe, and according to Adam, Gabe wet himself. It wasn't until fourth grade, after they beat the snot out of each other one day that they started to forge an alliance, with Stephan and Nick filling out the foursome. Neither of their mothers knew the true background of their friendship.

Gabe secured the Velcro end of the cotton at the top of his wrist and stood, flexing and throwing a few punches to test the wrap job. Adam finished pulling the wrap between his index and middle finger, wound it around his wrist and hand and secured it with a grunt of satisfaction. He made some practice jabs toward Gabe, dancing in front of the bench.

"You ready for an ass kicking?"

Gabe laughed. "To kick yours? Yep."

Adam swept an arm toward the door leading to the main room. "Lead on, Macduff."

"You just set yourself up for it, man," Gabe said with a shake of the head.

An hour and a half later, they'd stretched, shadowboxed, spent some practice time on the bags, and beat on each other in the ring. After quick hot showers, they headed for a coffee shop around the corner. Coffees in front of them, Gabe dug out the contestant bios, and Adam stretched his legs in front of him with a groan.

"Next time, we add in jumping rope," Gabe told him, idly flipping through the sheets. "Six sets, alternating fast and slow."

"Talk to me about Cat Woman," Adam said.

"Hmm?" Gabe looked up from the bios. "Talk to me about Tina."

Adam grunted. "Told you. She wants babies, and I don't yet. We split."

Gabe grunted back, but decided to give Adam a break for now. When his friend called after the breakup, he'd already drowned his sorrows and needed help getting home more than he needed to talk, so Gabe hadn't heard the whole story.

"Lily and I went out a couple nights ago," Gabe told Adam. "Matched me lager for lager." And she'd worn a thigh-skimming blazer with nothing underneath. Long, gold chains slipped in and out of its crossed lapels at her cleavage as she shifted closer to tell him about her background: the only Chinese girl in her suburban Baltimore hometown, moved to New York to dance and ended up as a waitress, but put herself through school and fought her way up from secretary to executive at CuisineTV. Renounced her Chinese name, Li Li Wen, and called herself Lila Winter for awhile.

"At some point," she said with a husky laugh, "I looked in the mirror and saw how very Chinese I was. Being ethnic was the rage then, so I compromised and changed Li Li to Lily and took Wen back."

Smiling at the memory of Lily's laugh, Gabe said to Adam, "I like her."

"It's about time." Adam took a long drink of coffee.

"What the hell does that mean?"

"You know, after Shatara and Cindy."

"Never date anyone named Cindy," Gabe said in a warning tone. "The name's deceptive. Every time."

"Yeah, heard it before. And you shut yourself off after Shatara."

Gabe pointed his coffee cup at him. "There was a lot more going on then and you know it." Hannah died not long before his divorce from Shatara.

Adam held up a hand in surrender. "Noted. You kiss her yet?"

"One date, man."

"O-ho." Adam leaned back in his chair with a chuckle. "She

wouldn't let you in. Losing your touch."

She had, in fact, refused to kiss him at the end of their date, and he admitted to noting a lack of warmth in her at times. But those peek-a-boo chains, the long, slow blinks when she stared at him like a cat. She fascinated him. Gabe gave the finger to a laughing Adam and returned to the stack of pages in front of him to signal the end of that topic.

He read the abbreviated bios and names on the cover sheet: professional chefs, private chefs, caterers, even a food distributor. Lynette, Tony, Teresa. Jonas, Rachel, MaryBeth. Karl, Antonio, Chance. Cookie, Ace, Aanjay. He smiled. As a writer, he loved names, assigning personas to them, and vice versa. A person's name could be descriptive or deceptive: Rachel sounded like an All-American girl; Ace, a hotshot with tattoos, and Teresa Steplowski was a short, dumpy pastry chef. Someone who liked to feed you babkas and fritters to fatten you up. At the same time, Aanjay could be blonde and blue-eyed while Antonio might be tall and skinny with glasses. Take his ex-wife for instance. Shatara's name was Hindi for good and industrious. She was neither.

"You're talking to yourself again," Adam told him.

"Names," Gabe replied, pointing to the list.

Even though he wrote academic papers and not novels, Adam was one of the few people who understood Gabe's idiosyncrasies regarding writing, names, and plotting. And how he often ended up thinking too loudly.

"Right." Adam scraped his chair back and grabbed his coffee cup. "Almost out of coffee and that cute girl behind the counter needs to be flirted with."

"Go get 'er," Gabe told him, not even looking up. "Demerits for the crappy grammar, though."

He turned over the condensed bios page and started reading Aanjay Ballal's full bio and "dream restaurant theme." He'd reviewed the majority of the contestants' mostly dull life histories when he flipped the page to Teresa Steplowski.

"Jesus Christ," he said aloud, and clutched at his chest. No one else paid attention, but Adam came at a gallop.

He slid into the chair next to Gabe. "What the hell? You look like you're having a heart attack."

Gabe could only point at the picture of the beautiful African-

American woman with the uptilted eyes and high cheekbones. She had a short afro instead of rows of thin braids, but he'd recognize her anywhere.

"Jesus Christ," he repeated, panting. "Teresa Steplowski."

"A stroke, then." Adam gripped Gabe's upper arm. "Do you know what day it is?"

"The day I tell you a story you're not going to believe." Gabe pulled from Adam's tight grasp, downed his coffee, took a couple deep breaths and added, "I need to make a phone call first." He pawed through the papers until he found the cover sheet from the Production Assistant, Katie Rand. He tapped in her number and waited, crunching his napkin in one hand while the phone rang.

"Hidey-ho, PA Katie here. Who's this?"

If he hadn't been so gobsmacked, he'd have smiled at her words and cheerful tone. "Gabe De Luca," he told her. "Listen—"

"Yeah, you're the blogger-slash-writer guy. Love your stuff, but your blog needs a little updating. I know this great web designer, she's my partner, actually, and we're having a baby soon, so you know, money's a big issue right now, but I promise she's a pro—"

"Yeah, Katie, sorry," he interrupted, "but I was reviewing the bios and I know one of the contestants. Conflict of interest?"

Adam raised an eyebrow. Gabe ignored him.

"Nope. It's not a newspaper, so no need for neutrality. We just ask that you watch any overt bias. It would be a problem if you were a judge."

A judge. Christ. Lily Wen. He shook his head; he'd deal with that later.

"Any chance you've got contact information for Teresa Steplowski?"

Adam glanced at the bio sheet Gabe had a possessive hand on, and raised his eyebrow higher.

"Sorry, no can do, can't give out any personal information beyond what's in the bios. But if you know her, can't you just—"

"No problem," Gabe said. "I appreciate the information."

"Any time. See you on the set!"

Gabe hung up and finally faced Adam, who grinned at him. "I can't *wait* to hear *this*."

CHAPTER TEN

The day before her flight to New York, Teresa showed up unannounced at her parents' to inform them and Mama Step she'd voluntarily entered a cooking show contest. Despite the awful dinner a few months ago and wondering if they'd consider her the family disappointment forever, Teresa knew she needed to tell them her plans. Her family might not understand her, but she wasn't ready to abandon them yet, and she would never leave Mama Step.

She wanted to snuggle with Mama Step in her chair, holding tight to her grandmother's hand. Instead, she sat upright on the couch next to her mother, listening to a ten-minute lecture on how her decisions were destroying her life and having disastrous consequences on her "impressionable" younger sister.

When her mother finally took a breath, Teresa charged in, her heart pounding hard. "I love you guys," she said in a shaky voice, "but I don't agree. It's my life to ruin, but it's also my success. I need to do this, so I'm doing it." She stood, having delivered her well-practiced speech, and not wanting to invite any more discussion. Her legs felt wobbly. "I wanted you to know. I'm leaving tomorrow."

Mama Step stood with her. "You need anything, baby?"

Teresa shook her head, biting hard on her lower lip. She hadn't realized how much she needed to hear those words. She hugged her grandmother and said, "Just your support."

"Done." Mama Step squeezed Teresa's forearms. "You need any recipes, you let me know. Now you go win that thing and don't worry about anything else."

Teresa walked out of the house without another word to her parents.

The next morning Kristen woke at 3:00 a.m. to see her off and held her so tight Teresa couldn't breathe. Kristen's tears wet Teresa's jacket, and her sobs set off Daisy, who turned purple in the face, her high-pitched screams causing dogs in the neighborhood to howl in response.

As Teresa disembarked at JFK, her ears still rang from the sobs and cries. Or maybe it was her guilt over leaving a new single mother with all the responsibility for the flat. While Kristen was quite capable, Teresa had seen the two of them developing into a little team. At least Frog seemed to like Kristen's friend, Indica, who was sub-letting.

Still, as Teresa wound her way to the arrivals level and waited at the luggage carousel, the guilt and sadness faded and a kernel of excitement joined the nugget of fear in her stomach. This could be such an adventure.

Pulling her luggage along, she rounded the corner of Central Diner toward the Information Center and saw two cameramen and three other people grouped together. She took a deep breath, held it in for three counts as Kristen had taught her to do, then let it out, and strode closer, head high. A very tall, pale man stood close to a chubby woman with long blonde braids, both clutching the handles of their suitcases as they listened intently to a beautiful Asian woman, bangs in her eyes, wearing…Teresa blinked, trying not to stare.

Yes, the woman wore a black catsuit with a high neck, three-quarter sleeves, platform heels, and a red belt. And she looked neither dorky nor stuck in the '90s. Teresa thought she looked fantastic.

Teresa paused and quickly reviewed her own hair and outfit: braids pulled back from her face, black dolman sweater, black and white striped wide-legged pants, and the charcoal military-inspired pea coat that Kristen had cried on that morning. She'd worn fuzzy boots on the flight, but changed into suede booties at landing, and was glad she did when the Asian woman turned and spotted her. She looked nothing like Victoria, being pale and slim with straight black hair, but her confidence reminded Teresa so much of her best friend, her heart twinged a little from homesickness.

"Lily Wen, CuisineTV," the woman said, in a clear, firm voice, smiling when the camera turned to her. She shook Teresa's hand.

"Welcome to New York."

"Teresa Step—" Something caught in her throat, and she cleared it before continuing. "Teresa Steplowski, thank you." She remembered to smile for the camera, too, and straightened her posture. "I'm happy to be here."

But Lily Wen had already turned back to the other contestants. "We're waiting for one more person, and then we'll be on our way." That hint of a smile made a brief appearance, then her face turned unreadable, if still pleasant.

The chubby woman with long braids beamed at Teresa, grabbed her around the waist in a bear hug, and shook her back and forth. "It's so lovely to meet you," she crowed. "I'm Lynette, and this is Tony." She released Teresa and patted at the tall man with glasses and a short-sleeved madras shirt.

Teresa shook his hand. "Nice to meet you. Teresa Steplowski."

"Where are you from, Teresa?" Tony asked. He had a surprisingly high-pitched voice for such a tall man, but it lightened his somber appearance.

"San Francisco," she replied with a smile.

Lynette clapped her hands together and crowed again. "Oh, I love San Francisco. Don't you go down to Fisherman's Wharf just all the time?"

"Ahh...well, not so much," Teresa replied; Fisherman's Wharf could be overrun with tourists. "So where are you all from?"

"Near Chicago," he said. "A small suburb no one's ever heard of."

"Oh? I have a friend from—"

"I'm here! I'm here!"

They all turned as a tall, willowy blonde raced toward them on heels higher than Lily Wen's. Her long wavy hair blew back during her run and settled perfectly around her face as she stopped in front of them.

Teresa tried not to hate her on the spot.

The cameramen turned to face the blonde, who executed a perfect pageant wave. "Hey, y'all, sorry I'm so late, my flight was delayed and they lost my luggage." She flung her hands out and produced a toothy smile. "But what are you going to do? Did I miss anything?"

Teresa pressed her lips together and tried to look approving and open-minded.

Lynette barreled into the newcomer. The tall blonde looked

slightly startled, rocking back on her heels from the greeting, but recovered admirably, hugged Lynette back, and casually flipped her hair over one shoulder.

Lily Wen clapped her hands once and everyone immediately turned to her except the blonde, who first gave the cameras another pageant contestant smile.

"Lynette, Tony, Teresa, welcome." She glanced at the newcomer, then down at a clipboard someone handed her. "And you must be Mary Beth."

"It's pronounced Mare-eh-beth. Three syllables, two names, one word."

"Yes," Lily said in a flat tone and made a mark on a piece of paper, then handed the clipboard back without looking at the assistant. She looked at each contestant in turn."I'm Lily Wen, CEO of CuisineTV, and I'll be escorting you this afternoon to meet the other challengers. You will all be learning a lot about each other in the next few weeks, both personally and professionally. My mother is Chinese, my father Irish, and I grew up in a suburb of Baltimore. I would rather have a big steak with a side of crispy potatoes and a good beer than Chinese food. I'm more of a red-blooded American girl than I look." She turned to the side. "Now, Lynette, tell us something surprising about yourself and a favorite food."

"Oh!" Lynette clasped her hands together and held them to her chest. "My name's Lynette Atkinson, I'm a caterer in Madison, Wisconsin, I have four children, three girls and a boy, Jessica, Hannah, Lila, and—"

"And what would surprise us about you, Lynette?" Lily asked.

"Oh, well, I got this tattoo last year of my cat…" She turned around and hooked her thumbs in the elastic of her stretch pants.

Everyone gave a collective "whoa!" and took a step back, including the cameramen.

Lily Wen brushed her bangs out of her eyes and said, "In regard to yourself and food, please, Lynette."

Completely unashamed, Lynette straightened, tugging her pants up, and turned back to the group. "I hate cilantro, I suppose."

Lily Wen blinked a few times, then turned to Tony. "And you, Tony?"

"I'm Tony O'Meara," he said in his high voice, glancing often at his feet and avoiding eye contact. "I'm from a suburb in Chicago called McCook. My grandparents were Irish immigrants. I don't hate potatoes," he said, glancing shyly at Lily Wen and pushing up his glasses, "but, um, I've been able to make an amazing chocolate soufflé since I was seven."

A dash of warmth for him rushed through Teresa; he seemed too kind and gentle to be in this competition. At the same time, she was furiously searching for her own "surprising" item. She wasn't clear on the point of this exercise, but had seen enough competition reality shows to know everything had a point.

Lily Wen glanced between Teresa and MaryBeth, and Teresa could swear she let out a sigh. "And MaryBeth? What about you?"

"I am a 'what you see is what you get' kind of gal," she beamed, tossing her hair over one shoulder. "Beauty queen, Miss Texas pageant winner, and personal chef to some of Hollywood's elite. I make an amazing soufflé as well." She held a hand out toward Tony, then to Lynette. "And I'd have to say, Lynette, you'd love my cilantro lime couscous with radish…"

While the others all stared, mesmerized by MaryBeth's speech, Teresa peeked at Lily Wen, and saw her do a quick eye roll. Before Teresa could look away, Lily caught her watching. Her heart leaping, Teresa smiled to show her solidarity, but Lily's expression went completely blank.

"So the unexpected thing about you, MaryBeth, is that you can make foods that change people's opinions about them for the better?"

MaryBeth flashed her supremely white teeth. "Why, yes, Lily, I would say that my cooking skills are such that I can make anyone a fan of an unpopular dish."

Lily Wen nodded at MaryBeth. "Wonderful." She glanced at the papers on her clipboard, made a mark and said, "Oh. And Teresa," without looking up.

Teresa's mouth went dry and she completely forgot her planned speech. She'd considered the bi-racial angle—Polish grandfather, black grandmother—as Lily Wen had done, but since Tony's attempt at using his Irish background fell flat, she scrapped that idea.

Then she remembered a few nights earlier, side by side with Kristen, searing a rib-eye steak for herself while the new mom whipped up a big batch of vegan mac-and-cheese. Kristen talked through each step as if to convince Teresa that this approach was preferable. Teresa hadn't been convinced, but she appreciated passion in cooking. She also flashed on one of her interviews with a producer, who told her she'd have to refine her restaurant's theme—classic comfort food—before the first challenge.

She cleared her throat and said, "The trend right now is for lean, spare portions, and comfort food is out. But I grew up with a big family, and some of my best memories are of big meals around the dining table, with seconds, and even thirds." This was true, as she'd loved to eat her grandmother's Polish treats. No one here needed to know any more details about her family's personal dynamics. "I believe you can enjoy comfort food, but it can also be healthy."

Lily stared at her as if expecting more.

A dish! She hadn't mentioned a dish. "And, so, um…I can make an amazing vegan mac-and-cheese."

Lily watched her for one more beat before turning away. "Thank you, everyone," she said. "We'll be heading out in a moment. Your luggage will be forwarded for you. You will be going directly to Studio A, where you will meet the remainder of the contestants, and face your first challenge."

Lynette, Tony and MaryBeth all made surprised noises at this, which Lily Wen ignored. She gestured for everyone to follow, which they did, the cameramen and assistants in silence, the contestants speculating on the challenge.

Teresa's stomach ached. She should have known to expect anything, but her experience with the world of reality TV production had made her overconfident and she hadn't thought everything through. She knew more about documentary type shows than contests.

On the way to Manhattan, Lynette chatted happily, playing with her long blond braids and throwing out idea after idea about the challenge. Tony nodded at each one, saying it was a possibility, but maybe there would be an added twist.

MaryBeth smiled at everything, but she disagreed. Oh, no, y'all, it couldn't be *that* complicated or *that* simple.

Teresa tried to look interested for the camera, but couldn't think of anything smart or coherent enough to add to the discussion.

What had she gotten herself into?

CHAPTER ELEVEN

Gabe paced the cavernous room of CuisineTV's test kitchens. He ran his hands through his hair, then brushed his palms along his thighs. Christ, he was nervous, like some teenage kid before a blind date.

Cameramen, Production Assistants, sound guys and other technicians bustled around finalizing the equipment set up. He edged around the crews to a small table in the corner. He could use a few swings at the punching bag right now, but writing would have to suffice for a distraction until the contestants showed up. He jotted a few sentences about the gleaming stoves, stainless countertops and lines of refrigerators.

Down the middle of the room, two parallel rows of counters held eight stations each with stovetop, oven, sink, cutting board, pots, pans and other implements. At the far end stood four refrigerators and shelving units with a variety of fruits, vegetables, nuts, grains, spices, condiments, and sauces.

After he started repeating descriptions of the gleaming appliances, he shut the notebook with a snap and reached for his messenger bag. He glanced around the room like a teenager hiding his copy of Playboy before sliding out the manila envelope with the contestants' biographies. He'd looked at Teresa's an embarrassing number of times. Now, he spread all the pages out in front of him—an even number of six men and six women.

A young woman with a fleece vest and large fanny pack, her ponytail pulled through the back of a Yankees cap stopped at the table and said, "Anything I can get you, Mr. De Luca?"

"It's Gabe." He shook her hand. "And I'm good, thanks."

"Katie. Everyone calls me PA Katie," she added, flashing a dimple.

PA, short for Production Assistant. Cute, he thought. Both the girl and the nickname.

"Thanks for your help the other day. I may take you up on your offer of the website update." He gestured toward her cap. "Too bad about Detroit."

She shook her head. "One, eight. Painful. But we'll get 'em next time." She gave him a wave and pulled out a walkie-talkie as she drifted into the crowd.

Gabe reviewed the contestants' head shots; he knew them by heart, but he needed another diversion. Multiply-pierced Ace fit his name, as did Antonio, with his suave good looks. Looking at her meaty hands crossed over her chest and spiked blue hair, he expected Cookie could kick his ass. MaryBeth's bleached teeth and shiny mane were more suited for *America's Next Top Model*. Aanjay had a beautiful exotic appearance, and Rachel exuded All-American sweetness with her cute brunette bob and pert nose.

Lynette and Tony seemed like a nice couple down on the farm, while Jonas reminded him of a Cosby kid, Karl like an Oktoberfest brewmeister, and Chance could be Gabe's kid brother. In fact, Chance barely looked old enough to be on the show.

That left Teresa Steplowski. If he hadn't had mind-blowing sex with her in an elevator, his persona for Ms. Steplowski would be as straightforward as the others. He remembered first seeing her name in the café with Adam, when he'd thought she sounded like a short, round pastry chef. He laughed out loud at that, sending an apologetic wave to the crew members that glanced over at his outburst.

Once he'd learned her name and hometown, he typed her name into Google every other day, but never hit Search. As far as he knew, she had no idea he worked for *Tasty Dish*; it seemed an unfair advantage that he even had knowledge of her contestant status. And her name. Or maybe she was the lucky one. Knowing he'd see her again in a few minutes had his guts tangled in knots.

"The teams should be here within the next few minutes," Katie said, startling him out of his reverie. "I'll just need to scoot you out of the way behind the cameras."

Gabe gathered his materials and he and Katie positioned

themselves between two stationary cameras to watch the doorway across the room. The show's host, Eric Wintersteen, entered first. A cameraman followed him, and then three other men and two women, all bunched together as they walked into the room. They stood in a clump, talking with the cameramen off to the side, then turned as a group to Eric, asked him a few questions that he answered with either a nod or shake of the head, then returned to their conference.

Katie leaned close to him and whispered, "Producers, their assistants and the director."

Gabe nodded, indifferent to this information; his mind replayed Teresa tossing her skirt over one arm, her thigh sliding against his right before he entered her. He blew out a breath and brushed his forearm over his brow.

Finally, one of the men, balding and with a slight paunch straining his blue oxford shirt, clapped his hands together once, said, "We're golden!" loud enough that it carried across the room, and positioned himself near Katie and Gabe, arms crossed.

Katie's walkie-talkie crackled, she spoke into it, and turned to the plump man. "They're on their way, Dan." She mouthed to Gabe, "Director."

He nodded his thanks for the information, still distracted, and crossed his arms over his chest, clenching and unclenching his hands.

Dan clapped once and boomed out, "Okay, people, they're on their way. Cameras A and B," he said, pointing to the stationary units that covered the row of stoves across the middle of the room, "you'll start to roll as soon as they come in. C and D." This time he pointed to the men waiting nearby with cameras balanced on their shoulders. "You'll take over for the remotes once our people are in the room. Everyone else? *Shut the hell up!*"

There was some last minute shuffling as lights were positioned, cables given a final taping down and cleaning supplies cleared out of the way. As things settled, Gabe heard voices in the corridor.

A cameraman backed into the room, filming a group of four people led by Joel Klein, the executive producer of the show. Gabe had met him at the same meeting where he'd met Lily Wen.

To cool down his fervor, Gabe mentally named the first contestants: Ace, tattooed and pierced; Jonas, a clean-cut African-American in a brightly patterned sweater. The third was Karl, a food distributor, and the fourth Antonio, a caterer to New York's wealthy and celebrities. In black slacks and shirt with a shiny black tie, Antonio was the only calm one, if his casual glance around the room was any indication.

The other three clustered together, arms crossed tight over their middles, eyes darting in frantic passes around the room. Gabe jotted quick notes on the backs of their bios.

Soon after they entered, another group of four came in, this time with Darren Michaels, star of *Light My Fire*. These were Chance, the one who looked too young to be here; blue-haired Cookie; Aanjay, elegant in traditional Indian dress; and All-American Rachel. Gabe added more notes to his pages, the tension in his body coursing from fingers to toes.

The third and final group arrived next, led by Lily Wen wearing tight black pants, a long gray sweater that reached to her thighs and clung as she moved, and high, high boots. Her style fascinated him, but she couldn't keep his attention today. He knew Teresa Steplowski was close, and his body strained forward, needing her appearance. He craned his neck, watching them enter, fingers tapping against his clipboard.

Lynette, the Midwest caterer; generic blonde beauty MaryBeth; very tall Tony; and the mysterious Teresa Steplowski, who seemed to be hiding behind Tony.

Gabe took a step to the right for a clearer view, and his breath caught.

His heart gave a mighty thump and he took a swaying step back, clutching his ballpoint pen so hard that it bent in half. All the memories of that brief time in the elevator crashed into his body.

"Jesus Christ," he said so loud that Katie gaped at him and Dan the director snarled in his direction.

At the other end of the room, Teresa caught sight of him and shrieked.

ALREADY UNSTEADY AND anxious about the first test, when Teresa spotted someone with feathered blonde hair across the room, a wheezy little scream escaped and she clapped a hand over her mouth. The host stopped talking and everyone turned her way.

"Sorry," she muttered behind her fingers.

"As I was saying," Eric continued, "we'll have you go back out to the corridor, you'll be assigned a station number, and we'll film you coming in. You go to your stations and I'll announce the rules of the challenge. Then..."

Teresa peeked around Tony at the man standing near Camera One. He stared at her.

It couldn't be.

She blinked a few times, knowing she was staring back, but needed to be absolutely sure it was her Elevator Man.

It *couldn't* be. What were the odds? Maybe it was someone who resembled him. In a freakish, doppelganger way. She had to admit the look-alike presented a yummy twin in gray slacks, black boots, and a dark green pullover with the sleeves pushed up. She tried to focus on Eric again but Mr. Doppelganger quirked up a corner of his mouth and lifted the fingers of one hand in an abbreviated wave. He flattened them so quickly against the clipboard held to his chest that if she hadn't been staring at him so intently, she'd have missed it. So, he could still be an especially flirty doppelganger.

She brushed her braids over one shoulder, about to wave back, when the other contestants turned en masse, pushing her toward the doorway. She let them, frantically trying to remember what Eric had said. Right. They'd be filmed coming back into the room as if it were their first entrance. She should have recognized the classic reality TV time shuffle. And she *would* have if Mr. Doppelganger hadn't distracted her.

She glanced at him before going out the door. Still watching her, he raised a hand and brushed it through his hair until the layers feathered back around his face. Exactly the way she'd described to Victoria and Kristen.

Teresa covered her mouth again to keep from shrieking. She hadn't told them she'd watched him make that gesture after buttoning up his shirt. After they'd had sex in the elevator.

She thought she might throw up.

She barely registered anything around her as everyone shuffled out to the corridor, got their assignments, then walked back in while being filmed, pretending they'd just showed up. Eric gathered them in a semicircle near the judging table for a special announcement. One of the executive producers of the show introduced himself, welcomed them all, and reminded them of the grand prize.

"What you all don't know," he said with what seemed like forced cheer, "is that the restaurant you'll win will be a..." He paused for dramatic effect. "A pop-up."

A variety of responses erupted from the other contestants, excited, but also annoyed. A far as Teresa's mindset was concerned, the executive producer might as well have spoken in Farsi. What was he even saying? She let someone shuffle her to the station, but to her horror, her spot was right between the two stationary cameras, facing *him*.

She kept brushing her palms over the apron she'd been given. She stared down at it. When had she gotten the apron? She vaguely remembered someone handing it to her, but she drew a complete blank as to when that happened or how she'd even gotten it tied around her neck or waist.

She wanted to rush over there, hear his voice, feel his lips on her collarbone to confirm it really was *him*. But she didn't need all that to be certain, did she? She'd spent maybe fifteen minutes in his presence, but she'd studied him well. She knew his deep brown eyes, that long hair framing his cheekbones, the fine blond hairs on his arms, the wide sturdy fingers that had swept over her skin, cupped her breasts, and brushed across her peaked nipples, shooting sparks of desire through her.

She knew that wide mouth, the way the upper lip had a slight cupid's bow, and the bottom a nice curve that made her want to run her tongue along its edge. It was a strong, generous mouth, as his kisses had been, whether against her own lips or trailing down her neck. She even knew his breath, as it increased in tempo with hers, growing more ragged as he pulled her tight to him before he came.

"All right, everyone!" a voice boomed around the room, and Teresa gasped, stunned back to the present. "You have sixty minutes to create your dishes. Starting…now!"

Teresa stood immobile. What? *What?! Oh God, oh God,* she thought, pushing away from the counter as everything exploded around her and her fellow contestants ran toward the far end of the room. She ended up in the back of the pack, her heart smacking around in her chest as she frantically tried to recall Eric's instructions.

Everyone else was grabbing what they could from the pantry and refrigerators, shoving vegetables and grains and meats into bowls and pans they'd gotten from the stations. Teresa had neither bowl nor pan, nor did she know what to grab. She vaguely remembered Eric talking about favorite dishes, but her panicked mind kept grasping at the sights and sounds around her rather than letting her ease back

70

into a few minutes ago to retrace what she'd heard.

MaryBeth bumped into her, muttering, "Steak with cilantro lime couscous," and something clicked in Teresa's head: Eric had said they should make their best version of the surprise dish they'd talked about with their hosts.

Oh no, what had she said?

Lily Wen had talked about beer and a good steak.

And Teresa? On her first day of the contest that could forever alter her life, she had talked about vegan mac-and-cheese.

CHAPTER TWELVE

When Teresa glanced up from dicing onions and saw Lily Wen whispering in Elevator Man's ear, her hand jerked and she neatly sliced her forefinger. She hissed in a breath as the onion juice seared into the cut, then set her knife down and raced back to the first aid station at the far end of the room, cursing her carelessness and men in general.

She didn't have time to worry about whoever he might be, or Lily Wen. Nor did she have time to get a cut bandaged. She seriously doubted her ability to make this a tasty dish, and might not even finish it, but she did know that if she dripped blood into her food, none of that would matter because no one would eat it.

She jittered one foot around while the tech cleaned her finger, making it burn even more, then wound a bandage around it.

"If you'd stop fussing, I could do this faster and get you back out there," he griped, but she couldn't obey his order.

She had too much riding on this and it had all gone very weird, very quickly.

The first aid tech yanked a rubber glove over her hand, and Teresa didn't wait for his all-clear to streak back to her station, narrowly avoiding a crash with MaryBeth, who flipped her hair forward and snarled something nasty at Teresa, hiding it from the cameras.

Teresa grabbed a spoon, scooped out a piece of elbow macaroni, blew on it, and burned her tongue anyway as she bit into it to test the texture.

Damn. Close to mushy. She thunked a colander into the sink,

grabbed the pot handles and dumped the noodles in, turning her head away before her face got steamed like a lobster.

Vegan-freakin'-mac-and-cheese. What had she been thinking? That would teach her to over-think and try to impress the CuisineTV staff.

Wait. Who was Lily Wen anyway? Why would the show's producers care that the group of people Lily had met at the airport make dishes that would impress Lily?

Teresa almost dropped the colander as she shook it over the sink to drain the last of the water. Oh God, Lily Wen was a judge. How had she not seen that before?

Teresa ran cold water over the noodles to stop them cooking, then risked a glance at...at...ugh, whatever the hell his name was. The guy who'd thoroughly disrupted her life twice now.

He wasn't where he'd been. Lily Wen, who had somehow changed clothes between the airport and studio, had dragged him back to one corner behind the cameras. Okay. Teresa didn't really know that Lily Wen had dragged him there, but she couldn't imagine her gentle Elevator Man willingly going anywhere with that wench. So maybe it wasn't him.

She rolled her eyes. Yeah, right.

A flurry of activity continued around her from her fellow contestants and the mobile cameramen, but as she stared into the corner, all of Teresa's senses narrowed down to focus on one thing: Lily Wen running a dark purple nail down from Elevator Man's collarbone and under the V of his sweater, where she popped the top button of his shirt.

Teresa couldn't see the little strumpet's face, but she was sure EM flushed, and took a step back. He smiled and maybe shook a finger at Lily—again, Teresa couldn't tell since Lily's body partially blocked her view—then redid the button and gestured with his head toward the contestants.

He caught Teresa staring and Teresa froze like a rabbit, unable to move even when Lily Wen turned to find the subject of his attention.

Someone bumped Teresa from behind and hissed, "Your tofu's burning."

Lily Wen's eyes narrowed at Teresa before the sights, smells and sounds of the rest of the room rushed back and she said, "Oh, shit!" very loudly before grabbing a pot holder and moving the tofu pan to a cold burner.

As she pulled out another cake of tofu and wrapped it in a dishtowel to absorb the moisture before pressing it between two plates, Teresa tried to channel Kristen and summon a few mantras.

I can do this.

I'm a good cook.

I'm a great *cook.*

None of this matters in the wider scheme of things.

But what was the wider scheme of things? Why in the world would the "scheme of things" have her seduce a stranger, land a coveted spot on a TV show, then be faced with said stranger only to find him involved with a judge in the contest? A judge she now had to impress with a vegan dish that might taste like tofu and mushy noodles.

That wasn't karma. That was screwed up.

Was she being punished? For not taking Cort seriously? For not taking the time to think all of this through and running away from everything, believing the show would solve her problems?

Probably that one.

But in the meantime, she was here, and she'd be damned if she would present anything less than spectacular to the judges. While she waited for the tofu block to drain, she prepped her faux cheese sauce.

Eric's voice boomed through the room. "Half an hour, chefs. You've got exactly thirty minutes remaining."

Teresa ran back to the pantry, praying for nutritional yeast, and dodged Lynette, to whom she owed a big debt of gratitude. Lynette had warned her about the burning tofu. At the spice racks, she bobbed and weaved, searching for the yeast. In desperation, she called out, "Does anyone have the nutritional yeast?" then immediately wanted to clap a hand over her mouth and take it back.

Who else would be using nutritional yeast, and if so, why would they help by giving it to her? Certainly no one else was making a vegan dish. The scent of grilled meat flowed throughout the room, making her mouth water.

How was she going to compete with a nice, juicy, medium-rare steak like Lily's Wen's favorite? And how was she going to impress Lily Wen after having caught her not once, but twice, at minor indiscretions. First she saw her rolling her eyes at MaryBeth's speech at the airport, and then flirting with…damn it, she wished she knew his name.

She poured marinade in a bag and added the cubed tofu to let it marinate for as long as possible before having to toss it on the grill. Again. She checked her "cheese" sauce—heated and blended potatoes, carrots and onions, and some spices—gave it a few stirs, and peeked into the corner where she'd seen Lily Wen and—

Well, she still didn't know his name, but that would change soon. And she supposed she couldn't call him "her" Elevator Man anymore. Whoever he was, he had returned to his former spot between the stationary cameras, and Lily Wen had disappeared.

He stood with that clipboard in one hand, staring at her. He caught her peeking at him and gave her a smile, then ducked his head. He actually looked abashed, although she wondered if that was conjecture on her part.

She couldn't help smiling back, ducking her own head in return. Her heart hammering hard, drowning out the other sounds around her, she decided she was going to make the best vegan mac-and-cheese with fake meat ever.

GABE COULDN'T TAKE his eyes off Teresa, the woman who had seduced him in an elevator almost four months ago. Situations like this didn't happen in real life. But then, having sex with a beautiful stranger rarely happened in real life, either, so what the hell?

Teresa was more beautiful than he remembered: taller, rounder in the hip, but still lean and toned, her skin that mouthwatering sautéed butterscotch color.

Once she lost the dazed look after Eric called "go," he saw panic take its place, then she gathered herself and the expression evolved into focus. Intensity.

Gabe's breath caught. Teresa Steplowski cooking looked a lot like Teresa Steplowski fucking him in an elevator. Passionate, intense, completely lost in the rhythm and heat.

Christ. He tugged at the neck of his sweater. Lily Wen and her purple fingernails on his chest had nothing on Teresa's intensity, but a crazy-stupid sense of betrayal plagued him at that thought. Whether he'd betrayed Teresa Steplowski with Lily Wen, or the other way around, he didn't know. Technically, Teresa had been there first, but he couldn't even say he knew the woman, beyond what he'd invented in his head.

He looked at Teresa's bio again while the other contestants were brought up one by one to present their dishes to the judges.

Born and raised in a suburb of San Francisco, twenty-eight years old, Polish grandfather, mother's family from Martinique, one of eight children, attended the San Francisco Culinary Academy, and worked as sous chef and server for Golden Gate Catering, with a burning desire to own her own restaurant and share her culinary loves with the world.

It explained a few things, such as her gorgeous skin and the shape of her eyes, and even why she was here. But it didn't tell him her favorite music, if she loved dogs, or why she had seduced him.

He ran a hand through his hair and sat next to Katie. This wasn't getting him anywhere. He wouldn't know anything until he could talk to her.

The judges were currently tasting Antonio's signature dish: wild boar with fig sauce. Joel Klein declared it wonderful, but perhaps a touch dry. Celebrity chef Darren Michaels disagreed. His was *very* dry and he wished Antonio had added a touch of vinegar to cut the sweetness of the figs. Lily Wen complimented his skills in combining ingredients, marrying the sweet with the spicy, but he'd overcooked the boar and added a little too much pepper.

Antonio stood straighter. "My clients love this dish, especially with the extra pepper, which provides bite without too much of the spice. I never have any complaints." He paused, and when none of the judges responded, he added, "Ever."

Lily Wen tilted her head to one side, and her long hair brushed against her shoulder. "You've never had one complaint about your food from any of your clients? In your entire history of cooking?"

Antonio shuffled, crossing his arms over his chest. "Not *never* never, no."

Lily Wen straightened, looking directly at Antonio without blinking. "Chef Antonio, our job here is to discover if you have the talent, skill, drive and business acumen to run a successful restaurant. To accomplish that, we will test you." She turned to address the other contestants. "All of you. And push you to your limits. No one is perfect here, and it is up to us to bring out your best and discover what areas need improvement, so you can build on those things."

Antonio waited, as if expecting more.

"Thank you, Antonio," Lily Wen finally said, in a clear dismissal.

"Tough crowd," Gabe murmured.

Katie, bent over her clipboard and making copious notes on a form printed on blue paper, nodded. "And it's only going to get tougher," she said, without looking up.

Gabe nodded. She was right. This might make for entertaining television, but everyone here took it very seriously.

He watched Lily Wen brush her hair back over her shoulder. And how seriously did Lily take not only this show, but everything else in her life? He hadn't missed the resolute expression on Lily's face after she'd invited him to her place tonight, then caught him staring at Teresa. But was her determination focused on him, or Teresa?

Lily called on Cookie, who marched to the judge's table and stood at parade rest, feet spread and hands clasped behind her back. Lily took delicate bites of Cookie's chocolate tart with crème anglaise, giving Cookie the occasional unreadable glance. Gabe liked Lily's nerve, appreciated that she could stand up for herself and took shit from no one, but he wondered if that attribute dominated her personality, to the detriment of others.

Gabe turned to find Teresa. She stood across the room, facing the judges in a line with her fellow contestants, but had her head turned slightly toward him. She had taken the band from around her hair and the braids hung about her face and around her shoulders. She faced him fully, and gave him a slight nod, the yearning on her face enough to make him shift forward in his chair, ready to answer it. He held himself back from rushing to her side, and instead returned her nod.

Lily excused Cookie and it was Teresa's turn.

CHAPTER THIRTEEN

Teresa stood tall while production assistants set individual servings of her dish in front of the judges. Lily Wen took a miniscule bite, made a mark on a card next to her plate, and looked up at Teresa. They locked eyes, and Teresa wondered what the judge was thinking, and if you had to be born with the ability to produce such a deadpan expression.

Eric gestured at the plates. "So, Teresa, what was your challenge?"

Teresa smiled at Eric, recalled the many episodes of cooking shows she'd watched, then turned to the judges. "Today I've made for you a vegan version of a traditional comfort food: vegan mac-and-cheese, with a side of grilled tofu. I believe you should be able to offer your clients a wide variety of foods in a range of…"

Lily Wen put her fork down with a loud clank against the dish and stared at Teresa, suggesting she would go no further until Teresa finished her sentence. Even as Teresa thought, *What a bitch*, she couldn't think what else to say.

"In a range of, um, health options," Teresa continued lamely.

"And is your restaurant theme going to be vegan, then?" Lily Wen asked.

"No." Teresa shook her head.

Lily scooped her fork through the pasta, lifting it up and holding it out for the camera until a fake-cheesy clump fell to the plate with a plop.

"Then I'm wondering why you chose to do a vegan version of this comfort food favorite. As well as add the superfluous side of tofu."

She lowered her fork, waiting.

Teresa looked to the other judges, but they remained silent, awaiting her answer. Teresa licked her lips, pressed them together, then did a side-to-side fidget before stopping to stand still. She clenched her hands tight together behind her back, trying to regain her poise, to summon Victoria's confidence or Kristen's ease. Or both.

She cleared her throat. "As I was saying earlier, I believe it's good customer service to offer your customers…to offer them a variety of healthy choices, vegan options being one of them."

Joel Klein asked, "Would you offer both options in your restaurant, one vegan and one not?"

"Yes," Teresa answered.

"And how do you believe that would be cost effective? What percentage of vegans over non-vegans would you have?" Lily Wen asked. "And would you have enough vegan patrons to make this option profitable?"

Teresa swallowed hard. They'd asked her a ton of questions about her dream restaurant "theme" in the interviews, but she hadn't thought of any of that. "I don't know," she whispered.

Lily Wen gave her a long, slow blink.

"You're here to prove you're capable of owning and operating a restaurant, and we are here to decide which one of you is best suited to that." Lily Wen swept her gaze along the row of contestants. "It would benefit you all to do your research where profit and loss are concerned."

"That said," Darren Michaels added, "you've done a nice job convincing me of this dish. It's creamy, has a nice texture, and is there…" He lifted up a forkful; no clumps plopped back on the plate. "Tomato paste in it?"

"Yes," Teresa whispered again. She cleared her throat and when she spoke this time, her voice came out louder and clearer. "Yes," she repeated. "The acidity of the tomatoes balances out the earthiness of the nutritional yeast, and gives it some tang. The paste contributes to the creamy texture. Then the saltiness of the tamari complements the nutritional yeast."

Eat that, she thought, glaring at Lily Wen.

TERESA WAITED WITH her arms tight around her waist while a friendly PA named Katie removed her mic pack. "No cameras, no need for a mic," Katie said as she pulled up the back of Teresa's sweater and disconnected the transmitter from her waistband. She moved around to Teresa's front, holding the pack out to keep the attached wire from getting tangled. Teresa lifted one arm to facilitate this, but lowered it again as soon as Katie unclipped the tiny microphone from Teresa's collar and pulled it down and out, wrapping it around the pack.

She barely heard Katie chattering about how relaxing it would be to have a simple interview now, no challenge, no one following her with a camera, just sitting back and answering a few questions from a nice guy. Teresa held herself tighter, even pushing her thighs together to keep them from shaking; the more Katie talked about the calm, relaxing interview, the faster her heart sped up.

"Go right in as soon as MaryBeth is done. Would you like something to drink? Tea, soda, water?"

A nice stiff brandy? Teresa wanted to say, but pressed her lips tight and shook her head instead. Katie patted her arm and walked back up the corridor, telling someone through the walkie-talkie that Teresa was up next, and to send Ace down in ten minutes. Katie's footsteps fell away and Teresa glanced up one side of the corridor and then the other. Bare, institutional walls and carpeting, lots of doors, no plaques. She could be anywhere. But she wasn't. She was in the heart of CuisineTV's studios, about to face the stranger she'd had sex with in an elevator four months ago. In her daydreams, she ran into him at a trendy café, he swept her off her feet and they lived happily ever after. She wasn't supposed to actually *see* him again, especially not after completely humiliating herself in the first challenge.

MaryBeth opened the door, her back to Teresa, and said, "Now you don't hesitate to call me if you have any other questions, sugar." Then she strode up the hallway without even glancing at Teresa.

Teresa took a step toward the door, one hand out to either knock or take hold of the knob, then turned on one heel and strode down the corridor, gasping. She couldn't do this. How could she face this man she didn't know, but had had thigh-weakening sex with? She had no idea what to say to him, and she certainly couldn't look him in the eye. At least she didn't know his orgasm face; they'd been pressed too close together for that.

God.

She forced herself to turn back. She had to do this, both for the show and for herself. Besides, it was kind of funny, right? The way life worked? She practiced a few lines in her head: she'd behaved inappropriately, let's be adults about the whole thing, consider the working relationship they had now and keep that to the forefront. Maybe they would even have a laugh over it all, and then move on. They owed each other nothing. They didn't even *know* each other, and had no hold on each other.

It would be *fine.*

She had reached the door again. Her hand drifted toward the knob while she willed her heart to beat normally and her mind to go blank—or to at least let go of the images of that time in the elevator with—

She smiled as her fingers caressed the smooth metal of the knob. Gabe De Luca. Gabe. His sexy name matched the rest of him. Would she have called it out in passion if she'd known it then? No. She made noises rather than words during sex, but...

She whispered it with a small moan to see how it felt. "Gabe."

Her throat and face flushed warm. She liked it; she wanted to try it out in action.

The knob shifted under her fingers and the door slid open. She jerked her hand back when Gabe came into view.

"Gabe," she whispered, before she could stop herself.

One hand on the door, he stepped toward her, and rested the other on the jam, eyes on her the entire time. He stood so close she could have risen up on her toes and kissed him. She remembered him as taller, but he was still quite a few inches taller than she, about five-ten or five-eleven. His eyes had a deeper cast to them, maybe from the green pullover he wore, and his hair brushed the collar of his shirt.

His gaze drifted down to the toes of her suede boots and made a lazy scan up her wide-legged, striped pants and dolman sweater, lingering at her neckline and mouth before stopping at her eyes.

"I didn't think it was possible," he said.

"What?" she asked, her lips tingling from the desire in his gaze.

"You're more beautiful than I remembered."

Her breath caught and shuddered as she forced it out. So many responses flew through her head, from neutral to flip to saucy, her brain stuttered to a stop.

"I searched for you, you know," he told her. "After." His soft smile suggested the memory was more lovely than lascivious to him. "I even finagled a list of attendees from a friend, but..." He shrugged.

Right, no pictures, she thought, but still couldn't speak. He looked so enticing, angled toward her, hands upraised, and close enough that he could swing his arms out and pull her close.

Jetlagged, shocked at finding him here, horrified at the challenge results, and overwhelmed by his scent, she lost all reason and, tipping up on her toes, pressed her palms to Gabe's cheeks and kissed him.

His unfamiliar yet recognizable lips touched hers, triggering a fleeting moment of panic, but then his arms were around her, his hands pressed to her back, squeezing tight, and all fear flew away. His lips parted and she flicked her tongue against his, deepening the kiss. Gabe eased her into the room, shutting the door behind them, and pressed her against the wall. As she caressed his cheeks, the rough and smooth of stubble electrified her palms, her chest absorbed the heat from his, and she reveled in the press of his thigh and biceps, the taste of his mouth, and scent of his skin.

She slid her hands around his neck, sighing when he broke their kiss to press his lips along her jaw and down her neck to her collarbone.

"Gabe," she murmured. A thrill of pleasure at knowing his name, combined with the physical thrill of his body, sent a shiver down her spine.

"Mmm," he moaned at her throat, flicking a tongue along her clavicle. One warm, firm hand swept around her waist to cup her breast and she gasped so loud she barely heard the brisk knock at the door.

Gabe's body stilled, then he pulled her closer, one palm along her lower back, the other still at her breast. His thumb grazed her nipple and she moaned, pressing her mouth to his shoulder.

"Yes," Gabe said in a curt voice.

"About another five minutes with Teresa," Katie's voice chirped, "and I'll bring Ace along."

"Great." He cleared his throat. "Thanks."

Listening to the thud of Katie's shoes as she walked back up the hall, Teresa watched Gabe absently thumb the lock. She stared between their bodies at her toes, missing his hand on her breast, her nipples tingling.

Staring at the door as if Katie still might burst through it, Gabe ran a thumb along his lower lip.

All awkwardness aside, Teresa still wanted to take a nip at that lip.

And that was what had gotten them here, wasn't it? Her inability to keep from throwing herself at him. She eased away from his arm, taking a few steps back.

"I'm sorry." She forced her gaze up to his.

"Don't be." He took a step toward her, then stopped and shoved his hands in his pockets. "I seem incapable of not ravishing you whenever we're within five feet of each other."

"That was going to be my line," she said. "Only you said it much prettier."

He smiled, ducked his head, then shrugged. "Writer. And I've been asking the contestants what they were thinking during the challenge, but..."

No way she was going there, she thought, and couldn't suppress a smile. Without quite knowing why she did it, Teresa held out her hand. "Hi," she said. "Teresa Steplowski. Cook."

He pulled a hand from his pocket and grasped hers; both warm and strong, it evoked the feel of it on her breast.

"Gabe De Luca. A pleasure."

A thrill at the way he said "pleasure" tingled all the way down to her toes, but she forced herself to say the next few words anyway. If she didn't, they would end up all over each other all the time—and kicked off the show. "I'm sorry, Gabe," she repeated. "I've behaved inappropriately the last two times we've...when we..." She waved her free hand back and forth between them; he still held her other one. "It was inappropriate and we should just pretend it never happened and move forward like adults." She couldn't look directly at him; that speech had sounded much better in her head. She waved toward the table and his computer. "Say I'm thrilled to be in the competition and looking forward to proving I'm worthy and capable of running a restaurant." Before he could respond, she pulled her hand from his and opened the door, barely making it past Ace before a tear slipped down her cheek.

CHAPTER FOURTEEN

G abe couldn't catch his breath.

Of all the scenarios he'd imagined since learning his mystery woman's identity, making out minutes into the second time they were alone wasn't one of them.

He wrapped up the other interviews, shoved his notes in a messenger bag, and headed out a side door to West 15th in a daze. He saw Katie on the way out and shook hands with Eric, the host, but saw neither Lily nor Teresa. He thought all of the contestants had been rounded up and driven to their house, the location of which was kept secret.

He bet he could find out where it was, if he wanted to.

Did he?

Hell, yes, he did. He'd been drawn to Teresa even before she seduced him. But that meeting had been a fluke, a one-time occurrence eventually slipping into the realm of fantasy. Then she popped back into his life, and while their second meeting hadn't been as dramatic as the first, he'd call it just as memorable. The way she'd gone up on her toes and kissed him, her hands stroking his cheeks, how their bodies remembered and drew together, his hand on her breast.

So what now?

He rounded the corner and strode up another block to 13th, its brick-lined street perpetually under construction. He passed Spice Market and pushed open the heavy green door of Louth's Pub, scanning the room. As usual, he was early and Nick would probably be late. He ordered a Guinness, exchanged banter about the Mets with Matt the bartender, then slumped into a booth facing the door to drown his—

Oh, hell, he was attracted to two beautiful women. He hardly had miseries to drown. Normally, he'd tell Lily about Teresa, and vice versa, but the contest screwed that up. What if it affected Lily's impartiality or Teresa's performance? He'd already witnessed evidence of those possibilities. Or what if it lost him the job?

He took a long swallow of beer, thudded the glass on the table, and rubbed at his forehead.

"Damn," he muttered. "Shit, fuck, damn."

"First day went well, then?" Nick slid into the booth across from him.

Gabe looked up at Nick, who signaled the waitress to bring him a Guinness, too, then sat back and grinned. Nick ruffled a hand through his jet black hair and said, "Well?"

"It's complicated."

"Okay, now, Nellie, tell uncle Nick all about it."

Whenever Nick noticed Gabe's cerebral side dominating or he thought he was being "girly," he called Gabe "Nellie." This alone disqualified Nick as first choice for discussing dilemmas regarding women. Stephan usually had that honor, but Steph was busy with Kaily, and Gabe wouldn't interfere with that for the world. Gabe had talked about women with Nick over the years—they'd swapped plenty of stories, and Nick knew all about Gabe's ex-wife Shatara— but he could predict Nick's advice here: keep his mouth shut and bang both of them. No harm, no foul.

Contrary to his reputation, Nick had a soft side. After Kaily's diagnosis and Hannah's death, Stephan first lost his job, then the chemo and radiation treatments ate his savings. Flush at that point, Gabe set up a fund for Kaily's medical bills, depositing what his financial advisor called an "obscene amount" of money, and Nick and Adam followed suit. During a drunken breakdown, Nick bawled about Hannah and Kaily and said he'd have given more if he could; he'd named a figure double Gabe's amount before horking all over Gabe's couch and passing out.

Though not exactly subtle, Gabe knew Nick's heart was in the right place, and maybe he could help out in this situation.

Gabe waited until the waitress brought the beer—and Nick finished flirting shamelessly with her—before saying, "I know one of the contestants. I met her in San Francisco."

"You bang her?"

Gabe sighed. Or maybe Nick wouldn't be much use. "Neanderthal."

"So that's a yes." When Gabe didn't respond, Nick added, "Don't much like San Francisco women. All that earnest political correctness and shit." The waitress brought a plate of assorted appetizers, leaning far over the table to set it in front of Nick; she added an extra sway to her hips on her return to the bar. "I just see hemp underwear and wanting to talk about my feelings." Nick shuddered and popped an onion ring in his mouth.

"You think women here don't want that?"

"Maybe, but they sure as hell don't have compostable panties."

Gabe couldn't help laughing at that and snagged a fried zucchini strip.

"So you met this girl in San Fran. And she's on the show. How'd that work?"

"God's got a funny sense of humor."

Nick grunted and finished his beer. After signaling for another, he asked, "Conflict of interest?"

Gabe shook his head. "I checked. But Lily Wen is a judge."

Nick nodded with a knowing smile. "Cat fight?"

Gabe knew if he let him, Nick would travel down the path of cat puns into next week. If he took charge of the conversation and showed his sincerity, Nick would follow suit. Mostly.

He bent forward and tapped a finger on the scarred wooden table, looking Nick in the eye. "Teresa deserves a fair shot at the contest."

Nicked raised an eyebrow. "So what are we talking about here? You like this girl enough that seeing Lily is a conflict? You were in San Francisco, what? Four days."

Gabe nodded. Along with his ability to switch from Neanderthal to modern man in a heartbeat, Nick also had an uncanny ability to home in on a situation's important aspects.

Gabe had spilled the story to Adam the day they boxed together and Gabe saw Teresa's bio sheet, but the entire situation had a surreal quality, and he couldn't have predicted they'd come together like magnets as soon as they were alone in the same room. Plus, Adam had a romantic side; he'd recognized the difficulty for Gabe.

"Yeah, I like her that much. But we didn't get a chance to know each other too well."

"You and Lily exclusive?"

"No."

"I don't get the problem."

"Even if I were the type to date two women at the same time—"

"Now you're talkin'—"

"We would all be working together. In the same room sometimes. And Lily is, in most ways, Teresa's superior in terms of the show."

"Tough day at the office in that case. Could you even see this Teresa? I thought the contestants were pretty much off limits during the shooting."

Gabe hadn't thought of this, but it was probably true, to an extent. He knew they had Sundays off, because he did as well. Could he see Teresa on Sundays? Hell, why was he even debating this? He was attracted to Teresa, but she'd been clear that she didn't want anything else from him.

He leaned back in the booth, one hand on his pint glass. "Shit, maybe not. She did suggest she wanted to concentrate on the show."

"I were a chick, I know I wouldn't want to see your mug first thing in the morning."

Gabe ran a hand over the side of his face, raising his middle finger to Nick. Maybe the Neanderthal had it right. Teresa probably did, too, and Gabe should just focus on his job.

Still, as he stroked his fingers around the damp glass, he couldn't help remembering the feel of Teresa's body pressed against his.

SOMEONE SHOVED A GLASS in Teresa's hand and another person toasted to everyone's success. She clinked with Lynette, Tony, and a young man she thought was named Jonas, and downed what turned out to be sparkling cider.

She wanted to run from her new home, a big brownstone in Manhattan, and try to get a grip. How was her mystery man *here*? She had signed up for an incredible opportunity, but hadn't thought the entire situation through. *Bad habit number two*, she told herself. That, combined with bad habit number one, dithering, had led her here.

But as Lynette gave her a sideways bear hug and one of the show's many PAs, a stern young woman named Chrissie, explained the living arrangements and the next day's schedule, Teresa knew running away to get a grip wasn't an option. She'd be living with some of these eleven people for six weeks—if all went well—and rarely have any time to herself. She hadn't realized they filmed multiple episodes within one week; two or three people would face eliminations every Saturday, but viewers would see those spread out over successive episodes. In between, contestants could win or lose a challenge, and that affected who went into elimination rounds at the end of the week.

She'd never have time alone with Gabe, a blessing in disguise, because her control clearly flew out the window whenever he entered her airspace.

Someone refilled her glass and she looked up at a bald man with multiple ear piercings and a tribal tattoo on one side of his neck.

He held out a hand. "Ace," he said with a warm smile.

"Tess—" She'd almost used Cort's nickname for her: Tessa. "Teresa," she told him. "I'm Teresa."

"I liked your dish today. I'm always looking for good vegan fare."

She stared at him, nonplussed. He looked ready to sling half a cow carcass on the table, butcher, spit and roast it, then consume the entire thing by himself.

She couldn't think of a single response, much less what dish Ace had made for the round.

"Thanks," she said. Then, to fill the awkward silence before it intensified, she added, "It's actually a recipe from a vegan friend. She made it for me right before I left for New York, and I really liked it, it kind of stuck in my head, so when they said to come up with a dish that was comfort food with a twist, along with..." She paused as warning bells clanged in her head, an indication that she was babbling and needed to shut up, right now. But her nerves took over. "Well, not really that, but what was it? Oh, yeah, with a twist but that also represented something about us, something surprising, that's what I went for. It didn't go so well." She wanted to crawl in a corner. "How did yours go?"

"Pretty decent," he replied. "That Lily Wen's a pretty tough judge, though."

His baldness emphasized his narrow face, but a ready smile and warm brown eyes softened everything. She appreciated his attempt at conversation, but embarrassment over her prattle flushed her face hot, and hiding in a corner started looking pretty desirable. She also knew better than to disrespect a judge, especially in this setting. Chrissie the PA could be listening, and Teresa knew reality TV producers hid cameras in plain sight. After a quick scan, she found one in the corner, its tiny red light blinking. During her mental search for a response, Ace jumped in.

"The other two judges really liked my Cajun blackened salmon, but that Lily Wen said it was a throwback to the '80s and she could pretty much see Don Johnson pushing up the sleeves of his pastel blazer before digging into it."

"Ouch."

"Right?" He shrugged. "I know it's good. And I'm not worried about the '80s thing. Everything old becomes new again." He gestured around them, encompassing the large living room with squashy green couches, adjoining dining room, and their happily chatting rivals. "So what do you think about the pop-up thing?"

Teresa smiled. Finally, something she could address with some intelligence. But before she could respond, MaryBeth darted out from behind Ace and said, "It's ridiculous. They're cheaping out. You know how easy it is to do a *pop-up*? There's a reason they're called *pop-ups*."

When Ace turned to MaryBeth and said, "Right?" Teresa stopped liking him. At least for now. She was too tired to fight MaryBeth for his attention to prove her restaurant knowledge.

If today was any indication, she wouldn't be around long enough to worry about it anyway. Between her terrible cooking today and Lily Wen's immediate aversion to All Things Teresa, her chances of winning this contest had decreased significantly.

Since PA Chrissie had threatened to take their cell phones after 10:00 p.m., Teresa decided to get some time in with hers. She slipped around Ace and MaryBeth, still agreeing with each other, and wandered up the hall until she found her room. An 8"x10" sheet of paper had been tacked up to the wall with names hand-printed in purple Sharpie:

Aanjay
Cookie
Lynette
MaryBeth
Rachel
Teresa

She sighed. It might only be the luck of the alphabet, but it depressed her that even her name was last. She looked across the hall and saw a similar sign:

Ace
Antonio
Chance
Jonas
Karl
Tony

This gorgeous old brownstone had to have at least four stories, with multiple bedrooms, yet reality TV producers were manipulating even this, as if it were a dating show: all of the women in one room, all the men in another.

Using her phone as a light, too weary to even turn on the overhead, she dragged her suitcase to a bed in the farthest corner and crawled into the lower bunk.

She plumped up a pillow and curled against it, waiting impatiently for her phone to start up.

It vibrated and beeped, and multiple email and text alerts popped on the screen. She tapped it and noted messages from Victoria, Kristen, her youngest sister Julia, her mother, friends from Golden Gate Catering, and...Cort. Which to open first? And would she tell Victoria and Kristen that her Elevator Man had miraculously shown up here? How would she even begin to explain that?

Better to get Mom's email out of the way: *Your father and I wish you well. Your grandmother plans to get a cell phone so she can be in direct contact with you. In the meantime, she wishes you luck. Be good, Mom and Dad.*

Teresa refrained from rolling her eyes, but loved the idea of Mama Step with a cell phone.

Julia's text: *Nockem dead sis I wanna meet Darren Michaels!!!*

Teresa quickly tapped back: *It's "knock 'em," doofus. And thanks! Love to everyone. Tell Mama Step it's great here.* She attached a picture of the front of the brownstone. She almost added "be good," but realized her mom had used that very phrase, and hit Send instead.

Her phone chimed a second later, with her sister's response: *kk*

She read the texts from her former co-workers next, more inspiration, but without family complications. She wrote back her thanks, then took a deep breath and opened Cort's message: *miss you darlin.*

"Moving on," she muttered, unprepared to address his loaded one-liner, and opened Victoria's.

Victoria: *How's it going over there? You kicking ass and taking names?*

Victoria: *Don't forget, you ARE an amazing chef.*

Victoria: *I mean it.*

Victoria: *Don't make me come over there. You know you are. You deserve this and you're going to get it.*

Teresa shook her head, fighting the habit to immediately respond. Victoria's very being demanded respect and attention and Teresa usually complied. But she was here to change her life, and she would reply—when she was ready—but she wanted to read Kristen's next, partly for a contrast between the sisters. And she kind of needed Kristen's patented blend of supportive and wacky right now.

Kristen: *Daisy and I love you!*

Kristen: *That out of the way, how are you? I'm so proud of you for doing this. Can't believe how tedious this texting thing is, but you're worth it. Saw my psychic friend Carlotta today and she said it's all going to work out for you and your dreams will come true. So, be your authentic self and everything else will fall into place!*

Comforted by her friends' words, Teresa opened a group text and typed a message to Victoria and Kristen: *Love you both! Thanks for the support. Crazy day. Lots to say, but we only get our phones for a short time at night.* She reviewed what she'd written, realizing she was procrastinating. She wrote a few more lines, deleting each attempt before finally writing: *It's insane, but my elevator guy is HERE. He works for CuisineTV. We kissed again, but no crazy sex in a small room. His name is Gabe De Luca, and he's still divine.*

Teresa waited for a response, but when nothing else came through, she sighed and scrolled back to review some earlier texts, letting Victoria's dry wit fill her brain and override her own situation. Well, mostly. Somewhere in the background, little creatures skittered around in her mind, feeding her anxiety, but hearing Victoria's Midwestern tone in her texts helped keep them at bay.

From her honeymoon: *Hawaiians are so CASUAL. No one plans anything here. It's all about enjoying the moment. Luke says he feels like Danny Zuko at the beach, a completely different person.*

Teresa had written back: *Do you sing* Summer Lovin' *together?*

Victoria: *<shaking my head> You and Kristen. She said the same thing.*

Teresa fell asleep with the phone clutched to her chest.

CHAPTER FIFTEEN

The next morning, Teresa stood with the other contestants in an empty field, blinking against the rising sun, and clutching a paper cup of coffee. They'd been roused out of their beds around 3:30, and stumbled into their clothes—"wear lots of layers," Katie had commanded—before gathering in the front room. To Teresa, they all looked how she felt: dazed. All except MaryBeth who either slept standing up in full makeup, or else woke an hour earlier and donned an impeccable outfit after applying flawless makeup and styling perfectly tousled hair.

Katie and Chrissie refused to answer any questions, other than to say this would be an overnight shoot, and their belongings would be taken care of, then hustled the contestants to three vans idling in front of the brownstone.

During the two-hour drive, the view from State Route 44 through the Hudson Valley mesmerized Teresa; she'd grown up in California and hadn't traveled farther east than Colorado. Her reference points were lots of hills and houses built close together. Here, very few side roads or interchanges interrupted the long stretches of two- and four-lane highways lined by rows of trees and interspersed with large houses on open lots. Along this route, she saw more greenery than buildings. She wasn't sure she wanted to give up California weather—drought, earthquakes and all—but this scenery was beautiful.

The procession of vans drove underneath a large wooden sign proclaiming the entrance to Big Valley Lodge, past a huge log cabin that looked like it could sleep 100 people, some smaller outbuildings, then onto a dirt road through swaying birch trees. The vans stopped within sight of a clearing, and everyone piled out.

A Production Assistant who introduced himself as Nicholas appeared from the end of the drive with an armful of coffees, followed by his twin Jeremy. Teresa noted the usual cameras, generators, cables and trucks associated with any shoot, but couldn't piece together their next challenge from the equipment.

Katie stepped in front of them, walkie-talkie hooked to her vest and clipboard in hand. "Good morning, everyone. Enjoy your coffee and this gorgeous setting. In a few minutes, Eric and the judges will arrive to let you know about today's challenge. They're still setting up for us, so please wait here until we're ready."

After Katie walked away with Chrissie, heads close together and pointing at something on the clipboard, the other contestants broke out in excited murmurs. Jonas took a few brave steps in the direction of the clearing, but paused at a stern look from Katie; he gave a jaunty wave, and returned to the group. Today he wore black corduroys and a patterned black-and-white sweater under a blue puffy jacket, and Teresa thought if she plunked him down in the middle of her parents' living room, they'd consider him a lost son. Then he sauntered over to Chance, who slid his a hand through his long blonde hair, letting it settle in perfect waves around his face, and Teresa started at his resemblance to Gabe. As the coffee started flowing through her system, she wondered for the first time that morning whether Gabe would be at all of their challenges, or only show up for a few.

And then she reminded herself that it didn't matter. She was here for a reason, and that reason did not include a man. Over and over, she'd allowed too many infatuations and other dalliances to divert her, using each relationship as an excuse to neglect her dreams.

No more. It was the Teresa Show, not the Teresa and Her Man Show.

As soon as she got her phone back, she'd text Victoria with everything she knew about the other challengers; V loved strategizing about different personalities.

Until then she'd have to be smart and focused, really concentrate on—

Oh, shit. She caught sight of feathered blonde hair in one of the lodge's picture windows before the door opened, and a cameraman walked out backwards, filming the three judges. Joel Klein, the executive director of their show, in a crewneck sweater and parka, complete with burgundy scarf around his neck. Darren Michaels, his signature Hawaiian shirt peeking out from his own parka as he stamped across the back porch in heavy hiking boots. And then there was Lily Wen in a block-print sheath of primary colors bordered in black and above-the-knee boots, her hand on Gabe De Luca's arm as she minced across the frost-dampened wood.

Teresa gritted her teeth. Anyone else would look like a big Rubik's cube in that dress. But Lily Wen might as well be on the catwalk, except for the helpless air she feigned so she could touch Gabe, who had his head bent and a serious expression on his face. Teresa's stomach almost turned over, except once Gabe lifted his head from the decking, his eyes locked with hers and a welcoming smile lit his face. She couldn't help smiling back, until Lily Wen noticed Gabe's attention had strayed, and her own gaze locked onto Teresa. Then a few of Teresa's fellow contestants turned to see the object of Gabe's focus.

And then the cameras turned on her.

Deflect, she thought, her stomach clenching, *deflect*.

She grabbed the arm of the person directly to her left and gushed, "Aren't you excited about this challenge? I can't wait to see what it's going to be."

Cookie rolled her eyes, but to Teresa's relief, played along. Sort of. "Should be pretty awesome," she agreed, and blew a huge bubble. When it popped, the sound echoed around the canyon, and a few people jumped or let out nervous laughter.

Dan, the director, shouted, "Quiet on the damn set!" even though they weren't on a set and it seemed like everyone had already forgotten they were being filmed. They all straightened at Dan's command.

The show's host, Eric Wintersteen, popped out from behind the judges and welcomed the contestants to their second challenge, then thanked the lodge's owner for hosting them today. Teresa snuck a peek at Gabe, who continued to smile at her, although he'd turned down the wattage somewhat. He'd also been separated from Lily, since the judges had to line up near Eric, and he now leaned against the deck railing, hands dangling and a light breeze brushing his hair across one cheek. Teresa shivered as the sharp air hit the back of her neck and exposed ears, then a rush of heat shot down her belly when Gabe's smile turned knowing, as if her shiver had been an invitation. She sighed. It probably had.

Cookie elbowed her in the side and muttered, "Pay attention," and Teresa reluctantly pulled her gaze from Gabe's and focused on Eric.

"So you'll be split up into three teams of four. When one team is up, the others will wait in the Aspen Cabin. After each team completes its challenge, it will be separated from the ones who have not yet gone, so everyone will have an equal chance. This is a very unique opportunity and will test not only your teamwork but your skills for invention and quick thinking, which will be requirements for any successful pop-up."

He paused to flip up the collar of his jacket as a stronger breeze flew across the clearing, then announced the teams: "Lynette, Ace, Antonio and Aanjay on Team One. Tony, MaryBeth, Rachel and Jonas are on Team Two. Team Three consists of the remaining contestants: Cookie, Karl, Chance and Teresa."

Teresa and Cookie glanced at each other and grinned. Teresa had seen Cookie's chocolate tart with crème anglaise yesterday and it had made her mouth water on sight. She worried about Karl, whose dish had flopped, but Chance's smoked salmon crisps got raves even from Lily. Teresa mentally snarked that it was probably because Chance looked so much like Gabe.

Eric continued his spiel, which took a few takes before he got it right, despite the fact he was reading from cue cards. This didn't bother Teresa; she was used to the "reality" of reality TV consisting of rehearsals, extra takes, and scripts.

He told them there would be one winning team and one challenge winner.

"Remember, the challenge winner can be on a losing team, but no one on the winning team will go home this week." He paused for the crew to reposition a camera and Dan to command the cast to shut the hell up, as they'd all started muttering and talking to each other. "So Team One," Eric said, louder than usual. "You'll come with me, the judges and Big Valley Lodge's owner, Duke, to the clearing through those trees. The rest of you can go over to Aspen Cabin to wait for your turn."

Those not involved with the first team's challenge watched as the others piled into vans and golf carts and disappeared around a bend in the deep forest of birch trees. Then they followed the twin Production Assistants, Nicholas and Jeremy, along a series of stepping stones, up a small porch and into Aspen Cabin.

On the way, Teresa glanced at Gabe to see which direction he'd go and was both relieved and dismayed to see him step in with Jonas and start chatting with him. She was too *aware* of him; if he'd gone with the others, she might be able to concentrate. She had to stay focused and find a way to shut off her body's insta-lust response to him.

To distract herself, she grabbed Cookie again and gestured for Karl and Chance to join them. They huddled close in the middle of the cabin's open living and kitchen area. Teresa noted a preponderance of wooden beams, squashy leather seating and wood paneling.

"We should go over our strengths and weaknesses," she said to the others. "Since we won't know what the competition is—"

"Campfire cookout," Karl said, hitching his pants up over his beer belly. "Isn't it obvious?" he asked when the others stared at him. "Lodge, middle-a-nowhere. I deliver to places like this all the time. It's about meat and grilled veg and s'mores."

"Okay, grilling," Cookie said. "Easy enough."

Teresa glanced at Team Two: tall Tony, beauty queen MaryBeth, All-American Rachel, and could-be-her-brother, Jonas. They sat around the long plank dining table, gesturing and muttering, faces intent. Gabe talked with Nicholas and Jeremy near the kitchen island, on which sat coffee, tea, other drinks and a variety of snacks.

Gabe had shed his parka and pushed up the sleeves of his plum Henley. He stood with one hip against the island, arms crossed, eyes focused on Jeremy as he spoke. Teresa noted his toned frame in softly worn jeans, and well-formed biceps in the shirt, before tugging her attention away and back to her crew.

She caught Cookie eyeing her and to cover said, "What if it's not grilling? What if they want us to assume the obvious and turn it on its ear? It happens all the time with these things."

"And you should know, isn't that right, sugar?"

Teresa turned to see MaryBeth now standing by the island, much too close to Gabe, a mug of something steaming cradled in both hands, a sticky-sweet smile on her face to match her tone. *Crap*, Teresa thought. *She knows something. How did she find out so fast?* Deny and deflect, or shrug and confess, possibly earning experience points for time on a reality TV show. Everyone was watching her now, including Gabe, and, continuing her new approach to life, she based a decision on her own feelings, and not on how anyone else wanted her to react.

She shrugged, as if MaryBeth's suggestion hadn't been laced with innuendo, then ambled over to the food, passing the ice queen on the way. "Well, we all watch these things, don't we?" She nibbled a piece of gouda, concentrating hard to keep her hand from shaking. "And the more information about how they work, the better our chances." She glanced over the array again, then asked, of no one in particular, "Do they have hot cider? That sounds really good right now."

Gabe pointed to her right. "In that carafe."

She gave him a grateful smile and noted his admiring expression. Acting nonchalant in the face of MaryBeth's derision had boosted her spirits, but Gabe's reaction added some icing to her victory cupcake.

"I'd say you have more *experience* than information about these things, wouldn't you?" MaryBeth said.

Persistent bitch.

Now Teresa's hands really shook, and the cup she pulled out of the stack clinked loudly against the others, threatening to topple a couple. Gabe slid the wayward ones from the island's edge and eased the mug from her hand. "Let me get that for you, I noticed the nozzle sticks."

"Thanks." They exchanged a warm glance that made her toes curl inside her boots.

"I guess y'all don't know we've got a bona fide reality television star in our midst," MaryBeth continued.

"What're you clappin' on about?" Cookie crossed her thick arms over her large chest and glared at MaryBeth. "You been on *The Bachelor* or somethin'? *Dancing with the Stars?*" She executed a clumsy pirouette, and some of the others laughed.

Color flushed MaryBeth's cheeks, but on her it only looked glowing instead of blotchy. Teresa shallowly wished that had happened to her. She hoped her history wouldn't come out here, but if it had to, she wanted her fellow contestants to know her better first.

Either way, she wasn't going to let this snotty beauty queen win.

97

Deliberately avoiding looking at Gabe, she said, "I worked in production on a show called *In Concert*. I dated one of the cast members and ended up on camera a few times." She finally glanced at Gabe, when he handed her a mug of hot cider, but she couldn't read his expression. "We broke up," she added, "and the show didn't go into another season."

"Hey, I've seen that show," Chance said, pointing at her. "Tyler Landry, right? Great fuckin' band, but I don't remember seeing you..." His voice trailed off and dark pink patches that matched MaryBeth's flushed his cheeks. "Oh," he said.

"Right." Teresa struck a pose with her mug. Had Chance remembered her half nude, straddling Cort in an easy chair? Or maybe upstairs in Cort's apartment, where they couldn't wait to go at it again, so just sprawled to the floor and did it right there? "Girls gone wild and all that." She took a deep breath and faced MaryBeth. "So, yeah, I have cooking experience, and I also know how these shows work." She gestured toward Karl, Cookie and Chance, who dropped his gaze to the floor. "And right now, my team needs to come up with a strategy." She lifted her mug at Gabe again, thanked him, and walked deliberately to the couch. After settling onto one plump cushion, she gave her teammates a stern look until they joined her.

She threw out a few other possibilities for the challenge and released a breath when the others jumped in, adding their own. She was proud of herself for not looking at the door when she heard Gabe excuse himself and slam it on the way out.

"SONOFABITCH," GABE MUTTERED, stomping through the grass behind the cabin to a break in the trees. He'd tried to stay inside, to act like Teresa's revelation hadn't affected him, but it had. And damned if he knew why. He barely knew the woman. They'd had "stranger sex" in an elevator four months ago and only a bizarre twist of fate brought them back together now. Maybe it meant something, maybe it didn't; but what might this latest revelation suggest?

As a writer, he added symbols and portents to his fiction, but rarely looked for them in real life. He lived it, grabbing that brass ring whenever it came near, no matter how tarnished it might be inside. He'd lived that way through his marriage to Shatara, both of them partying from one day to the next, until his income dried up and she filed for divorce on grounds of adultery.

At the time, he raged at the betrayal, and blamed her for leaving and swindling him for six figures. He took the asshole route, claiming all women left you in some way, by either dying like Hannah or taking the shirt off your back when you were down. Eventually he realized he held plenty of the responsibility, including cheating, and the rest was ego. He knew better now, but for awhile, he'd reveled in his misery. Then he'd punished himself by either ignoring women in general, or finding psychopaths who treated him as badly as he felt, like Cindy. All this happened in the few whirlwind years between the success of *Sonder* and the bitter humiliation of *Ennui*.

So he'd given up. Or thought he had, until a stunning woman approached him in an elevator and offered herself. And despite the insane circumstances, that experience brought him some hope.

A memory from that day flashed into Gabe's mind. "No cameras," she'd said. She only wanted sex, not a date with him. "Not exciting enough." She didn't even want to know his damn name. Then just yesterday, they'd crashed into each other again in the interview room. She'd apologized for being inappropriate. Was the "love 'em and leave 'em cliché" her modus operandi?

He slipped a hand inside his parka's inner pocket and searched for the phone he'd stashed there. He could tap into the lodge's wi-fi if he wanted. He'd seen enough reality television himself to know the producers twisted situations to fit their desired scenarios, but he could recognize a pattern outside the manipulation if he saw one. Did he want to look for Teresa's patterns?

He admitted to a prurient curiosity. She was beautiful, they'd had sex once and kissed passionately another time. Was she a rampant consumer of men? He hadn't thought so, even after their time in the elevator. There was a hesitation in her, some sort of melancholy. Hell, he knew enough psychology to realize she could be trying to fill a gap in her life with men, and sex. But he didn't want to believe it of Teresa.

But why did he care?

He pulled his phone out and opened a browser. What had Chance called the show? Landry something? No, that was the band. Something about a concert. He pulled up IMDB and typed "Teresa Steplowski" in the search box, then left his finger hovering over the screen, thinking.

His first novel hit the New York Times bestseller list and shot him to millionaire status. His second novel tanked, plummeting him to deep despair. In those few short years, he'd traveled the world, married and divorced, tried more drugs than he could name, and drove a fast car or two. He'd also become a world-class jackass, lost trust in women, and pissed away most of his money.

He liked to think he'd have returned to himself without the crash and burn, but he'd never know now because he'd had to rapidly recalibrate, for Stephan and Kaily, then for himself. It was much harder getting through life as an asshole if you had no money; people didn't put up with it the same way they did when they knew you had a roll of Benjamins in your pocket. It was even more difficult getting through life without friends. But his true friends had seen him through it all, and he liked to believe he'd regenerated a few good decision-making skills.

Teresa could very well have gone through her own jackass stage while filming *In Concert*, and was now a shining example of first-rate decision-making, their little tussle in the interview room notwithstanding. He'd call that lust, plain and simple. And lust rarely led to rational decisions.

Hell with it. He didn't want either of their histories to affect any future they might have, nor their present for that matter. He let the screen go black and tucked the phone in his pocket.

CHAPTER SIXTEEN

Teresa stood in front of a large outdoor stone fire pit with Cookie, Karl and Chance. Karl had been right: they were asked to do a cookout. But as with any reality TV competition, it wasn't that simple. Plank seating surrounded the pit and right behind them, a rock wall curved in a C shape about five feet high. Teresa and her team would have to scavenge wood, start a fire, and cook dinner and dessert for four in the pit. They would be provided with a selection of food and implements, but there was only one of each item: pot, pan, spatula, knife, etc. They were told the reasoning behind this was based on a pop-up often lacking in basic resources.

A nearby walkway paved in dark brick led to the lake; the sun shone through the trees on the western shore, and a long table for the judges faced the pit. They would have front row seating for Team Three's victory—or defeat. And of course, cameras, crew and equipment surrounded everything.

Dan the director did his usual striding around and yelling about something or other, and Teresa already found him tedious. But she had to tune him out as she and her crew huddled together, waiting for Dan's signal that they could start discussing their strategy. Teresa glanced at the judges: celebrity chef Darren Michaels was getting his makeup retouched, executive producer Joel Klein spoke to an assistant who crouched next him, and Lily Wen looked like she hadn't spent the entire day in chilly weather watching contestants scramble around, then eating their food. She looked striking and austere as she surveyed Team Three, and Teresa had to wonder if she knew about *In Concert*, whether MaryBeth had already spread the word, or if the producers had done their research on her and were waiting for the right moment to spring it.

On camera, of course.

Her bravado at the cabin was only to deflect MaryBeth; she knew very well that her days on *In Concert* might boomerang on her in one form or another. She had been naive to think that because it never came up in any of her preliminary interviews that no one knew about it.

Dan yelled for quiet on the damn set, then pointed at the team and said, "Go!"

They started talking at once and Dan shouted, "Quiet!" and they all shut up and glanced at him. "Cookie first, then Teresa, Chance and Karl. After that, you can talk over each other all you want. Go!"

And they went, throwing out ideas as if they'd come up with them that second, directing each other and offering to take over a certain task, then scrambling to execute it.

Teresa tucked her braids behind her ears, quickly sliced through an onion, then passed the knife to Chance, who waited to cube the steak they'd selected. Karl and Cookie concentrated on getting the fire started.

All that matters is here and now, Teresa told herself. *Here and now.*

Dan was grumbling about losing the light when they finally wrapped for the day and piled into vans for the return trip to the lodge. They gathered in the great room, huddling close to the huge fireplace and blowing on their frozen fingers when Katie reviewed the schedule. Tonight, their clothes would be collected and washed. Tomorrow, a 6:00 a.m. call: "that means awake, dressed, breakfasted and ready to go." A makeup crew on hand in the morning to recreate their hairstyles. Teresa and Cookie exchanged a grin at that. Teresa's braids pretty much always looked the same, and she expected that Cookie's short blue mohawk only needed a quick gel reapplication. Ace, with his shaved head, caught their look and grinned, too. One less thing to worry about.

They would film the judges' determination of the winning team the next morning, but the aired episodes would show the entire competition taking place within a few hours. The filming would take place outside, weather permitting, in the same area by the lake where they held the competition. The women would sleep in Birch Cabin and the men in Hickory Cabin. The rest of the crew would be dispersed among the other cabins, while the judges and Director Dan had rooms in the main lodge.

Cookie smirked and nudged Teresa. "Who you think's going to end up in whose bed tonight?" she whispered, lifting a chin at the grouping of Lily Wen, Darren Michaels, MaryBeth, and Gabe.

Teresa's heart dropped. MaryBeth flipped her hair back and practically shoved her cleavage in Gabe's face while chatting with him. She either didn't catch or ignored the death rays shooting from Lily's Wen's eyes.

"If I had to guess," Teresa joked to cover her anxiety, "I'd say Director Dan and PA Jeremy, with Dan shouting directions."

Cookie let out a whoop, actually slapping her hands to her knees, and everyone turned to them. She grinned and waved. "Just letting off some steam, folks. Crazy day."

Teresa made it through dinner, her thoughts wandering and eyes drooping, and didn't even complain when MaryBeth called dibs on the nicest bedroom, "graciously" agreeing to share it with Rachel and Aanjay. After brushing their teeth and changing into pajamas, Teresa, Cookie and effusive Lynette trooped into the smaller room, and dropped into bed.

But Teresa couldn't sleep. Lynette snored, the wind whistled around the cabin, and Teresa's mind raced. She'd responded to Kristen and Victoria's shocked responses to her text about Gabe, but tapping out a longer explanation to them only increased her restlessness. She couldn't stop thinking about Gabe, and suspected he was a convenient excuse to avoid facing the reckless decision she'd made by applying for this contest. Getting moony over a cute guy was so much easier than devising solutions for surviving *Tasty Dish*.

Of course, she realized with a start, she didn't have to. She could screw up on a regular basis and eventually get kicked off.

But no. She shook her head, her braids shushing against the pillow. She didn't have it in her. She might be quiet and unassuming, but her competitive streak rivaled that of a professional athlete, and she couldn't botch a challenge on purpose. She was here, and she'd fight to the finish.

In the meantime, though, she needed sleep. Tomorrow promised to be another long day, and the competition had barely started. She pulled the flannel sheets and down comforter closer to her face and snuggled into the bed, breathing deeply, counting sheep, thinking of calm, relaxing things: babbling brooks, reading in front of a warm fire, purring kittens curled up in a basket...

"Fudgesicles," she mutter-whispered. No go on the sleep thing.

She slid out of bed, pulled sweats over her flannel pajamas, and tucked her parka under one arm. She eased the door open, listening for the sound of disrupted breathing, then closed it and slipped her feet into her hiking boots without lacing them. Once outside, the frigid air hit her like a slap and she shoved her arms into the parka's sleeves and flipped up the faux-fur-lined hood.

Her laces clacked when she walked; the sound reminded her of Cort, who used to clomp around with his shoelaces untied. They clicked and clacked loudly, driving her to distraction, and he'd eventually agreed to start tying them. He said she'd changed him, and she believed him. But she'd changed, too, and knew they weren't right for each other. She'd told him that, but he didn't believe her.

She sat on the edge of an Adirondack chair and roughly tied her laces with freezing fingers. "Damn man," she muttered. "Damn stubborn-egotistical-can't-take-no-for-an-answer man. For that matter, damn *men*."

"All of them?" a voice asked from the darkness.

She jumped with a squeak and scrambled up from the chair. Another parka-clad person sauntered around the corner, lowering his hood as he got closer to the porch light.

Her heart jumped. Gabe.

"We're not all bad," he said.

Her heart sunk. Not Gabe, but Chance, his younger lookalike.

"No," she agreed. "Not all of you." She didn't think he was. He seemed like a nice guy, easygoing and enthusiastic. But young. And too focused on her since she confessed to her time on *In Concert*. "Great job today." He'd created their amazing s'mores.

"Thanks." He stood at the bottom step and looked up at where she stood on the porch. "Couldn't sleep?"

She shook her head.

"Me neither." He gestured to the path that led to the lake. "Want to walk?"

A voice from the opposite direction said, "She promised me a walk earlier."

He stood next to Chance, smiling up at Teresa, the steam of his breath misting in the porch light. Chance nodded and shrugged, then punched Gabe lightly on the shoulder in passing. The sound of his boots crunching on the gravel echoed in the quiet night.

Resist, Teresa thought, *resist*. "I don't remember you asking me to go for a walk with you." She crossed her arms over her chest with a rustle of material. "Maybe I wanted to go with Chance."

Gabe turned to the side and gestured at Chance's departing form. "Not too late." He faced her again. "But I'm hoping you'll choose me instead."

She studied him, his fair hair swept back in the breeze, face lifted toward her, brown eyes focused intently on her face. She'd noticed that before, how he gave people his complete attention.

"You know about my sordid past," she blurted, needing to know his reaction to that revelation.

"I only know what MaryBeth suggested, and how you responded. Sounds like an interesting experience. Most people don't go on one reality show, much less two."

"I wasn't trying to hide it. I just don't think it applies here."

"You don't have to explain anything to me."

"No," she agreed. The old Teresa would have; those days were gone. "I don't."

He smiled. "Teresa Steplowski, would you care to walk with me?"

She decided not to play coy. "Yes, I would."

Side by side, they headed for the paved path to the lake, where the day's challenge had been held.

Teresa shoved her hands in her coat pockets and shivered. "It's so crazy cold here at night, even in May. How can anyone stand it?"

"We're actually having a cold spell." Gabe shrugged, his parka making a whooshing sound. "I'm used to it. Although I wore shorts the first couple days in San Francisco, just because I could."

She heard the smile in his voice and stumbled on the brick, the memories of their brief, but crazy-hot time in San Francisco causing adrenaline to shoot through her system.

Gabe glanced at her, but she could only stare at her feet.

"Oh," he said. "Are we not talking about it?"

"Why not?" she announced, throwing her hands out in the air, then immediately replacing them in her warm pockets. Her attitude surprised her; Teresa Steplowski rarely gave attitude. She usually rolled along, avoiding conflict. And how boring was that? "It's all part of my sordid past, I guess."

Gabe stopped at a break in the trees, where the moonlight filtered down and illuminated the tops of their heads and sections of their faces. His eyes looked dark, and she couldn't quite read his expression, but heard the disappointment in his voice when he spoke.

"It wasn't sordid to me."

"I'm sorry." She didn't say it to appease him; she genuinely meant it.

"Was it to you?"

"No," she responded immediately, glad they shared that view of their time together. "No. I was talking about *In Concert*. But—"

"Then what was it? To you?"

"I'm not sure," she admitted. "Rebellion, maybe." She paused. How could she explain her inner turmoil during that time, that she never, ever propositioned men the way she had him? It would sound pretty false now that he knew about Cort. For all Gabe knew, she loved public sex, with lots of different men.

"I want to see your face when we talk about this," Gabe said. "Let's go to the water."

She nodded and they walked the path in silence, their boots chuffing along the bricks until they reached the fire pit and the walkway turned to hard-packed dirt. Gabe headed for a short pier, and the small lamp post at the end. She realized he meant it, he really did want to see her face. He sat and gestured for her to join him. They dangled their boots over the edge and the water shushed gently under them, soothing in its rhythm.

They both looked out across the lake, at the dark strip of land on the other side, and the moon hanging above the treetops, its glittering light shining across the water.

Gabe shifted to face her, leaning against the light pole. "No one's asked me for sex in an elevator before," he said. "It rocked my world. And I'm not just talking about the sex."

She stared at him. What was he trying to tell her?

After a few beats of her silence, he said, "Teresa. I don't know you. We shared something incredibly intimate and I could make assumptions from that moment, but I don't want to. I can only know you from observation and what you tell me. So tell me about yourself."

"I hate insta-bios." She wrinkled her nose. "They feel like dating websites, or a Playboy playmate's loves and hates list."

Gabe laughed. "Fair enough. How about I start? I have four best friends I'd kill for and we all had a small-town upbringing in Cold Spring, a little over an hour from here. My dad owns a hardware store and my mom has an antiques shop. I have two older sisters who are married with kids and they fuss over me like mother hens, when they can get hold of me."

"Is that why you don't live there anymore?"

He smiled. "No. I had big dreams. I conquered the world for about five minutes, until it decided to fight back. I got knocked down, and New York City has more opportunities than Cold Spring." He shifted on the planking, looking away before catching her gaze again. "I tried culinary school, but dropped out for a variety of reasons, mostly dumbass ones. I'm a writer now, a novelist when I'm not doing this gig. My first book shot off like a rocket, my second book tanked, and I made a lot more dumbass decisions."

She liked his candor. So many men she dated played games, excluding any mistakes while they talked themselves up, unless those mistakes made them appear sensitive enough to impress the woman. And get her into bed. And despite her own warnings to distance herself, Teresa was intrigued. She wanted to know more about his family and his childhood. Did he play baseball in his All-American town? Did he skateboard to the ice cream shoppe, stopping at his mom's antiques store to borrow five dollars?

Before she could respond, he added, "While I'm baring all, I was married for about eight months. That was one of my stupid decisions. So I'm wary about relationships, but not opposed to them. It's also partly why I believe in honesty right up front, whether something is going somewhere or not."

"What's the other part?"

"Small-town kid with a forthright mom. She didn't let me get away with anything."

She smiled. "But you still tried?"

He grinned back. "All the time."

He was so beautiful, with that generous smile, model-high cheekbones and long, wavy hair. "You're making me more curious about you with each piece of information you reveal."

He held his hands out. "Ask away. I'm an open book, no pun intended."

"I don't know where to start."

"Can I ask you one?"

She nodded. "Go ahead."

He leaned close. "Why?"

She could have pretended she didn't know to what he referred, but she *did* know. Why him? Why him in the elevator? Why did she ask in the first place? "You've never been propositioned in an elevator, and I've never done that before, either." She pulled her feet up to the deck and turned to face him, wrapping her arms around her knees. "I was caught in a life I didn't like. And it was my fault. Well, it was my fault I didn't like it, because I didn't speak up when something bothered me or I disagreed. But I was also surrounded by people whose lives were changing, and they were all so...so damn *happy*." Her throat caught on the word and she stopped, blinking.

"And you weren't," he offered.

"No," she admitted. "And I didn't know what to do about it. I felt so stuck. So I did something crazy to try to break out of it. Although, my choice wasn't completely spontaneous. I had seen you at the show earlier. You seemed nice." She cringed at how lame that sounded.

Gabe pulled his boots up, too, copying her pose. "You risked a lot on what you thought you saw."

"It was really stupid." She rocked back, then forward, and tapped her toes on the boards, then against his. "Thanks for not being psycho." *And for the amazing orgasm.* They might be sharing a lot, but she wasn't sure she could go so far as to admit that yet. "I almost thought you were going to say no."

"I almost did." He touched her knee. "It was extraordinary. But I shouldn't have done it."

She shifted back from him. "What?"

"You were irresistible, Teresa. You're beautiful. Once you suggested it, I knew I couldn't say no, but I don't want to start a relationship that way. And by 'relationship,' I mean getting to know someone, whether it leads to more or not." He brushed his fingertips across the back of her hand. "But I am not, by any means, sorry."

She covered his hand with hers, enjoying the contrast of his warm fingers against her freezing ones.

Gabe shifted forward and wrapped both of his around hers. "What you said yesterday." The tips of his fingers gently stroked. "In the interview room. About pretending it never happened and moving forward like adults. Did you mean it?"

Her hands were warming from his touch. She squelched a ridiculous desire to ask him to warm up her frozen nose. "Yes and no," she replied. "I was so shocked to see you. I really don't believe in sleeping with someone before you know them." She wanted to add *really, I really mean it*, but they were being honest and straightforward here, without embellishments. And besides, it would sound like she was covering up.

"Me, too."

"Except we've both done it, haven't we?" she said with a laugh.

He laughed, too, giving her hands a squeeze before letting go. "I like you, Teresa. I want to learn more about you. I know these are crazy circumstances, and I don't want to distract you from the contest."

An image of Lily Wen possessively touching Gabe at yesterday's challenge flashed into her mind. What to address first? Lily, or the fact that she liked him, too? She took a deep breath of the frigid air, reminding herself why she was here: to change and improve her life, not get a man. But she couldn't deny that every time Gabe was around, she was like a compass and he was true north.

She steeled herself; she had to know. "What about Lily Wen?"

"Ah." He leaned back. "We met when I got hired for the show. We went out a couple times."

Teresa waited, to see if Gabe would say more without any prompting.

"I haven't officially broken it off with her, but I was considering it. Even before I saw you again."

"She already suspects something."

"I know. I'm sorry if it's affected how she treats you."

"I'm a big girl," she said with a show of bravado; Lily Wen scared her, a lot. "I can handle it."

"I don't doubt that." He shifted closer, until their knees bumped. His face was very close. "I'm not sure you can handle the cold, though. You're shivering." He stood and held a hand out to her. "I'll walk you back."

She took his hand and let him help her up and tuck her close to his side. For warmth, she told herself, then admitted she wanted to touch him as long as possible. "I still don't think I'll be able to sleep," she told him, their hips bumping as they wandered back up the path. "I'm really wired."

He let out a breath and they watched it stream upward. "Don't tempt me to help tire you out," he said. "It's too cold, and there are no private indoor spaces available."

She bumped his hip on purpose, warming at the thought, but his words also reminded her of something. "Thanks for talking with me," she said. "For clearing some things up. But I still don't know where we stand."

They reached the outer corner of Teresa's cabin, and he pulled her around the side, out of the chilling breeze. The back porch light illuminated the deep brown of his eyes when he tilted his head a certain way.

"I'll tell you what I'd like. I want to get to know you better, but I don't want to interfere with the contest. And I'm going to break things off with Lily. I'm neither a multiple nor a serial dater."

"So we'd be dating?"

He stepped closer. "Tell me what you want," he murmured, skimming his hands up her coat and along her neck, to cup her jaw.

Everything, she thought. *Right here and now, and damn the cold.* Her breath shuddered. "I want to get to know you better, too. But you're a distraction, plain and simple. So if we find..." Damn, was this right? Would he run away from her demand? If he did, then he wasn't right for her, no matter their attraction. "If we find ways to see each other while the contest is happening, then no sex."

His fingers paused, but didn't stop. He nodded. "I still want to kiss you." He brushed one fingertip around the edge of her ear and she shivered.

"Danger zone," she admitted, but could hear the hesitation in her own voice. She wanted him to. She pushed a hand against his chest, to get his attention rather than stop him. "Give me your phone." She tilted her hand, palm up. Another test, she realized.

Without hesitation, he fished it from an inner pocket and set it on her palm. As she entered her information to his contact list, she said with a smile, "We'll get to know each other the old-fashioned way." She handed the phone back. "Our phones are confiscated most of the day, but we get them for awhile at night. Text me."

He slipped the phone away and tilted his head toward hers. "Done. But for now, I want to..." His lips were so close. "...kiss you."

She nodded and the movement brought her mouth against his, so she kissed him, their lips warming at the contact. His arms swept around to pull her against him, and his tongue tickled her lips apart. She felt his fingers stroking down the back of her neck to the tops of her shoulders, his mouth so warm, his tongue against hers, and their breath mingled as it steamed in the cold night air. But she couldn't feel his body. And damn her earlier declaration, she wanted to, she wanted that more than anything right now. She fumbled between them, yanking at his coat, her numb fingers unable to grasp the zipper.

Her scrabbling increased her rapid breathing and in her desperation, she kissed Gabe harder, with more fervency; her face heated up and her heart pounded. She clutched the material of his jacket in both hands and rotated them both around until his back bumped against the wall of the cabin, and finally, sweet blessed everything, *finally*, she found the zipper and yanked it down. His rapid breathing matched her own and he clutched her shoulders; his fingers tightened even through the heavy jacket when she slid her hands down his chest. Her thumbs brushed against the waistband of his pants and she inched his Henley up enough to slide her fingertips against the hot skin of his taut belly.

He gasped and pulled away from her. "Jesus, your hands are freezing," he panted.

"Sorry." She drew them back from his skin.

"No." With his own palms, he pressed hers back to his belly and the muscles tightened under her fingers, then relaxed as he warmed up again. "You touched me there before," he whispered, his face close to hers. "I like it," he breathed, and kissed her temple.

She closed her eyes at the soft press of his lips and her lashes brushed against his jawline. Without any fumbling on his part, he drew the zipper of her coat down, eased her hands around to his bare back, then spread their coats open so they could press closer to each other, most obstructions gone. His hands went around her waist, too, under her shirt and at the waistband of her pants, warm, comforting, strong.

She sighed when he rested his cheek against hers, the gentle sway of their bodies lulling her. Their hearts beat in rhythm, their skin heated up wherever it touched, and a gentle lassitude suffused her body. She could sleep standing up right here with him.

"I really am incapable of not touching you whenever you're near," he murmured in her ear.

111

"Mmm," she said as his fingers pressed into the small of her back, easing the tight muscles there.

"Which is why," he said, lifting his head, "we need to stop." Hands still on her waist, he took a step back.

He was right, and she knew it—it had been her idea in the first place to slow down—but he was a reassuring calm in the midst of her stormy life. Which was why he was very, very right. "I know," she agreed. She squeezed his wrists, then set them away from her; the cold air rushed to take their place, and she hugged her coat around her.

"You were right, what you said earlier. If we're going to find out if anything exists between us beyond the physical, we need to slow it down."

She nodded. She also needed to stop using other people as a distraction for overcoming her life's obstacles. Wasn't that one of the reasons she'd entered this contest in the first place?

He pressed a gentle kiss to her temple, whispered, "Sleep tight. See you tomorrow," and slid away around the corner.

CHAPTER SEVENTEEN

Gabe suppressed a yawn and noticed Teresa doing the same. She stood in a grouping of her fellow contestants, facing the judges in a re-creation of yesterday's challenge as they awaited the team verdicts. He stood behind the line of cameramen and other crew, PA Katie by his side with her clipboard and headset, his gaze frequently straying to the dock where he and Teresa had sat and talked. It had been ages since he'd shared that much about himself with a woman he barely knew. He still vibrated at the memory of Teresa in his arms, the smooth skin at the small of her back, the slight indents above her ass, and the feel of her tiny braids bumping through his fingers as he caressed them. He wanted her to brush them over his bare skin, for the loose feathery ends to dance over his body, waking up his senses as the two of them basked in naked bliss.

"Shit," he muttered, dropping his hands to his thighs, his head drooping.

Katie touched his shoulder as a reminder of "quiet on the set," and he nodded, still bent over.

She leaned close and whispered, "You okay?"

He nodded again and rose with a quick, but quiet outrush of breath. He held up a hand in apology, and she nodded back with a shrug and a smile. He brushed his hair from his face and focused on the scene in front of him. *Easy, De Luca, you haven't lost your cool because of a woman since you were thirteen.* But that had been for Winnie McCallister, all dimples, freckles, and yes, pigtails. When she'd turned her sweet smile on him in front of his dad's hardware store while selling Girl Scout Cookies, the same swooping sensation overwhelmed him then as when he thought about Teresa now.

Jesus, but he was a goner, and he barely knew her.

When Eric announced Team Three as the challenge winners, Chance, Cookie, Karl and Teresa cheered and hugged each other. Cookie did a little dance, and fist-bumped Karl. Chance held Teresa longer than necessary, and Gabe narrowed his eyes. He gestured to Katie that he was going to watch the rest on the monitors and she handed him a set of headphones. He nodded his thanks and joined Monica, the assistant director, at the setup well back from the action. Monica plugged his headset in and clicked her fingers for Jeremy to bring up a chair. Gabe thanked her with a smile, declining with a shake of his head and cutting motion of his hands. He preferred to stand at this point, too antsy to sit in one place.

He positioned the headset over his ears and heard Eric congratulating Team Three again, then asking them to step back into line with the others while he turned the next phase over to the judges. The three of them praised a few individual standouts—-Antonio for his soft-shell crabs, Aanjay's take on grilled corn curried up, and MaryBeth's succulent babyback ribs—then turned to those that didn't work out as well. Feeling bold, Gabe sent Teresa a saucy text, already anticipating her similar reply when she got her phone back that evening. He tuned back in in time to hear the judges call out Rachel for burning her buttermilk biscuits, Jonas' lack of seasoning, and Lily Wen noted Teresa's lack of originality. Lily bashed the shish kebabs as too easy, and their s'mores cliché, as if the entire meal had been Teresa's responsibility.

"What the eff," Gabe sputtered. If Lily was already gunning for Teresa, would splitting with her only increase her animosity? He had to make the break; no matter his feelings for Teresa, he couldn't be with someone who got petty revenge this way—but damn if it didn't put them all in a bad spot.

Eric called the three forward to stand in front of the judge's table and reminded them being in the bottom three didn't mean automatic elimination. He noted that since Teresa was on the winning team, she was exempt—at least this week—from elimination.

The judges then announced the winner of the entire challenge—MaryBeth, who would get an advantage in the next contest—but Gabe unplugged his headset at that point, returning it to Monica. He stomped up the path to the main lodge, and to the small conference room set aside for his interviews. He paced, angry at the circumstances, and the trouble he'd unwittingly caused for Teresa.

And now he had to interview her as both a member of the winning team and a challenge "loser."

He ran his hands through his hair. "Shit."

"Hey." Katie poked her head around the door jamb; she'd obviously heard his outburst but kindly ignored it. "Whenever you're ready, I've got Team Three here for you. How'd you like to do this? Teresa, Jonas or Rachel first, then the group, or vice versa?"

He pretended to ponder the options, but knew immediately he needed to talk to Teresa first. He didn't always wear his heart on his sleeve, but he wasn't much for all that manly bullshit about not showing your feelings, either. It came from growing up with two older sisters and a dad who masterfully straddled that line between classic macho and sensitive male. He wanted to live an honest life, so he worked at addressing conflict as soon as possible.

Life was fucking hilarious sometimes.

"Let's start with Teresa, then Jonas, and Rachel. I'll talk to the whole team last."

Katie gave him the "okay" sign, and he heard her boots go from hardwood to carpeting, so he knew when she'd reached the area in front of the fireplace. A few murmurs, then two pairs of shoes made their way back to the room. Gabe stared out the window at the lake, the tops of nearby trees swaying in the gentle breeze, and considered how best to handle this situation.

"Teresa for you," Katie announced, and Gabe almost laughed at the unintended entendre.

He lifted a hand to her in thanks and she shut the door. Teresa stood in front of it, watching him, then pivoted on one foot, flicked the lock, and turned back to face him. "I can't do personal right now," she announced, then flinched, as if the admission hurt her in some way.

He held his hands out from his sides. "Whatever you need. I just wanted to be sure—"

"I'm fine."

"—that you know what happened just now sucks the big hairy eyeball."

She gaped at him, then barked out a laugh and covered her mouth with one hand. "I didn't expect that. I thought you were going to get all serious and sorry on me, and I didn't think I could handle that."

"I am serious," he told her, mentally noting that neither of them had moved yet, maintaining the distance between them. "Seriously pissed about what happened, and sorry, too, but not in a pitying way. And I couldn't interview your team without you knowing that first."

She brushed a foot along the tile floor in a small arc. "Oh. Well, thanks. But the big hairy eyeball thing was still pretty funny."

"It wasn't planned. I regressed for a second there."

Her shoulders lowered a fraction and she took a step forward. "Did you and your friends say that when you were younger?"

"Yeah, that and a few other choice phrases that would offend your mother."

Another couple of steps. "Believe me, it's not so hard to offend my mother."

"Oh?"

"Staunch conservative."

"So she can't take any credit in raising an amazing, open-minded daughter?" She stood in front of him now, and he shoved his hands in his pockets to keep from touching her.

"Unless she did it on purpose so I'd rebel against her, no. That was all Mama Step."

He tilted his head; the name sounded familiar. "Mama Step?"

"My grandmother." She wrapped her arms around her waist. "The most amazing person I've ever known. My grandfather was white and Polish, and they left Virginia so they could marry legally. They raised three kids, started a deli, and she said she'd do it all again in a heartbeat, despite their shop getting torched, crosses burned on their lawns, and my grandmother herself getting beat up more than once."

"Christ," Gabe whispered.

Teresa nodded. "She's my idol. Every time I think I have something tough to face in my life, I think of her. Today was nothing compared to that." She narrowed her eyes. "Nothing. That's my official quote."

"You want me to use that for the interview?"

She nodded. "Any of it you want. I got sidetracked for too long, forgetting who I was and who I wanted to be. I can't do that anymore."

"What are you saying?"

"Have you broken up with Lily Wen yet?"

"There hasn't been time."

"I hate conflict," Teresa said. "I used to go out of my way to avoid it, sometimes literally running in the other direction to get away from someone I had a conflict with. I can't do that anymore," she repeated. "I *won't* do that anymore. Our food wasn't unoriginal, but your girlfriend—"

"She's not my girlfriend."

"Your whatever. Did you see her face at the verdict? She enjoyed telling me that. She's caught us watching each other. If she considers me a threat, I'm not going to get a fair chance in this contest."

"I am breaking it off with her. But if she's as vengeful as you think, I don't want her to take it out on you."

"I can handle myself. And just to be clear, I'm not mad at you, I'm mad at her. But I'm also really pissed that I was called out that way. You can't use that in your interview," she added, then spun around and swept out the door, slamming it behind her.

"Well, hell," Gabe said.

He somehow got through the interview with Team Three, then walked around the main lodge in search of Lily Wen.

AFTER THE LONG DRIVE back, the cameras followed the contestants into the brownstone, so Teresa had to maintain her stoic appearance when all she wanted to do was crawl into her bunk and hide. She'd built up a lot of steam between the time Lily Wen blasted her dish for being boring and when she charged into the interview room to confront Gabe. She'd practiced her speech a few times, and it still hadn't come out quite right, but she meant it. And now she needed to live it. No more running and hiding.

So she stayed in the living room with everyone else, chatting about the gorgeous location, the challenge, and what might happen next. She let other people complain about the judges, not saying a word against them herself. Finally, PA Chrissie said they were on their own for the evening, but they needed to be ready to go at 5:30 a.m. for the two eliminations tomorrow. Then Chrissie, Katie, and the crew left, and a few people headed to bed, since it was already 11:30.

Ready to make her own way to sleep, Teresa stood, but paused when Rachel approached her.

"That judging stank." Rachel held out a drink for Teresa. "It's just wine. They don't let us have anything stronger. This isn't *The Real World*."

Teresa smiled and took the drink. "Thanks. Sorry they blasted you, too. I bet they've all burned things themselves."

Rachel scrunched up her face. "Yeah, but probably not during the most important competition of their lives."

This statement surprised Teresa. Rachel had a sweet quality about her, and seemed competitive in the way of someone used to getting things because she was pretty, but not especially driven. Teresa took a sip of wine and said, "Oh?"

"Totally. Other little girls dreamed of weddings and sweet sixteen parties and all that, but I dreamed about my own cupcake shop." She tucked her bobbed hair behind one ear. "It's all I've ever wanted. It's the *only* thing I've ever wanted." She downed her wine and swayed closer, tilting her head up since she barely reached Teresa's shoulder. "I took cooking classes, graduated from the CIA, the Institute of Culinary Education, and Johnson & Wales, you know, where Emeril Lagasse went? But every single thing you can think of happening got in the way of my actually getting a shop. My dad died, I got pregnant right out of high school, my husband got arrested for dealing meth and had all these attorney fees, I mean, he didn't *do* it, right? But we still had to deal with all the legal stuff. We're *still* dealing with it. I had to use the money I'd set aside, my 'pin money,' as my mom used to call it, the money for my *shop*, for the lawyers and bail and all that." She stopped abruptly, staring into her wine glass, and Teresa thought maybe she'd wound down when Rachel said, "I need more wine." She pointed at Teresa. "Don't go anywhere."

Teresa commiserated with Rachel, but she didn't need to hear anymore about her sad life right now, and didn't have anything to contribute to the conversation. "Sorry, Rachel, I really need to get to bed." She set her glass down on the kitchen island and fast-walked up the hallway to the bedroom. Everyone else was asleep except Lynette, who sat on a lower bunk next to Teresa's, brushing out her hair.

"Rachel cornered you, too?" she asked in her normal loud voice.

Teresa nodded, grabbed her toiletries case, and started to back out of the room.

"I just want to give that girl a hug," Lynette said. She bent over to pull something out of her own bag and Teresa saw the tattoo she'd mentioned the first day. It was a cartoonish tabby, sitting face forward like a person, with huge round eyes, shimmery angel wings, and a pink halo. "No one should have to live through all she has," Lynette continued. "And to lose her dad. No girl should have to go through that, either, especially when she's trying so hard to open her own business—"

"Oh, who cares?" MaryBeth grumbled from the top bunk. "She'll drink herself to oblivion and shrink the competitor pool even more." She leaned her head over the edge and eyed Teresa in the dim light from a lamp on a table by the door. "Of course, some of you are taking care of that in other ways."

Teresa paused, her bag clutched to her chest, unable to come up with a brilliant response. "Oh, just...just shut up," she said, and marched out.

MaryBeth's nasty laugh drifted after her.

Teresa took a quick shower, brushed her teeth, and changed into leggings and a long t-shirt. If they were surprised by a camera crew in the middle of the night, she didn't want to be wearing some tiny nightie or an equally embarrassing outfit. She usually wore a t-shirt and panties to bed, but the t-shirts didn't always cover her rear, and that wouldn't work here, either.

By the time she got back inside, Lynette had turned out her light and Rachel snored on top of the covers in the remaining bunk. Aanjay and Cookie had apparently slept through everything. Teresa covered Rachel with a blanket, then crawled into her own bed, grabbing her cell from the pillow where Chrissie had placed it. She turned it on, unlocked it and waited impatiently for the connections from her loved ones to come through.

She heard rustling from one of the bunks and used her phone's light to illuminate Cookie stooping by her bunk.

"Shove over," she whispered. "I hate sleeping alone."

Teresa straightened, but didn't move otherwise. "Uh."

Cookie rolled her eyes. "I'm not a lesbian," she said, as if tired of the suggestion. "You're gorgeous and all, and if I was a lesbian, you should be flattered, but I like men. I especially like *my* man." She held up her own phone, as if that proved all she said. She looked over her shoulder, but Teresa knew it was all but impossible to tell if anyone was eavesdropping. "Look," Cookie continued, still whispering, " I helped you out earlier when you were all gaga over Mr. Hot Blogger and almost got caught not paying attention, and when the prom queen started yapping about that show you were on, and I hate sleeping alone in strange places, so..."

Teresa shoved over.

"Thanks." Cookie slid under the covers and gestured at Teresa's cell. "Who you waiting to talk to?"

Teresa shrugged. "Anyone at this point who can remind me what real life is like."

"It's only been three days," Cookie reminded her.

Teresa snorted out a laugh and covered her mouth. "I know. But you have to admit this is pretty..."

"Immersive, yeah, I know." Cookie's phone buzzed. "Sweet Jesus, finally," she muttered, and read the text.

In the phone's light, Teresa saw Cookie's round, rough face soften and a smile form at the corners of her mouth. She sent a rapid-fire text back, still smiling. Teresa's own phone buzzed, but she ignored it for the moment, wondering if she'd ever feel so strongly about a man it would change her entire countenance when she thought of him.

"What's your man's name?" Teresa asked Cookie.

"Huh? Oh, Thomas, but we all call him Urgayle, or Urg." She stroked the edge of the phone with one thick, blunt finger.

Teresa blinked a few times and Cookie turned to her, laughing quietly. "He's a Navy SEAL. He looks like the Viggo Mortensen character in *GI Jane*." She thumbed through a few items on her phone before showing Teresa a picture of herself and a buff guy with a chin dimple, dark sunglasses, a green tank top and shorts that revealed super-toned legs.

"Holy shit," was all Teresa could say.

Cookie smiled at the picture. "Right? Sometimes I feel like putting this picture on a t-shirt that says, *Really, I'm not a lesbian*." She lifted a chin at Teresa's phone. "Your turn."

Teresa glanced at it, and after telling herself to get over it when she didn't see anything from Gabe, identified each person for Cookie. Youngest sister and rebel, Julia; Kristen, a new mom and one of Teresa's best friends; her grandmother, Mama Step; and Libby, a friend from the catering company.

"And..." She scrolled down. Victoria was conspicuously absent. But then... "Um."

Cookie read over her shoulder. "Cort? *miss you pretty darlin do good.*

Leaves something to be desired in the grammar department, but he clearly likes you."

Teresa closed the text, but the icon of Cort's face stayed on the screen. "That's kind of the problem."

"You don't like him back? You want Mr. Hot Henley more?"

"Mr. Hot Henley?"

Cookie shrugged. "We're working on something better."

Teresa stared at her, horrified. "*We?* We who?"

"You're not the only one who's noticed his hotness. Me, Rachel, Chrissie, Karl, even Aanjay got a little hot in the sari. And we know *Mary Beth*," she added, separating the two names, "and Lily Wen were duking it out for him earlier, even if it was just via nasty expressions."

"Wait. Karl is gay?"

From across the room, MaryBeth snarled, "I don't know what you two dykes are yapping about, but you need to shut up."

"Oh, cram it up your poop hole," Cookie shot back. She shrugged at Teresa, kissed her phone, and rolled onto her side.

In the silence, Teresa sat clutching her own phone, just as she had before Cookie showed up, but now her mind raced in twenty more directions. After going off on Gabe, she hadn't expected a text from him, but his silence still disappointed her. She decided to answer Kristen's text, because she honestly didn't know what else to do or think at that point, and she certainly couldn't *sleep.*

She gave Kristen the full scoop, including her decision to stop running from conflict. She meant it this time, damn it, but it seemed like that opened the door for opportunities to stand up for herself. *Shoved right in my face*, she wrote. She admitted she hadn't done such a great job dealing with those opportunities.

Kristen responded with: *Welcome to the Universe making sure you really want what you say. Remember the parental dinner? Get ready for more challenges, if you're determined to live this way.* She added a smiley face, possibly to lessen the pain. Teresa wasn't sure if it helped.

She wrote back: *When do the challenges stop?*

Kristen: *Oh, honey, they never stop. That's life. But for your particular declaration, they probably stop once you've integrated the decision in your life and no longer have to decide to be/act a certain way. You just are. Daisy and I fully support you.* She attached a picture of a smiling, fat-cheeked Daisy in a "Peace Love Veggies" onesie.

Now *that* helped.

CHAPTER EIGHTEEN

Gabe sat on a stool at Pete's, the bar located under the CuisineTV studios, waiting for Lily. After scanning the dim room, heavy on brick walls, cast-iron fixtures and a painted ceiling, he checked his phone for the fifth or sixth time. No return text from Teresa, and almost 11:15 p.m. Not late for New York, but late for him these days. He didn't have to be at *Tasty Dish* filming until later tomorrow for the elimination rounds, and everyone had Sunday off. He'd use that time to check in with his friends and family, talk to his editor Ondrea, and work on the edits she'd given him. He had a lot to fit into his "weekend," and he'd take as long as necessary to work things out with Lily, but he'd breathe easier after ending it with her.

He took a sip of Belgian ale, scanning the bar again, and when he saw a few heads turn in the direction of the door, he knew Lily Wen had arrived. And he had to admit the woman knew how to make an entrance. Red purse tucked in the curve of one arm, form-fitting black capris, and a blouse tied off at the waist so a hint of bare skin at her midriff peeked through. Her long hair swayed as she walked toward him in red platform pumps.

Her gaze stayed on him the entire way as she wound her way through the tables to his spot at the bar. Fuck me shoes, but "fuck you" eyes. He hopped off the stool as she got closer, and said, "Here or a table?"

"What about your place?" she challenged.

"Not a good idea."

"Why not? You mad I blasted your girlfriend today?"

He refused to respond with "she's not my girlfriend," especially since that's what Lily anticipated, but he'd be damned if he denied Teresa, either. Plus, it echoed Teresa's earlier words. No winning that one, so he kept it simple. "We need to talk."

"Always such a good beginning." She thumped her bag on a nearby table and snapped her fingers at the bartender while addressing Gabe. "Buy me a drink."

He paid for her whiskey sour, which she sipped for awhile before turning to him. "You're done, aren't you?"

"It's not working between us," he told her.

"I saw you with her," she said, her glass close to her face. He could still see her cold eyes, though. "Last night. Groping each other like a couple of hick kids against the side of the cabin. Tacky." Another sip before she set the glass down. "Did you decide it wasn't working between us before or after you met her?"

He wasn't about to get into the specifics of when he actually "met" Teresa. "Before."

"And you didn't tell me, because...?" Before he could respond, she said, "Because I have more balls than you?" Her cell buzzed and she pulled it out of a side purse pocket. She glanced at it, and that little cat's smile he'd liked early on appeared, then disappeared just as quickly. It no longer charmed him. "We're going to have some fun surprise guests on the show." Her long black hair swung forward as she stood and bent over him. "I won't fire you," she hissed, "for groping a contestant. But you and your little pet might not be enjoying yourselves so much from now on." She slammed down the rest of her drink, then stormed out of the bar.

Gabe gestured for a shot.

TERESA PRACTICALLY SLEEPWALKED through the next few days. She observed the two eliminations on Saturday with a combination of guilt, fear, and relief. She'd placed last with her vegan mac-and-cheese in the first challenge, but her team's win at Big Valley Lodge exempted her from eliminations this week. Her exemption threw Aanjay into an elimination challenge instead. When Aanjay's take on curried spaghetti and meatballs failed to wow the judges, Teresa's stomach dropped. If her team hadn't won, she might be the one going home.

After they said goodbye to Aanjay, Katie directed everyone to change into the extra set of clothing they'd brought. That way, the afternoon's elimination challenge would look different from the morning and could be shown as happening in a completely separate week when the series aired. Rachel and Jonas faced off next, and while Jonas made an impressive batch of chocolate-dipped pistachio truffle cookies in half an hour, they didn't match Rachel's bite-sized lemon cream pies. When Jonas went home, the second elimination of the day, the reality of how quickly any of them could be kicked off hit Teresa like a sucker-punch.

She didn't have time to linger over it, though, because their challenges over the next two days occupied all her energy. First, they boarded a cruise ship and were directed to create a dinner menu that was judged by both the main panel and cruise guests. Teresa was not surprised her seafood paella fared better with the guests than with Lily Wen, but it was enough to keep her out of the bottom two. That went to Lynette, whose spinach soufflé fell flat.

Before they'd recovered from that competition, sadistic PA Chrissie commanded them out of bed at 5:30 the next morning for a challenge at the Bronx Zoo. Each team of two collected clues along the Activity Trail that gave them ingredients for their children's menu meal. Teresa could swear her teammate Chance pinched her ass at the Bug Carousel, but he blamed it on a group of passing Kindergartners. They didn't do well in the challenge with their personal pizzas, but Karl and Ace came in last place for their unimaginative and messy grilled cheese sandwiches with avocado.

Both days, Teresa saw Gabe taking notes as well as texting and laughing quietly to himself over things he saw on his phone. Yet when she checked her phone each night, nothing from him came through. Their gazes locked plenty of times, but no opportunity for talking privately came up.

Teresa bonded more with Cookie, and they shared texts and pictures when Cookie slept in the same bunk. They exclaimed together over Mama Step's charming texts, a picture of Kristen's new, short haircut—*harder for sticky fingers to grab!*—perfected a simultaneous flip-off whenever MaryBeth called them Dykes for Diners, and surprisingly found themselves drawing Rachel into their small inner circle. Rachel was very funny and loyal, and happily shared humorous stories of her various culinary schools experiences.

Lynette and Tony spent time together connecting over their Midwest backgrounds. MaryBeth, Antonio and Ace huddled together a lot as if they were on *Survivor*, setting up alliances and pitting contestants against each other. Chance continued to approach Teresa as if he might want to ask her out or maybe relive her time on *In Concert* with him, and she continued to avoid him as much as possible.

But Teresa would gladly take Chance and his weird flirting over Lily Wen's passive-aggressive behavior any day. Kristen's prediction that the universe would send more challenges her way was starting to come true. Teresa had no clue what the point of the conflict with Lily Wen was, but it definitely existed. Lily went out of her way to sidle next to Teresa, smirking and looking like a model in her outrageous outfits.

Without any information from Gabe, Teresa had to conclude he'd decided to stay with Lily.

"Maybe for the best," Cookie said one night as they shared texts from their friends and family members. "Hot men aren't always faithful."

Teresa raised an eyebrow at her.

Cookie raised her own eyebrow back. "Urg knows I'd kick his ass if he cheated. But I'm a firecracker in bed. He has no reason to cheat."

Teresa believed all of that.

On Wednesday, Teresa stood in the back of an empty storefront while a food truck operator described his journey from unemployed to pop-up restaurant owner in six months, with the help of family, friends and a small business loan. His story inspired her, and she wanted to kick Lily Wen in the shin when the other woman sidled up to her in yet another pair of impossibly high heels and whispered, "He's great, isn't he?"

Teresa crossed her arms over her chest, nodding in agreement, but refused to look Lily's way.

Lily leaned so close, Teresa couldn't avoid seeing her. "I love overnight successes," she said, her eyes on Patrick, the owner.

Nostrils filled with the scent of Lily's Chanel perfume, Teresa took a step away, but she was blocked by a prep table behind and Tall Tony next to her. And Lily knew it.

"That can happen a lot on reality TV shows," Lily continued in a low voice. "One day you're languishing in obscurity and the next, catapulted to celebrity status. Just because you're on a television show." She snorted. "And it can happen to anyone. Swimmers, biologists, musicians. Even people who think they can cook."

Teresa shot her a look, and was about to defend herself when Lily Wen turned and clicked away. Teresa's heart skipped a beat as Lily walked toward three people: Gabe, holding hands with a pale, fair-haired little girl in a blue Elsa costume who in turn held the hand of the man on her other side. He was tall, with casually tousled black hair, and wore a black on black suit. He was model handsome, and knew it. He looked nothing like mini Elsa, but she certainly resembled Gabe, with dark blonde hair and wide-set hooded eyes.

Behind her, the group clapped and PA Katie announced a break, but Teresa couldn't take her eyes from Gabe, who had caught her watching him. He gave Teresa a hesitant smile, then nodded at Lily when she stopped in front of the trio. Lily said something, but Gabe shook his head, gestured toward the girl and other man and took a couple of steps in Teresa's direction. He was forced to stop when the man held out a hand to Lily and grinned at her like he knew what she wore to bed at night. Gabe then introduced the girl, and Lily crouched down to shake her hand and exchange a few words.

The girl smiled, but sidled closer to Gabe, hugging his leg, and hid her face behind him. Lily straightened, dug in her purse, and handed a card to the handsome friend before clicking her way to the door and outside. The friend held a finger up to Gabe and followed Lily.

Gabe spoke to the girl and she nodded, took his hand again, and followed to where Teresa now stood alone, her fellow contestants talking to the food truck owner, gathered in small groups or taking a quick walk outside.

"Hey," said Gabe when he and the girl stood in front of her. He swung the hand of the little girl. "This is Kaily. Kaily, this is my friend Teresa."

Teresa crouched in front of Kaily, reminded of Lily having done it, too, but she wanted to treat Kaily like an equal. "Hi, Kaily. It's very nice to meet you."

Kaily glanced up at Gabe, who nodded in reassurance, then she held out a hand and said, "Very nice to meet you, too, Teresa," in a sweet, solemn voice. Then she perked up. "I'm almost five!"

Teresa shook. "You know, I was pretty sure your name was Elsa when I first saw you in your beautiful blue dress."

Kaily's face brightened. "She's my favorite," she gushed. "I'm going to Disney World soon and meet her, and I guess I'll meet Anna, too. She's okay, but Elsa is the best. And I'm gonna meet Mickey, too!" she crowed. "And he's going to make me all better forever." She beamed at Gabe, who smiled back at her even as his eyes tightened at the corners.

Teresa wobbled on her heels and stood up to keep from falling on her butt. Before she could find a way to ask what Kaily meant by *better forever*, Gabe said, "Kaily's in remission from Acute Lymphoblastic Leukemia, so she's already better."

"Yeah, but I need to be *forever*, so Daddy won't be so sad no more."

"And she breaks my heart on a regular basis," Gabe whispered to Teresa before swooping down and flipping Kaily over his shoulder so she shrieked with joy. He righted her, straightened her dress, and held her in the crook of one arm. She set a small hand on his shoulder and he gave her cheek a noisy kiss. "Kaily's daddy is my friend Stephan. He had to go into the office today, so Kaily gets to hang out with me."

"No, Gabe. *You* get to hang out with *me*," she said with a giggle.

They high-fived each other and Teresa smiled, both in pleasure over their camaraderie and relief that Gabe hadn't been hiding a secret love child from her. She still didn't know why he hadn't been in touch the past few days, though.

"And we *both* get to hang out with Nick," Kaily added.

"And a pleasure that is for everyone," said Gabe's handsome friend as he strode back inside, easing his sunglasses on top of his head. "Hot, hot number," he stage-whispered to Gabe, before turning to Teresa. "But, then, it looks like that's going around. Hi. I'm—"

Gabe interrupted. "It's Bring Your Neanderthal to Work day. And mine is called Nick."

"And we all know what Neanderthals were known for, right? Their really big—"

"Nick," Gabe warned, with a glance at Kaily.

"—brains," Nick finished, reaching for Teresa's hand to shake it. "A pleasure."

"Hey, caveman," Gabe stepped between them so Nick had to release Teresa's hand. "How'd you like to show Kaily the food truck and get her some falafel?"

Kaily bounced in Gabe's arms and clapped. "Ooh, falafel." She batted her eyelashes at Nick. "Please, caveman, please?" She dove at him and he caught her, flipping her around and up so she sat on his shoulders. "'Sides, Gabe wants to talk to Teresa about 'portant matters."

"Indeed I do, wise one." Gabe lifted a chin at Nick. "Thanks."

Nick gave them a knowing look and bounced out with Kaily, neighing and stamping his feet like a horse.

Gabe waited until the door closed behind them before saying, "Katie said you were on a lunch break." He glanced around. "Everyone's outside. So can we? Talk?"

She shrugged. *You have my phone number,* she thought. *We could have talked any time.*

He tilted his head at her response. "Are you mad at me?"

"Yes," she said, but without much heat. She was too tired to be mad. Disappointed, maybe?

"I was hoping to hear from you. And then I had a scintillating texting session the other day with someone named Gladys who said she'd be happy to take me up on my offer if I really had that much stamina."

Teresa blinked at him. What was he talking about?

He waved the phone at her. "You gave me the wrong number."

"What?" She grabbed it from him and scrolled through his contacts. "Oh, fudgesicles, I gave you the wrong number," she repeated, staring at the screen, embarrassed but relieved that he actually had tried to contact her.

"Well, Gladys didn't seem to think so."

She corrected the number and returned his phone. He slipped it in his pocket and held out a hand. "My turn."

Bemused, she handed hers over, glad she had it today since they didn't have a challenge, and watched him input the information. "Gladys will be sad," Gabe told her, "but I'll be very, very happy." After giving her phone back with a smile, he said, "That out of the way, would you like to start? Or shall I?"

Teresa smiled, remembering an exchange Victoria shared between her and Luke, before they started dating. In his charming Southern accent, he'd said, "I do like the way you talk." Teresa said the same to Gabe now, minus the accent.

"Did I say something especially clever?" he asked, with a hint of a smile that told her he knew what she meant.

She shook her head, gesturing toward the appetizers that had been set out. "Let's get some food."

They filled up their plates with sweet potato fries, grilled zucchini rolls, watermelon skewers, and mini bacon maple cupcakes; each grabbed a water bottle and sat on top of a picnic table set in the window, their feet on the bench.

Teresa stared at the outside scene: her fellow contestants lined up at the three food trucks, Nick dancing a jig with Kaily still on his shoulders, the masses of people in suits weaving around each other on the sidewalk. New York's female population seemed to exceed that of men, and they all dressed beautifully. Compared to San Francisco, the energy here made Teresa jittery, and she wondered if she'd ever adjust to it if she lived here long-term.

She finished a bit of watermelon and said, "Can you tell me about Kaily?"

Gabe let out a sigh, but his expression brightened when he caught sight of the little girl skipping in a circle around Nick's legs. "She's the best thing that's happened to all of us."

"Who's all of us?"

"Her dad, Stephan. Me, Nick. And our other friend, Adam. We were the fantastic four growing up. But we're the fab five with Kaily." He stopped, his expression conflicted. "Her..." His voice sounded gruff and he cleared his throat. "Her mom died a few minutes after she was born. Eclampsia, which led to a heart attack."

Having witnessed Daisy's birth, Teresa couldn't imagine that joyful occasion forever altered, with Kristen taken away from them, and from her baby. Thinking of her life without Kristen, and that chubby-cheeked little one never knowing her mom made Teresa's heart ache. She blinked back tears.

"I'm so sorry, Gabe."

He'd set his plate down and his hands dangled between his knees as he stared outside. "I wasn't there. I was off playing celebrity millionaire with my new 'friends.'" She heard the quotes around the word, and could guess those "friends" had only been around Gabe because of his money. "I wasn't even in the country and kept forgetting to charge my cell." He glanced at her, and Teresa saw the guilt he carried with him before he turned his head away again. "I didn't know about it for five days. Nick had to fly in and track me down, get me sober enough to travel, and kicked my ass all the way home."

"Are you still kicking your own ass over it?"

He gave her a small smile and slid his fingers around hers, letting them rest on the table between their thighs. "Every day. But that's not why I help Steph out with Kaily, or why I love her so much. That's just...family."

Still thinking of Kristen, Teresa asked, "What was her mom's name?"

"Hannah. She was part of our group growing up. She was smart and feisty, with this really raunchy sense of humor that came out when she got drunk. I think we all had a crush on her at one point or another. But she was fiercely devoted to Stephan and didn't see anyone else after we turned fourteen or so."

Still holding her hand, Gabe slid off the table and stood in front of her between her knees. She caught a glimpse of Nick peering in the window at them, then sweeping Kaily away. He might be a caveman, but he had some tact. And then Teresa only saw Gabe, his wide-set almond-shaped eyes, feathery blonde hair and full lower lip. "How did things get so intense between us?" he asked.

"I'd say they've been intense from the very beginning."

He stepped closer, prevented from coming right up against her body by the bench she rested her feet on. "Hell, yeah." His voice lowered and he dipped his head toward her. "Have I told you how good you tasted that day? When I licked you. Right. There?" With his free hand, he traced a circle around her clavicle, and across her collarbone. "Like nutmeg, only sweeter."

He kissed the side of her neck, his hair brushing her cheek. She closed her eyes against the rush of sensations: the soft brush of hair; warm lips tracing a path to her ear; his fingers tightening around hers; the pulse of blood in heart, temples and between her legs; the friction of her hard nipples against her bra when she arched toward him. His lips reached her jaw line and made their dangerous way toward her mouth. She moaned in anticipation, shoving forward on the bench to be closer, desire arcing between them like lightning, scorching her skin wherever they touched.

She wrapped her legs around his thighs and squeezed when he finally tilted his head just enough and their lips met. She inhaled a rush of breath through her nose and flicked her tongue across his lips. He growled in the back of his throat, and circled one arm tightly around her shoulders while cupping the back of her head with his free hand. His lips parted and he met her challenge, tongue caressing hers, mouth hot and insistent, full of promise she knew he could fulfill.

"Jesus, I'd love to join you, but I don't think there's any room for me."

Teresa and Gabe broke apart, gasping, to see Cookie at the front door, a big grin on her face. "Sorry to interrupt," she said, "because that was the hottest thing I've seen in a long time." She tilted her head toward the street. "But we're being called back to the vans. I'd say you've got five minutes, max." She pointed at them. "Make it count," she demanded, and popped back outside.

Teresa let out a breathy laugh, and Gabe dropped his head to her shoulder. "Well, that's it, then."

"What's 'it'?"

Gabe straightened to look at her. "Whenever you're around, I get lost in you. And when I touch you? The rest of the world doesn't matter. And I can't not touch you." He stroked a thumb over her knuckles.

"I'm like a horny teenager when you're around," Teresa admitted.

Gabe laughed. "Yeah, that, too." He cupped her face and gave her a gentle kiss. "I wish we had more time, and not just for the obvious reasons. To talk to you, too." He let her go and stepped back. "I broke things off with Lily on Friday night. She didn't handle it well, and I'm worried she'll take it out on you." He reached for her hand again and helped her down from the table. "You'll let me know if she does?"

"I told you, I can take care of myself. And I think involving you would make it worse."

"I still want to know." He pulled her close for another kiss. "You devastate me, Teresa Steplowski."

This time they were interrupted by Nick and Kaily. "I think your ride is leaving, beautiful," Nick said.

"I think they love each other," Kaily said simply.

"I'm not touching that one," Nick said with a grin.

"In your best interest," Gabe advised him with a sock on the arm, his other hand still wrapped around Teresa's. He crouched in front of Kaily. "I'm going to walk Teresa to the car, and I'll meet you guys back here. Then we can go to your dad's office and release him from the shackles of employment."

Kaily shook her head. "Big words again." She peered up at Teresa, who crouched next to Gabe to be at the little girl's height. "Gabe is a very nice man," she said solemnly. "I don't want him hurt."

"And I don't plan to do so," Teresa responded, just as solemnly.

Kaily brightened. "Can I get boots like Teresa's?" She pointed to Teresa's purple cowboy boots.

Nick laughed and swept Kaily up to peer down at her own sparkly Mary Janes. "What's wrong with these?"

"These are cute. But *those* are *cool.*"

Gabe and Nick exchanged an "oh boy" look. On the sidewalk, Gabe stopped a few feet away from the line of vans for the show, and pulled Teresa under an awning, out of the way of pedestrian traffic. "Let me cook for you," he said, his expression earnest. Before she could respond, he continued. "I know how busy you are, and I don't know when we'll find the time, but I want to do that for you. A date, at my place." He made the Boy Scout sign of a promise. "No sex. Just dinner. Talking."

She gave him a spontaneous kiss, said, "Yes," and bounced to where Cookie waited to get into the van with her.

CHAPTER NINETEEN

Math had never been Teresa's strong suit, but she knew the number of remaining challengers didn't divide evenly into the three food trucks parked in a row across the street from Washington Square Park. This was their third challenge this week, and Teresa had now reached the level of exhaustion she heard about from new moms, the one where you started hallucinating.

But then Lily Wen stepped out of her warm trailer to address the huddle of shivering contestants, and Teresa got her answer.

"Good morning," Lily said cheerfully for the cameras. "You can probably guess from the food trucks that this will be today's challenge. You'll once more be split into teams, and will cook enough to feed the office workers and many students that attend nearby NYU." She held a hand out to MaryBeth, who stood off to the side of everyone else. "As a two-time challenge winner, MaryBeth is not only safe from elimination this week, but she will select the teams, choose your themed menu, and...lucky girl...gets to sit this one out."

Next to Teresa, Cookie muttered, "Does she get to use your monogrammed dildo, too?"

Rachel snorted a laugh and Lynette squeaked in protest at the profanity. She'd been trying to clean up Cookie's language since the start of the competition, but Teresa could have told her it was a losing battle.

Another fight none of them seemed able to win was the one against MaryBeth. She smiled sweetly and her accent grew thicker as she teamed them up and selected their menu themes. MaryBeth's own "alliance" team of Ace, Antonio, and Chance were given Mexican. The second team, consisting of Cookie, Tony, and Karl had to work with eggs, and Teresa was teamed up with Lynette and Rachel and...popsicles.

A couple people laughed, Cookie said, "*What?!*" and Teresa smiled for the cameras. Actually, she smiled because Gabe strolled around the corner behind the cameras, notebook in hand. He looked so delicious in his boots, worn jeans, and another hot Henley. Gabe's thoughtful look vanished, replaced by a smoldering one, and Teresa flushed head to toe even as she scrambled with her teammates to their assigned truck, a Pepto-pink concoction that was even now being assigned the name Popsicle Heaven by a crew member.

"I love popsicles!" Lynette gushed, as they crowded into the narrow interior.

"Of course you do," Rachel snarled. "Can we do a vodka one? I may need it."

Teresa gave the equipment a quick review, then peered out the window. A cloudless May day, and they might be lucky to break seventy-five. She took a deep breath, ignoring Lynette's speech to Rachel on what she thought might be a "teeny-tiny little drinking problem," and looked around the truck again. Something flashed outside the small service window on the sidewalk side and she caught Gabe holding his clipboard up with a handwritten sign. He had to walk by twice before she caught each word: KNOW STONER HANGOUT.

She gave him a thumbs-up and squeezed by her bickering teammates. "I have some marketing ideas," she said above their raised voices. "You two come up with flavors! Think NYU students, grumpy businessmen!"

She jumped down to the sidewalk right as Gabe stepped into a building with a large "public restroom" sign next to the door. "Bathroom," she announced to the crew, and flew inside, knowing she had very little time before either she'd be missed or her teammates would fall apart. Plus, they had a lot of prep and creating to do before noon unleashed the hungry customers they needed.

In the dim lobby, she squeaked when Gabe grabbed her around the waist and practically carried her into a tiny, empty office nearby. He locked the door, and Teresa, recovering quickly, pushed him by the shoulders up against the wall. She pressed against the length of his body, reveling in every hot, solid inch of him, then raised up on her toes to kiss him. He matched her enthusiasm, his arms circling her body to keep it pressed close, and they lost some time to their mutual desire.

Gabe broke it off first. "That's not why I brought you here."

Still on her toes, she nuzzled his neck, breathing him in. "I don't care," she said, and for that one moment, truly nothing else mattered except the feel of his hands on her and his warm, heady scent.

"I thought we agreed hands-off," he said, but she could hear the humor in his tone.

"*I* thought we agreed we couldn't help ourselves, that we were slaves to our baser natures." She kissed him just below the ear.

"Jesus, you smell good," he breathed. "Like coconut."

Her lips moved down his neck, her destination the section of chest above the V of his shirt.

"Stoners," he gasped, then grasped her upper arms and gently eased her away.

She raised her head and stared at him, stupid with lust. "What?"

"The challenge, Teresa," he said, clearly fighting for clarity himself. "Since you got screwed with popsicles in the challenge, your best bet are the students and the stoners in the park."

She took a deep, shaky breath. "Right." Reluctantly, she increased the space between them.

"The cops are all over the park these days," Gabe continued, "but there's a contingent fighting to make it legal that hangs out here." He gave her a small, handwritten map with directions from where they stood.

Teresa didn't have an objection to pot smoking, per se, but she didn't want to be involved with it herself, or with someone who did it. Her lust-filled brain cleared rapidly. "How do you know this?"

"I have a professor friend at NYU. We run in the park sometimes."

"You jog?" She couldn't picture him in little shorts and tennis shoes. She glanced down the length of his legs. Or maybe...

He gave her a quick kiss. "When I have to. Otherwise, I box."

"You *box*?" Now that was incredibly sexy, and one part of her started scanning the room for a horizontal surface. Maybe she could claim stomach upset and buy them some time.

"Babe, I need you to focus."

Teresa froze. "Did you just call me babe?"

"I did. Term of endearment. Do you prefer sweetheart? Pumpkin? Baby-cakes? My little lemon bar of love?"

She knew he was joking, but kind of liked the last one. "No one's ever called me babe before," she admitted. "Say it again."

One hand flat against her lower back, the other wrapped tenderly around her neck, he eased her toward him. Lowering his face to hers, he looked straight in her eyes, and she watched his pupils dilate with desire. "Babe," he said, his voice husky.

Her lips parted, her breathing sped up, and she got wet at the promise in his voice.

"Go make the best damn popsicles anyone ever lovingly sucked on."

She laughed, her own voice husky, then gripped his shoulders hard, and kissed him harder. "Thank you," she said. She punctuated each "thank you" with a kiss. "Thank you, thank you, thank you."

"Sunday," he said.

"What?"

"Sunday. For our date."

She nodded, this time stupid with glee. "Text me the details."

He led her to the door, unlocked it, and waved her ahead of him. She ran back outside, the map tucked in one hand, ready to kick some ass with the food truck challenge.

GABE RE-LOCKED THE DOOR of that day's interview room, taking time to come down from the high Teresa always gave him. He'd acted like a Neanderthal himself, grabbing her in the lobby and carrying her inside, but she felt so damn good in his arms. Then she'd turned the tables, pushing him against the wall and taking charge until he thought he'd go off right then.

He took several more breaths, then pushed through the glass doors; Teresa's job today was harder than his, but he still needed to fulfill his commitment of writing a blog post about the challenge.

Well back from the frenzy of activity, but close enough to hear the contestants cheering each other on as they planned and prepped, Gabe took a lot of notes. Already attuned to Teresa's voice, he heard her calling out instructions. "We need more shredded coconut. Not so much lavender in that mix, or it'll have a weird aftertaste. Do you have the zester? I need it for the lemon."

He also heard Rachel, whose voice reached an un-naturally high pitch when she got upset. "Are you kidding? We're actually going with peanut-butter-and-jelly popsicles? That's so pedestrian! This is New York, not the middle of your nowhere-ville home town, we might as well do macaroni and cheese ones!"

Lynette's response came in a softer voice, so Gabe didn't catch the actual words, but Rachel's pitch rose even higher. "No, we are not making macaroni and cheese popsicles just because the two things are your daughter's favorite food! Teresa, can you reason with this woman, please?"

As Teresa played peace-maker, Gabe resisted writing up the exchange. He'd refrained from bias as much as possible in his work for the show, but he wouldn't embarrass Teresa or her team, as much as the dialogue amused him. He moved to the truck manned by Ace, Antonio, and Chance, who prepped their fish tacos and enchiladas in a well-choreographed dance. As with many of the other challenges, Ace gave him a sample so he could include a description in his write-up, and he couldn't help a moan at the exquisite combination of fried cod, pickled onion and jalapeño cabbage slaw.

A sticky-sweet voice in his ear said, "I could make you do that if I was your main course."

MaryBeth. The only contestant who hadn't realized he and Teresa had a thing for each other; or maybe she knew and didn't give a damn. He did, though, and having already witnessed her hypocritical side, he decided enough was enough.

He finished his taco and said, "Appreciate the thought. Not interested."

"They're *all* interested, sugar. Even Karl. He just don't know it yet." She brushed a hand along his upper arm, giving it enough of a squeeze with her talons to make a point. "You'll come around, too."

"I'm even less interested than Karl, *sugar*." He knew, because Karl had confessed a thing for Antonio, knowing full well he had no chance with the suave chef. Gabe didn't know why the contestants felt comfortable divulging their secrets, given his position could lead to exposing them, but he'd heard plenty during his interview sessions. "I am, however, interested in that egg stromboli Cookie's offering up."

He sauntered toward The Egg Wagon, reflecting that the show

really needed to come up with more original names, and accepted the cardboard container from Cookie with a wink and his thanks.

"Don't you mean, 'thanks, *sugar*?'" Cookie corrected with an exaggerated version of MaryBeth's southern simper.

Gabe roared out a laugh and high-fived her after tucking his clipboard under his arm. "You get five stars for *that*, screw the stromboli."

"That's what the little strumpet was hoping you'd do, wasn't it?"

Gabe dug into the pastry filled with eggs, spinach, bacon, mushrooms and cheese. He savored the flavor combination, the flaky texture of the pastry, the salt from the cheese, and sighed in satisfaction. "Cooks, you know I wouldn't get near her stromboli with a twenty-foot pole."

"How 'bout our west coast woman?"

"That's between me and her, and you know it."

Cookie leaned far out the window, her blue mohawk brushing the top of the service window, her breasts crushed against the bottom, and crooked her finger at him. Curious, he stepped closer until they were almost face to face. "She says your name in her sleep, you know." She pressed a palm to his mouth before he could say anything. "I'm only sayin' it because you mean something to her, and if you hurt her, both me and Urg are gonna take turns kicking your ass into the next century."

Students started to stream across the park to the trucks then, and Gabe was so flabbergasted by Cookie's words, not to mention wondering who the hell "Urg" was, that he didn't even get a sample popsicle.

This turned out to be a good thing, because halfway through the challenge, with lines for each truck snaking down the block, Rachel finally broke and yelled at Lynette to just shut the hell up, causing both of them to storm out. Teresa served the last of the popsicles with at least twenty people still left waiting outside the truck, then chased after her teammates in an attempt to reconcile them. They eventually returned, but ran out of time before they could produce more key lime/coconut, Thai iced tea, blueberry lemon or peanut-butter-and-jelly pops.

At the judging, Joel Klein told Teresa her team-building and effort at reconciliation helped save her, but Lily Wen reminded her this was the second time she'd been called to the mat for food-related issues, which was the contest's focus. Their team lost, and Rachel and Tony ended up on the bottom two. Even though the judges had enjoyed the egg team's stromboli, Tony kept bumping his head on the truck's ceiling and burned a few omelets. MaryBeth's "dream team" won the challenge.

After Dan called "cut" on that segment, Teresa stormed out to the van and Gabe missed talking to her since he was busy interviewing Tony, who cried when Gabe asked him to recount his experience of the challenge. At a loss, Gabe gave him a few pats on the arm and poked his head out the door to ask Katie for some tissues. He shoved them in Tony's hand and Tony clutched them to his chest, then pulled Gabe in for a bear hug.

He blubbered a few incoherent words, blew his nose in an extremely noisy fashion, and told Gabe he was the best. "The absolute best," he repeated. Gabe didn't think they'd exchanged two words other than question and answer sessions, but nodded and thanked him. They finished the interview and by the time Gabe got outside, the other vans had gone.

TERESA STARED AT THE cryptic message on her phone.

Since coming to New York over a week ago, she hadn't slept more than five hours a night, so maybe she was hallucinating. Or a bit drunk. It was Friday, their first free night in ages, and she'd had quite a bit of wine with the others before she and Cookie trooped to the bunk for some alone time with their phones. She re-read the text from Victoria again, very slowly: *Ethics say no, friendship says yes. Prepare for surprise guest on your show: CL.*

Her world went sideways. She couldn't mean Cort Landry. That was insane.

She tried to call, but the phone went to voicemail. So she wrote: *WTH? Details would be more helpful.* Reviewing her words, she thought it sounded too harsh, so she deleted it and tried to think of a nicer tone. Then she checked herself. No, she really did mean "what the hell" are you talking about, and more details really would help. Because...Cort? Here? On *Tasty Dish?*

While reality television had a poor reputation for ethics, Victoria held herself to a high standard. She set boundaries for her cast, the crew and herself, sometimes to the detriment of her social life and friendships. And then Luke Tyler came along. Teresa and Kristen watched her struggle to keep the relationship professional, but she'd fallen hard for him, and lost her job over it.

Realizing how hard it must have been for Victoria to share this information, but still angry and scared, Teresa retyped her message and hit Send. She wondered if she should interrupt Cookie's rapid-fire texting session with Urg to discuss this. How much should *she* reveal?

Her phone buzzed. Victoria: *Sorry, at a club, super loud. Need me to call you?*

Teresa typed back: *No. Too many ears here. Is it really Cort?*

Victoria: *I'm SO sorry. We all tried to talk him out of it. He's going to guest judge. Not sure of the timing, but we're all coming (no Kristen) to support and see you.*

Teresa stared at her phone so long, it went black. A few minutes later, it buzzed again.

Victoria: *You ok?*

Teresa shook her head at the phone. *No. Shocked. Can't think or talk right now. Thanks for letting me know.*

Victoria: *I had to. Let me know if you need anything?*

She was about to shut her phone down when another text came through. When she saw the words, "Sunday's menu," her mood lifted and she sighed in happy anticipation.

"Hot Henley?" Cookie asked.

"Hot Henley," Teresa admitted. "He sent a menu for our date Sunday." Thankful for the distraction, she read it aloud to Cookie: seared scallops with herb butter sauce, grilled asparagus, sauvignon blanc and pomegranate palmiers for dessert. She sighed again, but not in pleasure this time.

Cookie rested her own phone face down on her chest. "Sounds delish. Why the angst?"

She wanted to tell Cookie about Cort as a guest judge, but couldn't. It was bad enough that she knew. She gestured at the text. "It's...fancy."

"And that's bad because?"

"I'm not sure how to explain it." Teresa turned on her side to face Cookie. "We're doing this challenge, right? Everything we do has to be larger than life in some ways, we have to impress people who do food for a living. All you and I do, all day and night, is fancy food.

Even our dumb popsicles were fancy."

"Peanut-butter-and-jelly?"

Teresa scowled at her. "Don't get me started."

"Sorry. So what you're saying is, you'd like a big medium-rare burger with all the fixin's, some fries and a beer?"

Teresa collapsed into her pillow. "That sounds like heaven."

"So tell him that."

Teresa stared at her phone, even though the screen had gone black. "I can't. He wants to impress me. I don't want to squash that."

"You're a really good not-girlfriend, you know that?"

But wouldn't a truly good not-girlfriend tell Gabe she didn't want fancy? She sighed and typed back that she was looking forward to it, then spent the rest of her allotted phone time flirting with her not-boyfriend and trying to forget that her ex-boyfriend was showing up in New York soon.

CHAPTER TWENTY

Teresa braved her first subway ride from Manhattan to Brooklyn, but took a taxi from the station to Gabe's apartment. She stared up at the six-story brick building, and then at the small Queen Anne houses directly across the street. Except for the wider sidewalks and low fencing around front yards, she could almost be in San Francisco. It was clean and inviting, with older trees along the front of a neighboring apartment, and still she hesitated at the front steps.

She took a quick peek at the encouraging texts from Kristen and Victoria, reminding her she was smart, beautiful and worthy. Then she examined the outfit it seemed to take hours for her to select: black halter-style dress with vertical pink stripes down the front, close-set horizontal ones at the tucked-in waist and wider ones down the skirt, which ended at her knees and flared out a little. She'd traded in her purple cowboy boots for black flats and carried a dusky pink wrap.

She took a bracing breath, tapped up the steps, and pressed the buzzer. The front door buzzed in response a second later and she'd barely stepped into the warm hallway before Gabe came pounding down the stairs.

"Hey." He closed the gap between them and kissed her before she could greet him back. "I promised no sex," he said, his face so close she could see a dusting of flour over one eyebrow, "but I don't remember promising not to touch you."

She smoothed her fingers over his eyebrow to brush away the flour smear. "One often leads to the other."

"Especially with us." He took her hand, and led her up the stairs. He glanced at her as they reached the first flight, stopping her at the landing. "You look beautiful, by the way."

She shook her head, but couldn't resist a smile, dipping her head. "We're never going to get to know each other."

"I've learned a lot about you from our texting sessions." They walked side by side up the next flight.

"The whole point of this was to get to know each other better, in person, without sex getting in the way. I hadn't taken touching into account."

"Does it bother you that whenever we're around each other, I want to touch you?"

She stopped him at the landing this time. "No. As long as you don't get obsessive and creepy about it, I'm flattered. I can't do obsessive and creepy. But I can't go forward with you if we don't spend some time together actually talking. The physical side of things is good, we've proven that. Let's just...talk."

"And eat."

She nodded, then gestured up the stairs. "How many more flights?"

"Just one." He patted his belly. "Helps keep me in shape."

At his door, he gestured her ahead of him while Al Green's "You Ought to Be With Me" beckoned her inside, but she stopped when a woman popped out of the adjacent apartment and exclaimed, "Oh, sweet darling, I am so pleased."

Teresa didn't know if the older woman in a multicolored gypsy dress and scarves was addressing her, Gabe, or the man who slipped out from behind her and stood beaming around the hallway. Maybe all three, she thought, as Gabe pressed a kiss to her cheek, and shook the man's hand.

"Teresa," he said, "my good friends, Natalia and Raul." He slipped an arm around Teresa's waist. "And this is Teresa."

"Darling," Natalia said in a Russian-sounding accent, and Teresa started at the warmth of Natalia's use of the term "darling," as compared to the distant way her mother said it. Natalia held both hands out and caressed Teresa's cheeks. "We are so pleased at your appearance."

"Thank you. I'm happy to meet you," Teresa told them both.

Raul nodded and adjusted his skinny tie.

Still holding Teresa's face, Natalia said, "You are making our Gabriel the happiest, and for that, we are the happiest."

Teresa caught Gabe's eye. "He makes me the happiest, too," she admitted.

Natalia finally released Teresa and stepped next to Raul, who was about two inches shorter. She clasped his hand and said, "We are dining at the new Vietnam restaurant so you may have the loud sex if you wish."

Teresa gaped at her and could swear Gabe choked back a laugh.

He waved at Natalia. "This is the getting-to-know-each-other date, remember, Natalia? No sex tonight."

"Oh darling," she said. "Never waste an opportunity for the good sex. You can still talk during." She winked, Raul waved goodbye, and they made their way down the stairs.

"I can't explain them," Gabe said with a grin as he led her inside.

"I don't want you to. They're lovely. And I can't disagree with her. But..."

He closed the door and laid her shawl across the back of the couch. "They've been together thirty years, and spent the previous twenty as part of a community outreach group for immigrants. They talked to each other for *decades* before falling into bed."

She nodded, relieved that he understood. She was determined to keep this the getting-to-know-each-other date, as he'd told Natalia.

"Your place is so charming." She twirled to look at it, her skirt flaring out. "And I don't mean that in a real estate agent way to cover up that it's small."

He smiled. "It is small. But I've been happy here for quite awhile. It has everything I need. Maybe someday something bigger." He shrugged. "Would you like some wine?"

She nodded. He led her toward the café table by the window near the kitchen and gestured for her to sit. She perched on the tall chair, crossing her legs, and peered out the window while he poured.

"I'll get the asparagus going, then the scallops won't take too long after that." He filled a pan and set the steamer basket inside. "So what would you like to talk about?"

She swiveled toward him, wine glass in hand. "Can I help you with any of that?"

He shook his head. "Not allowed. You've been cooking on demand for weeks now. You get to relax and enjoy." He set the clean asparagus on the prep area and began snapping off the ends. "Should I have put together some conversational topics?"

"You've told me a lot about yourself, including your family and friends, and where you grew up. I've told you a few things about me, but..." She took a breath, then a sip of wine. "One of the things I've done in my life that I want to change is that I can dither about something for ages, then I get tired of my own dithering and jump in just to stop the madness. In the meantime, I sidestep things a lot." She set the glass down and stood across the table from him. He rested his hands on the edge of the wood block, letting her take her time before continuing, one of his aspects she appreciated. "I don't want to do that anymore."

"It can be scary to commit."

"You're not a commitment-phobe, are you?"

He set his elbows on the table, his face now closer to her. "Not for the most part. But I know it can be scary to jump in with both feet, especially if you're not used to it."

Teresa reached for his hands. "Can you pause your cooking enough for me to say something?"

When Gabe's warm hands circled Teresa's, she almost lost her nerve. But if she couldn't say this one little thing to him, if her only accomplishment was pushing him up against a wall and seducing him, then that's all they had. Not a bad accomplishment in itself, but she wanted more. Her stomach went squishy at that, but she took a deep breath and forged ahead. "I don't want scallops for dinner."

"You don't like scallops?"

"I love scallops." But she hated the defeated expression on his face. He looked like these confused rabbits she'd seen in a YouTube video after getting separated from their herd. "Please don't be a sad bunny," she said before she could stop herself.

Gabe glanced at her still-full wine glass before looking back at her. "You need to help me out here."

"I don't want to disappoint you."

He shook his head. "Not possible."

"*So* possible." She backed away from the counter, reluctantly dropping his hands. "The better people get to know and like each, the easier it is to disappoint them."

Gabe stepped around the counter toward her, but stopped when she held her hands up to him, palms out. "And it's easier to forgive each other," Gabe added to her statement.

"Because they care," Teresa added. "The more you care—"

"The less important the small shit becomes." He leaned against the counter and crossed his arms, waiting. Without touching her. "And I care about you, Teresa. So what is this about scallops and sad bunnies?"

"Filming this show has taken over my life." As she spoke, she couldn't help noticing how hot he looked in his worn jeans and a white button down with the sleeves rolled up to his elbows. She shook her head. "This would be so much easier if you could tone down the sexy."

One side of his mouth twitched in a quick, lopsided smile. "Can't change nature, babe."

A shiver ran through her. "As I was saying." She cleared her throat. "After only three days of filming, I told Cookie I couldn't even remember what real life was like." This shouldn't have been so difficult; none of it was coming out right. "We do fancy all the time." She gestured toward the bowl of scallops, the waiting asparagus. "I appreciate the effort, but..." She dropped her hands to her sides, feeling like a complete jerk. "Fancy," she whispered.

Gabe straightened, shoving his hands in his front pockets. "I am an asshole." He shoved his hands through his hair, paced a couple steps away, then came back to stand in front of her. He held up his arms as if about to reach out to her, but slipped his hands back in his pockets. "You deserve to be spoiled," he told her. "I wanted to take care of you, and, yeah, to show off a little. But I didn't ask what *you* wanted."

What she wanted was for him to take his hands out his pockets and touch her all over, but that wasn't sad-bunny on her part, that was just slut-bunny. So she recited the menu Cookie had mentioned. "I'd love a burger and fries, maybe some onion rings and a good amber ale."

His shoulders lowered and he smiled. "Bacon cheeseburger? Medium rare?"

"My mouth's watering."

He stretched for his phone on the counter, but it was just out of his reach. As he slipped by her, he casually brushed a kiss across her temple, as if that happened every day. She dropped onto the stool, watching as he ordered "two of the usual, loaded." During the call, he kept his head down, but shifted nearer to where she sat. When he finished, he said, "There. No more sad bunny."

No, but slut-bunny still lingered. Desperate for a distraction, she asked, "Can you give me the tour?"

He cocked his head, then swept an arm out. "It's pretty much as you see it."

She stood and tucked her hand in the crook of his arm. "Show me anyway."

"The kitchen, as you can see. New Yorkers don't cook much. They store their sweaters in the oven and bananas in the microwave. When I really want to spread out, I go to Natalia and Raul's. But for everyday cooking..." He pointed toward the prep table. "This folds down and I keep it and the wooden block in the closet."

He walked her past the refrigerator and a cupboard to the loveseat, edging around the coffee "table," which was a chest on wheels. He pointed out the bathroom and closet next to it.

"This is my favorite part," he told Teresa, pointing to a large desk surrounded by shelves. He pulled a handle above the desk; the desk remained level, but shifted down and back, tucking itself underneath a bed.

"That's amazing. Can I try it?" She shifted the bed all the way down, up to its desk position, and back down, before returning it to the desk. "It makes bed fun," she said, then clapped a hand to her mouth with a giggle. "Sorry. Innuendoes should be banned tonight, too."

He gently wrapped his hand around her wrist and pulled her hand from her face. He pressed a kiss to her palm, then let go. "Let's not ban spontaneity."

She stepped toward him, then shuffled back, turning to the shelving around his desk. *The Chicago Manual of Style*. An old-school thesaurus. What looked like his childhood baseball mitt. Some CDs and a few movies: *Chinatown, Singin' in the Rain, Don Juan DeMarco, Gladiator,* and *Fight Club.*

"I like your movie selection, a little bit of everything." She pulled out *Don Juan DeMarco*, with its cover of a partly bare-chested Johnny Depp bookended by Marlon Brando and Faye Dunaway. "Are you a secret romantic, Gabe De Luca?"

"Not so secret."

He shifted close and she held up the DVD as if that could deflect the sparks arcing between them. "I never had a dog," she blurted when he raised his hands to her face as if to pull her close and kiss her.

"Pardon?"

She placed the DVD between his upraised hands and let go so he'd have to take hold of it. "We're getting to know each other," she said. "Remember?"

"Right." He shelved the DVD.

Relieved and disappointed at the same time, she turned to the framed pictures next, picking up the first one she saw.

"I recognize you, Nick and Kaily." Gabe and Nick crouched next to each other at the top of a large boulder. One man stood in front of the boulder, Kaily on his shoulders. Her hair was in pigtails. A fourth man, with sandy blonde hair and a friendly face, held one of Kaily's hands, as if to help her stay balanced, and they grinned at each other. "This must be Stephan." She pointed to the one with Kaily. "Is that your friend Adam?"

"Yeah. He's a professor of archaeology at NYU. This is at our favorite vacation spot, Cranberry Lake in the Adirondacks." He took the picture from her. "I really want to kiss you."

"And I really want you to." She left the "but we agreed not to" unsaid, holding her ground.

She picked up another picture. "Your family?"

"My parents and my sisters, Nancy and Ellen. We were celebrating the publication of my first book."

Gabe's family members were all blonde and lovely, more America's heartland than New York. They sat at a long farmhouse table, Gabe leaning back and resting an arm across his sister's chair back. "They must be so proud of you."

He nodded. "They were. Then they were disappointed. Now, they seem...resigned."

She set the picture back in its place. "Why?"

One side of his mouth tilted up in an ironic smile. "They don't understand what I'm doing with my life. It's not stable enough to them. I think they'd feel better if I was still in Cold Spring, with a wife and kids and a minivan, having Sunday dinners there like my sisters." He sounded matter-of-fact instead of bitter, and she found the idea of disappointing your parents—but still having a good relationship—fascinating.

"You don't want that kind of life?"

"Not yet. Whatever I end up doing, the decision will be mine."

"Independent," she said with a smile.

"Speaking from experience?"

"I guess so," she said, surprised by the realization.

He gestured around the entire apartment. "That's my tour. Not too many skeletons, since there's no room for them."

She reached for his hand, uncertain of her motivation, but the buzzer rang. He squeezed her fingers before letting go and jogged the few steps to the door. While he waited for the delivery guy in the open doorway, he said, "So far, so good."

"With what?"

"Talking instead of throwing you on my desk and ravishing you."

She could swear she saw a twinkle in his eye as he said it. The delivery guy bounded to the top of the stairs, and Teresa watched Gabe take the food and share a joke while he paid, enjoying his ease with the world in general. Had he always been this way, or had some of it developed out of the heartache he'd encountered along the way?

She'd never experienced such mutual comfort with a man, both of them sharing at a deeper level, like they'd been in an intensely passionate relationship for many years. With profound pleasure, she watched his hands as he unrolled the tops of the paper bags and sniffed appreciatively. She liked the feeling. She liked *him*, but she was only now figuring out herself and her life. And she didn't want to make any more bad choices.

Mama Step had told her to trust her instincts. Kristen suggested that if you have to question something too much, maybe it wasn't right for you.

She didn't doubt Gabe, a man mature enough to be willing to set aside the plans he'd made to impress her. As much as she wanted to tear his clothes off with her teeth and rub her naked body all over his whenever she saw him, the thought of talking to him excited her, too. Maybe not as enthusiastically as the thought of his warm, bare skin, but excited nonetheless. She liked where her instincts were taking her in regard to Gabe.

He looked up from the bags and smiled. "Since sad bunny and his date are no longer doing fancy, we need to switch things up." He hustled around the small place, pulling out plates, cloth napkins, a long-sleeved t-shirt, pint glasses, and a large plaid blanket. He wheeled the trunk coffee table to one side and spread the blanket in the middle of the living area. "You sit, I'll get the food, but first..." He held the shirt out to her, gesturing toward her dress with his free hand. "These things can be messy."

When he turned away, she held the shirt to her face and inhaled, giddy at his scent. She pulled the shirt over her head, then sat on one end of the blanket, watching as Gabe set down burgers, fries, onion rings, beer and condiments before settling across from her himself.

"Bon appétit," he said, and they dug in.

Her first bite had her swooning almost as much as his shirt had. "*Thank* you."

"My pleasure. And I may have given in on the scallops, but Al Green stays, and we're keeping the dessert."

"The pomegranate palmiers?"

"Mmm hmm," he murmured. "Golden brown, flaky, melt in your mouth, sprinkled with sugar."

Eyes closed to appreciate the full flavor, Teresa popped a fry in her mouth and chewed. Hot, salty, with a slightly crisp outer edge. "Mmm." She hummed to herself in happiness. "Divine," she sighed, slowly opening her eyes. Lost in the food, she started when she caught Gabe watching her. Her gaze drifted down to his mouth, wide, with a slightly fuller bottom lip, the corners that easily lifted into a smile. She enjoyed the dinner, seductive music, and promise of palmiers, but the combination of comfort and arousal this sexy man sparked was the main cause for happiness surging through her.

She popped across the small space and pressed her lips to his, lingering long enough for a taste of him, then sat down again and ate a couple more fries. Just as good as the first time, both the kiss and the fries. "I know. I broke my own rule. But you're hard to resist."

He set a hand over hers and squeezed, then let go to eat his own food. "I can't argue. You tempt me to do the same."

They continued their meal, covering other topics, like yesterday's eliminations of Lynette, Karl and Tony, who had cried even more than when Gabe interviewed him. They also discussed more general things like New York weather, good museums, and the latest Broadway musicals.

Toward the end of their meal, Gabe said, "Tell me about the people in your life."

She'd texted a few things about her friends and family, but hadn't gone into too much detail. "Well, I've told you about Mama Step. She's the main reason I cook. And when I was growing up, she was really good at both cheering me up and telling me to pick myself up by my bootstraps at the same time. She still is. But my friends..."

She told him about Kristen, free-spirited, funny, and the most capable new mom she'd ever met. "She's very open, she'll say whatever's on her mind, but she's not judgmental. She truly sees everyone as a friend, and life is amazing to her, on so many levels. I really admire her." Then she talked about Victoria, strong, capable, who often shot first and asked questions later, but always, always was there when Teresa needed her. "She's recently married, but she's never going to be a typical wife. The two of them are in Nashville, working on a documentary about Luke's band. Recording their album and going on tour."

"So that's Tyler Landry?" Even though he sounded casual, she caught a hint of tension underlying the question.

"Yes," she said without hesitation. With another man, she might be reluctant to discuss a former boyfriend, but she wanted to be clear with Gabe about her relationship with Cort. At the same time, she knew to keep her own tone neutral. "My ex-boyfriend Cort is the Landry part of the band. As you heard, we met on the set of their TV show. We broke up about six months ago."

He had stopped eating, focused only on her as she spoke. "Was it a tough breakup?"

"It was," she admitted, drawn by the intensity of his gaze. Normally, her own eyes bounced all over the place when she talked to someone, especially about difficult situations, but now she found herself unable to look away. "But it's over now, and I've moved past it."

He smiled and reached for his beer, breaking the spell. "Lessons learned?" he asked, and before she could respond, he added, "I learned enough for another novel from my ex-wife. Plenty of mistakes I'll never repeat."

"You said you were married about eight months?"

He nodded. "She was fascinating and gregarious and I thought she loved me for myself, but it was all about money and lifestyle. And when that situation dramatically altered, she found herself much more interested in someone else. Not the oldest story in the world, but one of them."

"I'm sorry."

"I'm sorry things didn't work out with you and Cort." He smiled at her again. "But only the painful parts. I'm not sorry you're here with me."

He gathered the detritus from their meal and she followed with the plates and glasses, too restless to sit. He set everything in the sink and tossed the garbage. They danced around a little in the tight space, brushing close at times, smiling at each other; Gabe brushed his hair out of his eyes, Teresa wanted to push him to the blanket and have her way with him. She was hopeless.

Gabe nodded at the loveseat in the "living room." At her return nod, he said, "Go ahead, I'll bring everything in."

He really was going to behave himself. How extraordinary.

She watched him set their ales on a tray, then take a warming pan from the oven and slide the cookies onto a decorative plate. Not wanting him to catch her peeking, she dropped her eyes to a picture on the small side table. A tiny black, white and tan puppy sitting in the middle of a tucked up blanket, a white stripe down its nose and little arches of tan eyebrows above its round black eyes.

She picked up the frame, remembering Gabe saying he loved his dog, that day in the elevator. "Your dog..." she said with a catch in her throat. "He was so sweet."

Gabe rolled the chest in front of the couch again and set the tray on it. He took the photo from her hand, then sat next to her, hip to hip, thigh to thigh, looking at the picture with a melancholy expression. "He was a great dog. I think about getting another little guy sometimes, but Moody'd be hard to beat. And I'm so busy these days, I don't have the time to spend with him. I'd have to pawn him off on Nick a lot, and he'd learn a lot of bad habits." He reached over her to return the picture to the table.

"Or she."

He straightened to look at her. "Or she."

Teresa wanted to slip off her flats and tuck her legs over his, to curl against his chest and eat pomegranate palmiers all night. Which reminded her. "I'm sorry to tell you this, but you spelled it wrong."

He looked surprised. "Spelled what wrong?"

"Pomegranate." She pulled her phone from her bag and scrolled through the long text threads. "There's no I in it."

He scooped the phone out of her hand and stared at the screen.

"I'll be damned." He laughed, gripping the phone in one hand. "That's embarrassing. The literary guy misspelling something."

"I'm kind of a terrible speller myself," she said. "But I had to write up some of the menus at the catering company and someone ordered pomegranate and lemon bars." She leaned against his shoulder to finish her story. "I spelled it wrong, too," she said with a giggle. "But my friend Libby pointed it out and we fixed it in time. Sorry," she added, tilting her head toward his. "I thought you should know."

He set the phone on the side table. "Well, that's a story we can tell our grandkids."

"Except they'll only want to know one thing."

He shifted, his shirt warm under her cheek. "What's that?"

"What they tasted like."

His lips brushed the top of her head, then he rested his cheek there. "I don't want to move now, and they're too far away to reach."

She slipped her arm around his biceps, shifting closer. "Is this breaking the rules?" she whispered.

"Hell, I hope not," he said in a heated rush.

She slipped her shoes off and tucked her legs over his, leaning her head against his chest to hear the soft, steady beat of his heart.

"The cookies can wait."

CHAPTER TWENTY-ONE

The remaining seven contestants stood in a line in front of the judges, who all perched on tall stools. Lily Wen sat up straight, long legs crossed, short skirt somehow not riding up her thighs like it would if Teresa had worn something similar. Teresa's disgust with Lily had not abated, especially since Lily continued to make snide comments to her off camera and away from any witnesses.

Lily waved away her makeup artist, Dan called quiet on the damn set, and the cameras rolled.

Darren Michaels read off a cue card, praising them for their determination, stamina, and amazing meals in the previous seven challenges. Yesterday's had been for a secret supper club and the day before they'd put together appetizers for an art gallery opening.

"It's only going to get more difficult as we get into it," Darren continued. "Each one of you is going to have to pull up your socks and..." He peered past the cameras to Dan. "Really? 'Pull up your socks'? What does that have to do with cooking? In fact, if you think of socks and food, it's—"

"Cut!" Dan yelled. He stepped between two stationary cameras and approached Darren. They whispered to each other for awhile, Darren gesticulating toward the cue cards and then himself.

If viewers only knew the amount of waiting done on the set of a reality TV show. And how *un*real so many of them were. Teresa wondered why people continued to participate in them, considering the drawbacks, but then checked herself. Everyone wanted their 15 minutes, and not many participants discussed the "reality" of their experience, even on social media. Of course, a lot of them signed contracts preventing them from this, herself included.

She sighed, and it came out louder than she meant.

"Right?" Ace muttered to one side of her.

On her other side, Cookie whispered, "What d'you think the next challenge is going to be?"

Teresa shook her head, trying to forget Victoria's text. "I'm almost afraid to know," she said, feeling bad for the deception.

Dan finally straightened, and clapped his hands once to re-focus everyone. He told them all to shut the hell up, a few people scurried around changing the cue cards, and they started filming again, with Darren reading new lines. They still sounded cheesy, but Teresa didn't care. Her feet ached in her cowboy boots, and at this moment she'd trade in her 15 minutes of fame for a 15 minute nap. She took a quick peek around and saw Gabe in the corner, standing next to PA Katie. He winked at her and she heated right up. Well, maybe five minutes of sleep after a spicy ten minutes or so with Gabe.

Joel Klein said, "We take this show, and your careers, very seriously."

"But we can't always be serious," Lily Wen added. "In fact, we're going to have some fun this week, and we think you'll really enjoy the next challenge." She beamed brightly, looking at each of them in turn.

When her gaze landed on Teresa, all Teresa saw was a row of shark's teeth.

"Why is she talking like that?" Cookie whispered out of the side of her mouth. "It's freaking me out."

Lily Wen continued. "We've all heard stories of what it's like for a musician on the road—"

Even though she'd had warning, something swooped through Teresa's entire body, top to bottom, and she even swayed toward Cookie, who put up a reassuring hand. *She couldn't do this. She couldn't fake it or face it.* Her head buzzed so loudly, she missed the rest of the intro, but it didn't matter, because she did hear Lily Wen say the name *Tyler Landry*, and those shark teeth made another appearance. She found herself grabbing for Cookie's hand to help ground her.

Cookie gave her a questioning look, then said, "Whoa. You've gone the black girl equivalent of pale. What's wrong?"

Teresa shook her head, pressing her lips tightly together. "Later," she whispered. She knew Lily Wen was getting great satisfaction out of this, but Teresa refused to give her any more ammunition. Keeping hold of Cookie's hand, Teresa took a deep breath and let it out to the count of five. Then she took another, and tried to smile brightly for whatever cameras might be on her. Or just for Lily Wen.

Then she focused on Joel's information. Tyler Landry was the opening act on Jason Aldean's summer tour, and the band wanted some interesting, healthy options for their time on the road, so each contestant needed to create a dish that was not only quick, filling and easy to make, but also healthy and as "low cal" as possible.

Her equilibrium returning, Teresa dropped Cookie's hand and tried not to roll her eyes. Since when had Cort Landry cared about calories?

"You'll have two hours to come up with your dishes, then we'll film your prep of the dish this afternoon. After that, you'll present the dish to us as well as a member of the band, who will be an honorary judge of this challenge."

"Jesus Christ," Teresa spit out.

Everyone turned to her.

She pressed a hand to her mouth, then lowered it. "Sorry. I'm sorry." She flashed her bright camera smile again. "I'm just excited," she told them.

Someone snorted and another person laughed.

Dan called cut again, and asked what was bothering the miscreants.

Everyone shuffled around and stared at the floor.

Finally, MaryBeth said, "She knows the band, she'll get an unfair advantage."

"It's like nepotism or something," Chance added.

"That's when people are related," Cookie told him.

"It's actually both relatives and friends," MaryBeth said in her know-it-all way.

Cookie waved her away. "Whatever. The point is, they wouldn't let that happen." She looked at the judges. "Right?"

The judges shifted in their seats, not meeting anyone's eyes, and MaryBeth glared at Teresa.

Teresa glared back. "Believe me, I didn't ask for this." She couldn't quite lie about having previous knowledge of the situation, but her stomach still roiled as if she'd only learned about it today.

Cookie took a step closer to Teresa. "I saw your face, girl. I believe it."

"And *we* saw the clips," MaryBeth said, pointing between herself, Ace, and Chance. Chance at least had the decency to look chagrined. "They're all over YouTube," MaryBeth continued. "You and the cowboy."

"Holy shit," said Rachel.

"Does your new boyfriend know?" MaryBeth continued her taunting.

Teresa glared at MaryBeth and then at Lily Wen for good measure. "He does. Sounds like you might like to have a few YouTube clips yourself."

Hands on hips, MaryBeth took a step closer to Teresa. "You shouldn't be involved in this challenge at all."

Teresa stood her ground.

Lily Wen chose that moment to intercede. "I understand the concern over fairness. If we can continue filming, you'll all have your answers."

The cameras rolled again and Lily Wen continued as if they'd never stopped. "We're all so excited to have Cort Landry, part of this up-and-coming band, taking time out of his busy schedule to join us in our endeavors. Now, one of our very own is a close and personal friend of the band members and their manager, isn't that right, Teresa?"

Teresa had been expecting this. She waved to the camera and pointed first at herself and then at Lily Wen, giving her a jaunty smile.

"We hold ourselves to a very high standard here at CuisineTV," Lily continued, "and would never want anything to interfere with a fair judgment in this contest. For that reason, Teresa will be sitting out." A lot of people gasped, and Gabe took a step forward.

Lily gave a fake, tinkling laugh and pressed a hand to her chest. "Sorry, sorry. Just kidding. To maintain fairness in the judging process, this will be a blind challenge. We've polled our guest for his favorite dishes, and those will be on a forbidden list. Mr. Landry won't know who created which dish and he will not be allowed to visit with any of the contestants—" she looked at Teresa when she said this "—until after the end of the challenge."

CHAPTER TWENTY-TWO

Gabe wished he had time to talk to Teresa, but she and her fellow contestants were in the prep room. The scents of garlic, roasting meat, tomatoes, lemon, and cilantro mingled in a heady cloud throughout the building. He stood in the doorway, watching everyone gather materials, check temperatures, frantically stir simmering pots, open and close oven doors in rapid-fire fashion, taste and grimace, or taste and nod, all with suppressed anxiety. Overlaying that, though, he could sense the dedication and drive of the seven remaining contestants. He'd known the challenges would increase in difficulty, but he'd had no idea how ugly things could get with this type of competition.

"It wasn't my idea, you know," Lily Wen said from behind him, before she brushed against his shoulder to join him in the doorway. She wore what he thought of as her trademark catsuit today, and it did nothing for him anymore. He moved away from her to find PA Katie, but she spoke again. "All of the producers knew she'd been on that other show."

He looked at her, and she relaxed back, her spine against the doorframe so it pressed her breasts out. How had he not seen earlier what a manipulative bitch she was?

"And you gave them a little nudge toward having her old boyfriend here."

She shrugged, glancing into the room before looking back at him. "They planned it as soon as they got her entry and started researching her. CuisineTV spends millions on these shows and the winners. You think they're going to bring on just anyone?"

"I think they *make* millions on the hype they create around personal dramas."

She pushed away from the doorway with a huff of disgust. "Don't be so naive."

"Don't be so ugly," he said with a shake of the head, and walked away. If he had to listen to another word, he'd throttle her. His phone buzzed and he pulled it out. Stephan, asking if he could bring Kaily by for a couple hours.

At the studio, Gabe wrote back. *Ok for today.* Gabe checked in with PA Katie on a regular basis in case Stephan needed someone for Kaily and none of the other guys could do it.

While he waited, he lounged against the front of the studio building, alternately watching the variety of New York life pass by and researching girls' shoes on his phone. Kaily's fifth birthday was coming up, and, as they did every year, his parents were hosting a big party at their place. Stephan's parents were older, and Hannah's parents lived in a small apartment in town.

Kaily had *Frozen* fever, and loved everything Elsa, Olaf, and Sven, but he wanted to get her something special, to find the perfect gift for his favorite girl.

His thumb paused on the screen, where he'd been scrolling through ballerina flats.

His favorite girl.

Kaily touched his heart like no one else, for so many reasons, but Teresa...she'd become his favorite woman, and she left him breathless. She only had to lean against him, as she had on Sunday night, and he simultaneously relaxed and gasped for air. Like everything in the world was as it should be, but also too much to take.

"Great writing, De Luca," he muttered, going back to his phone. "Why don't you put that in your next book."

A Town Car pulled up to the loading zone and he glanced at the beautiful woman passenger as she stepped out, phone to her ear, auburn hair loose around her shoulders, in a pink and gray suit, and high heels bringing her up to a good five-seven or so. Last month, he would've given her more of a look, maybe even offered his assistance so he could usher her ahead of him and check out the sway in her hips. But now? He'd still appreciate her beauty, but had no desire for anything else.

Hell, that was something. He was already anticipating the ration of shit from Nick once he found out, and laughed as he returned to the screen.

"Now, darlin'," a deep voice rumbled out, "I'm sure they've got it taken care of. No need to run this show."

Gabe looked up again, curious now about this particular show in front of him. The tall cowboy who'd spoken had just untucked himself from the car, clapped a black hat on his head, and slung an arm around the woman, who gazed up at him with a sweet smile. Now that Gabe looked closer, he noticed both of them wore wedding rings. She rang off and slipped the phone in her purse while their fellow riders followed them out of the car. A young guy in jeans and a flannel jacket looked around in awe, head craned every which way. A slim guy with long, straight black hair tucked his hands in the pockets of his baggy khakis and strolled up the street to look at a display in an antiques store. And another cowboy, a big blonde who put on his own white hat, took a deep breath as if ready for anything and announced, "Bring on the food, I've got myself a big appetite."

Gabe straightened. Christ. This must be Tyler Landry, including Teresa's friend Victoria, recently married to the lead singer. And the hungry cowboy had to be Cort Landry, Teresa's ex. He took a step forward to introduce himself when Kaily burst from behind the group and launched herself at him.

"Gabe!" she cried, and he caught her up and swung her around, making her giggle and say, "Again!" So he did, catching Stephan winding around the band members, too, and Luke Tyler giving Kaily a winsome look.

Kaily caught sight of Stephan and threw an arm out to him. "Daddy, too! You're slow today!"

Stephan gave Gabe a half-hug and Gabe saw the wear on his face. "Busy?" he asked quietly, aware of the crowd on the sidewalk now watching them.

"Lots going on," Stephan said. "No worries, though. We'll talk about it later." He kissed Kaily's hand, then her cheek. "Be good, pumpkin."

"Not a pumpkin!" She pouted. "A princess!"

"Princess, yes," Stephan said, "but we don't do spoiled. Do we, Gabe?"

Gabe hefted Kaily higher so she could look in his eyes. "We don't."

Distracted by PA Katie now ushering the band inside, Gabe still appreciated that, despite his exhaustion, Stephan refused to let Kaily's attitude slide.

Kaily lowered her head and pouted a little longer before lifting her gaze to Stephan again and saying, "Sorry, Daddy. I'm your pumpkin." She shrugged, head turned so her shoulder lifted toward her chin. "Just wanna be a princess, too."

"So you're Princess Pumpkin?" Gabe asked.

She crowed with laughter, and Stephan joined in. "Thanks, man. I'll see you in a couple?"

Gabe nodded and brought Kaily inside, the two of them inventing different configurations of Princess foods.

"Princess Cupcake, obviously," she said, as they headed up the hall to the judging and prep rooms. Various people scurried past them, looking harried and distracted.

"Princess Parmesan?"

"Princess Panfiglio!" she announced, one fist in the air.

Gabe stopped at the doorway to the main room, laughing. "Is that a food?"

"No, but my friend Joey Panfiglio said 'eat me' to some big boys at school."

"Oh. Huh." Gabe looked down at her innocent face. "That's..." *Something to discuss with your father*, he wanted to say. But he, Nick and Adam had been substitute parents since the day Kaily was born. They'd never overstep their bounds, but Stephan depended on their help. And someday, he hoped, he'd have a child of his own. Never hurt to have some practice.

"From *Alice in Wonderland*," Kaily supplied while Gabe struggled to find the right words.

"It is," he agreed. "But if someone says it in a mean way, it's also...not nice."

The door opened and Gabe took a step back. Cort Landry popped out and said, "Hey, you know where the toilet is?"

Gabe gestured behind him with one thumb. "First left, then another left and a right. Just past that. It's kind of a rabbit warren in here."

"Thanks, partner," he said, but he was smiling at Kaily. "You've got nice daddies there."

Oh, hell, the guy thought he and Stephan were partners.

"He's the best!" Kaily crowed, before Gabe could respond.

"Stephan and I aren't together." He stuck out his hand. "Gabe De Luca. Her godfather."

"Cort Landry. Taken," he said with an apologetic shrug. He glanced toward the door behind him, where Gabe knew the contestants must be working in a frenzy, perfecting their dishes. And this was only the first round of cooking they'd have to do today. "She's in there cooking her heart out. Can't wait to see her."

He grinned at Kaily and clapped a dumbfounded Gabe on the shoulder before sauntering down the hall, whistling what sounded like the theme from *Smokey and the Bandit*.

Kaily bounced in Gabe's arms. "I changed my mind. I want to be Princess Cowboy!"

Gabe bit back an oath and opened the door to the anteroom, which was more crowded than usual. All of the Production Assistants were in, even those with the day off. And they all clumped around the remaining three band members, chatting and laughing as if they'd never seen musicians before. Far from looking put out, Victoria stood to one side with Katie; they both glanced at the crowd before sharing knowing smiles, and continued their conversation. Teresa was right: Victoria was a strong woman. He thought he'd like her.

Gabe pointed at the closed door across the room where the red light mounted next to it glowed. "Remember what we talked about?" he said to Kaily. "They're filming a television show in there, so we have to respect what they say. We can make noise out here, but not too loud, and if they ask us to leave for whatever reason, we can go to the canteen, or maybe downstairs to the market. Capisce?"

She gave a nod. "Capisce," she said in a solemn tone. She pointed to the door, too. "Is Teresa cooking in there?"

"She is, but I don't know what she's making."

"Can we see her?"

"She's pretty busy, but once they're done, hopefully we can have a couple minutes to hang out with her. I don't know how long she'll be in there, though."

Kaily glanced around the room, then leaned close and whispered in Gabe's ear as if they were grand co-conspirators. "Do you think she'll want to come to my birthday party?"

"You want her to go to your party?" he asked, before he could stop himself. He was the adult here, and Kaily obviously felt insecure about asking or she wouldn't have whispered it to him.

She nodded. "Do *you*?"

"I'd love to have her there, K. I'm not sure if she'll have the time. You remember we talked about the competition she's doing on the TV show?"

"Like *Survivor*," she said with a nod, still solemn.

Sometimes that brutal, he thought. "Right. They get really busy, and sometimes they have to work on weekends. I don't know her schedule, but we can definitely ask her."

Kaily bounced in his arms. "Okay," she said, cheered again.

He set her down, and they wandered to the craft services table, where she asked him questions about every item there, from the bagels and lox to crudités, doughnuts and empanadas. Right as he thought she'd never tire of asking how things were made, what went with what, where did they come from, was it all organic, why would someone want to eat *that*, and how come she couldn't have doughnuts for breakfast every day, the crowd of PAs pulled themselves away from the band members and bustled toward the prep room. While he'd been educating Kaily on the various food items, he'd also been very aware of Cort Landry returning to the room and chatting up both PA Katie and Chrissie. He was starting to piss Gabe off.

Now, as the door opened and the contestants filed out, Gabe took Kaily's hand so they wouldn't be in the way, but Landry charged right past them, bellowing, "There's my girl."

He wrapped his arms around a very surprised-looking Teresa and lifted her up, twirling her around in the same way Gabe had twirled Kaily earlier. Everyone else stared at them, and Gabe charged forward to intervene, even as Teresa told Landry to put her down.

He did, but kept his arms around her waist. She twisted sideways, and added, "Cort, please."

"Hey, darlin', didn't you miss me just a little bit?"

"That's enough," Gabe commanded. "Let her go."

Landry turned to him as Kaily pulled her hand free from Gabe's and threw herself into Teresa's arms, breaking Landry's hold.

"Will you come to my party?" Kaily asked Teresa, patting at a dusting of flour on her shoulder. "There'll be balloons and maybe a pony and maybe you can make my cake, too? Gabe says you cook real good and—"

Gabe and Landry glared at each other while Teresa stared between them, backing up a step and holding Kaily out like a shield. "Uh, I'd love to come to your party if I can. Um...Gabe De Luca, this is—"

"We've met." Gabe gave Landry a curt nod. "Kaily, we need to let Teresa go. She's working."

Landry circled a finger from Teresa and Kaily to Gabe and back again. "What's the story here?"

"We're dating," Teresa told him tersely, and handed Kaily back to Gabe.

"Now, darlin', that's—"

She rounded on him and hissed, "I am not your darling. Stop." Gabe saw her fighting back tears, and he stepped in again, but Teresa glared at him, too. "I have to go." She managed a smile for Kaily. "I'll try really hard to make it to your party, honey."

Then she whirled and stomped away, stopping briefly to hug Victoria and the band members before Katie finally pulled her from the room. Landry turned to Gabe now and they eyed each other.

"Told you earlier I was taken."

Kaily shifted in his arms and twisted so she hung halfway over his shoulder. Hard to have a stand-off with a four-year-old hanging over you like a sack of flour. "Sounds like you had it wrong," Gabe replied, keeping his tone even.

"We got something special, me and Tessa."

"Tessa?"

"My special nickname for her." Landry flicked a thumb against his hat, pushing it up slightly.

"I'd say she's done with special nicknames."

"Not 'til she tells me so, son."

"Son?" Gabe shook his head. "Sounds like you've got 'special' nicknames for everyone."

The sharp click of a pair of heels came their way and Teresa's friend Victoria stepped neatly between them, holding out her hand. Gabe automatically shook.

"Victoria Clausen Tyler." She tilted a head toward the green room door. "Teresa had to go, but she said you've been dating and would like us all to have dinner tonight if there's time. Here's my cell." She held a card out to him tucked between two fingers, and the tall man standing behind her—Luke Tyler—smiled.

She smiled back at him, a charming shade of pink tingeing her cheeks; their exchange looked very much like a married couple private joke.

"If you've got another one of those," Gabe told her, "I'll write down my cell for you."

She tucked the card in his palm, which he then slid into his back pocket. "PA Katie already gave it to me. You've got your hands full," she added, smiling at Kaily.

"Hello!" Kaily chirped. "I'm Kaily. I'm almost *five*."

A little formally, Victoria replied, "Hello. I'm Victoria. And this is my husband, Luke." Another of those secret smiles. "And I see you've met Cort." Gabe didn't miss the withering stare she gave cowboy Cort, and his already high estimation of her increased a few points.

Luke reached around and gave Gabe a firm handshake.

"Well, now, Miss Victoria," Cort said, "I assume that dinner invite includes everyone."

"Of course, Cort," she replied. "But don't you think that would be awkward?"

"No, ma'am, I do not," he said, and Gabe recognized the stubborn set to his jaw, thinking it reflected his own expression. He couldn't blame the guy—much. He wouldn't let go of Teresa so easily, either. And it took this stubborn cowboy's appearance to make him realize he really did want to hold onto her. Before, he'd been attracted, fascinated, enjoying getting to know her, but still going day-to-day. Now, no way in hell this bozo was coming back into her life. Her "something special" now was Gabe.

"I'd like to interview the whole band for a piece on the show's web mag." He addressed Victoria more than the others; he could tell she was used to being in charge. "Let's have everyone at dinner." He shrugged at Cort, as if it were no big deal. "Two birds, one stone, all that."

Cort turned to Victoria. "There you have it."

The guy clearly wasn't big on subtlety.

Victoria glanced at Gabe. "You know the area. Any suggestions?"

He named an Italian place a couple blocks down and she had her iPhone out before he finished describing it. "Great. I'll make reservations."

Kaily was wriggling in his arms, and he set her down. "I want to see PA Katie."

"She's working right now, sweetheart."

Katie walked by, ubiquitous iPad in one hand. "But I always have time for Miss Kaily," she said with a grin. "Want to see some of the stuff we filmed today?" She waved the tablet. "Teresa's in it."

"Yes!" Kaily jumped up and down, then sobered, and looked at Gabe. "Is that okay?"

Gabe nodded, but told Katie, "Pass her back if you have to leave or she gets to be a handful."

They trotted to a corner with two chairs and Gabe found himself facing off with Landry again, Luke standing to one side and eyeing them warily. Victoria wandered around the room, phone to her ear.

Gabe sized up Cort. Taller, but no more broad in the shoulders or across the chest. He could take him in a fair fight. But would Cort Landry fight fair? Gabe gave an internal shrug. The guy seemed like a straight shooter, so yeah, he probably would. Still...

"Sorry you came all this way, but it's not gonna happen," Gabe told him.

Cort straightened, increasing his height, and this time Gabe gave an internal head shake. "Could say the same to you," Cort replied.

In a level tone, Luke said, "Not here."

Gabe kept his eyes on Cort's. Crossing his arms over his chest, he said, "No. Not here," because he knew at some point he and Landry would have a face off.

"Well, now, I'm a here-and-now kinda guy," Landry replied. "Maybe we should settle this and be done."

"Nothing to settle," Gabe told him. "Teresa's decision."

"Decision was made a long time ago."

"Oh, God, give it up or go pee on each other outside," Victoria demanded, charging up to them, cell phone in one hand. She glared from one to the other. "Normally, I'd love a good man-fight, especially if you put a camera in my hand and I can get some interviews with you later, but this is not the time or place, and Teresa is not the girl. And by that, I mean, some women thrive on being part of a love triangle, having two men fighting over her. Not T. It's not her thing, and she has too much going on in her life right now to have to deal with the two of you in a caveman contest. She doesn't like conflict, she doesn't deserve to be torn apart, and I won't, I will not, sit back and watch if the two of you continue with this peeing contest and it ends up hurting her in any way."

Gabe believed her.

Cort held up his hands. "No harm, no foul."

Gabe nodded. "Fair enough. Teresa's health and happiness is paramount."

"Well, now you're just sweet talkin'," Landry said. He pointed at Gabe. "Two can play at that game."

Luke clapped Cort on the back. "C'mon, son. This really isn't the place." He tipped a hand to his hat. "Nice meeting you," he said. "We'll see you at dinner." He led away both his wife and Landry, to join the other two band members.

CHAPTER TWENTY-THREE

As she prepped for dinner out, the day's events ricocheted through Teresa's mind.

Her draw to Cort had existed from the moment she saw him playing a small club in San Francisco with Tyler Landry. When he held her tight and twirled her around today, she remembered how protected she had felt with him, how safe. With everything so crazy and unsettled and *scary* right now, safety and protection sounded comforting. But Teresa knew it was a false safety, so she firmly told Cort that she wasn't his girl and, to back that up, that she and Gabe were dating. But she shouldn't have used Gabe as a shield and a buffer against Cort's doggedness.

Her hand shook as she tried to apply mascara, and she lowered her arm, studying herself in the mirror. Reasonably pretty, good cheekbones, tall and mostly slim, but a bundle of confusion and contradiction.

Stripping away attraction and insecurities, what did she want?

She didn't know. And *that* was really scary.

She'd prefer to crawl into her bunk with Cookie, share some texts, and sleep, especially after losing today's guest judge challenge to MaryBeth. But the band was flying back to Nashville tomorrow, so tonight was their only chance to spend time together. And despite the odds, Teresa was still in the competition, so she might not see her friends again in a long time.

Gabe had offered to share a cab to the restaurant with her, but she declined. He'd sounded disappointed, but she needed to be independent this evening, for everyone to see her as Teresa, the person who entered a cooking competition and moved to New York all by herself. Not as Cort's ex, or Gabe's current squeeze, or Victoria's friend. Just Teresa, known for her accomplishments and not her connections.

Cookie knocked on the bathroom door, startling her out of her reverie. "Cab's here."

Teresa swiped mascara over her lashes, told herself sternly to pull up her big girl panties, did a quick turn and look over the shoulder to make sure everything was okay front to back, and opened the door.

She held her arms out. "How do I look?"

She wore black, heeled boots with pointy toes, slightly flared black pants, and Rachel had lent her a shiny gold, sleeveless top that dipped low in the front.

"Knockout." Cookie nodded with approval. "That blouse not only shows off your amazing shoulders, but it gives your skin a golden glow. You make me a jealous bitch, you know that?"

Teresa smiled. "I think I'm supposed to say 'thank you' here, but it doesn't sound quite right."

"It's right," Cookie reassured her. "You got a jacket for in between? It's cold out there."

Teresa shrugged into a long black leather blazer, Rachel and Cookie saw her to the door, and she spent the cab ride continuing her pep talk. This dinner was about spending time with her friends, enjoying them, not about soothing—or pushing away—Cort. Nor was it about showing off Gabe.

Although, how could she not, she thought, as she opened the door and saw him at a table across the room. He sat facing the door, and at the sight of her, a knowing smile lit up his face. He flicked his long hair from his eyes, excused himself to Victoria, and strode to meet Teresa at the hostess stand. In black slacks and a dark gray sweater that hugged the planes of his chest, his body long and lean, shoulders broad and demeanor relaxed, he radiated confidence. He'd pushed the sleeves up to just below his elbows and his muscled forearms devastated her. *He* devastated her. He stood staring into her eyes, and she couldn't look away.

"Every time I see you, you look more enticing than the last."

A voice boomed next to her, "That's because Tessa's a natural beauty." Cort reached her other side in a couple steps, and her mind went blank at his appearance. He'd ditched his cowboy gear and wore a dark suit, the white shirt open at the neck, revealing a peek at his toned upper chest. "Stepped away from the table a second and missed your grand entrance, but now I'm making up for lost time."

"I've never seen you in a suit," she said inanely.

"Clean up pretty good, don't I?" He swept a hand in the air from top to bottom, indicating his transformation from urban cowboy to dashing gentleman.

"I..." She turned to Gabe and her chest tightened. What was the protocol for being in the same room with two men who were vying for you? She looked to Victoria for help, but Luke had wrapped an arm around her shoulders to whisper in her ear, and the two of them were lost in each other.

Gabe took a step in front of Teresa toward Cort. "Look, Landry—"

"No," Teresa told them, her voice low but firm. She stepped between the two men. "No, none of that. No competition, no...just don't."

"Why don't we sit down and enjoy a nice dinner?" Gabe gestured her ahead of him. She didn't miss the quelling look he gave Cort, but ignored it for now. She hugged Marty and Parker, then Victoria and Luke, warming from their embraces and happy smiles. Despite her best intentions, she found herself between Gabe and Cort at the round table. Marty and Parker were on the other side of them, and Victoria and Luke sat across from her. When she draped her blazer across the back of the chair Gabe held out for her, Cort let out a low whistle.

"Tessa, you look just like a New York woman. You fit right in here."

She smiled at his compliment but searched the table for neutral ground to discourage further discussion on that topic. She leaned over Gabe to ask Marty about his son, Alex, a couple months older than Kristen's daughter, Daisy. After Marty updated her on Alex's latest accomplishments—holding his head up, rolling over, eating solid food—Luke added that he'd watched the little tyke for Marty and his wife, Miranda, one day and couldn't wait to do so again.

Surprised at this admission, Teresa looked at Victoria, and saw that baby Alex's sweetness and light had not swayed her best friend. "Did you share in the babysitting duties, V?"

"I did not," Victoria said, and Teresa almost laughed at the similarity in her tone to Luke in stubborn mode. "That was all Uncle Luke, all day. Diapers and everything. And it didn't cure him of baby fever." She took a long sip of wine.

"One little baby's not gonna do that, darlin'," Luke assured her, and brushed her hair behind one ear, stroking her shoulder along the way.

Despite a visible shiver that ran up her spine, Victoria said with authority, "Don't worry, I'll figure out something that will."

Teresa decided to avoid pursuing that subject, too, and this time leaned over Cort to ask Parker about City Lights, the bookstore he used to manage in San Francisco.

"Divine," he said. "We're currently busy with the album, of course, but the store holds group meditation sessions now. I try to do it at the same time in Nashville, to connect to that positive, life-affirming energy. We meditate and pray for the planet, for the souls upon it, for all of life to converge as one, instead of working against each other and splitting us all asunder."

Without irony, Gabe said, "A noble cause," and Teresa's resolve to remain aloof melted. She had a soft spot for Parker, a gentle being blissfully unaware that he sounded like a San Francisco cliché. She defended him fiercely, even though she knew he didn't care, and could defend himself if needed.

Gabe and Parker spent a few minutes discussing the state of the planet and Teresa ping-ponged between them, trying to find a way to include Cort in the conversation without inappropriately encouraging him.

"... group meditation has been shown to make a distinct difference in locations where it's practiced."

"I read an article recently by Ravi Shankar..."

"Quantum physicist John Haglin purports that..."

Once they got into physics, Teresa gave up. She sat back in her seat and found that Cort had draped his arm across it. She gave him a look.

"I sure have missed you, darlin'," he said, either completely unaware of her silent admonition to him, or completely ignoring it. His arm moved up to enclose her shoulders.

She leaned forward. "I'm sure you've been busy."

"We have, settin' down tracks, figurin' out tour stuff, haven't sang this much in years, and that's just from the rehearsals."

She noticed the broadened accent. That only happened when he was playing it up for someone mocking him, or to impress a woman.

Damn.

The waiter set down a basket of warm, yeasty bread and cold butter pats, and took their drink orders. Teresa ordered a Bellini, and picked up her napkin in anticipation of devouring some of that delectable bread. She spread the material across her thigh, and warm fingers grasped hers and lightly squeezed. She looked at Gabe, but he was paying attention to the waiter while ordering a vodka martini.

One corner of his mouth tilted up, though, and he squeezed her fingers again. She returned the gesture. Finished with his order, he leaned back in his chair and looked in her eyes. "The aroma of that Anadama is ambrosial," he said, and flicked his eyes at Cort's arm on the back of Teresa's chair, his hand wrapped around her upper waist.

"Fancy words ain't everything, professor," Cort said mildly and took a piece of bread before handing the basket to Teresa. He spread a thick pat of butter on his slice, one-handed.

"He's a writer," Teresa corrected.

Cort took a huge bite and chewed. He swallowed and gave her a charming smile. "I know," he said, and took another bite of bread.

"Passive aggression is often misinterpreted," Gabe said in his own mild tone as he selected a piece of bread and passed the basket to Marty. "Frequently to the user's detriment."

From across the table, Victoria set down her wine glass and said, "You know, usually I encourage this sort of behavior, at least for the camera, but don't you two think this is a little much?" She gave both Cort and Gabe stern looks.

Gabe brushed a thumb along the back of Teresa's hand before letting it go and sat straighter. "You're right. I've been disrespectful. Of everyone here, but especially Teresa." He turned to face her. "It's your life and your choice who you end up with, and I fully support and respect that." He looked around the table at each person in turn, including Cort. "In a short period of time, I've realized how special Teresa is. And she's become special to me. I want to know the people who are important to her, in her life."

He stood and stepped behind Teresa's chair to hold a hand out to Cort. "That includes you, Landry."

Cort scraped his chair back and eyed Gabe. Teresa's heart

pounded hard as she twisted her head back and forth to watch them.

"Pretty speech, professor," Cort said without sarcasm. "I mostly agree on it, only I'll add that I aim to get Tessa back, and after tonight, I won't play fair about it."

Gabe nodded at this, and they shook hands, then resumed their seats.

Breathless, Teresa sat through the rest of the meal, from her *frito misto* to the honey glazed pork chop and the slice of chocolate and walnut torta she allowed herself because the last few weeks had been hell. And tonight hadn't helped one iota. Two men had never competed over her before, let alone in the same room. And when each had been touching her at the same time? Well, despite her stints on reality TV, she knew how sheltered her life had been up to that point, because the naughtiness exhilarated her, her body heating in all the right places, her nipples hard.

Between Luke's obvious lust for Victoria, and Gabe and Cort's sparring, the testosterone pumping into the air gave her a head rush. She tingled all over, even after Victoria halted the standoff, the food arrived, and the conversation turned to Tyler Landry's tour.

After their breakup, even when Cort pursued her with songs and texts, she hadn't believed him to be completely serious. She knew she'd hurt him, but from their first meeting he'd been both self-contained and enjoying the attentions of many beautiful women. She assumed he'd collect himself after their split and move onto the next beauty, not because she wasn't special to him, but because the latest adventure waited.

So was tonight's show a statement of his sincerity, or did it rankle his ego to see another man step in? The tug-of-war only added to the confusion that had been swirling around her for months now. Sex with Cort had been explosive, and the side of her tired of being a good girl had craved his caveman. The heat between her and Gabe easily roared into flames with just a look. But now she realized that when she'd propositioned Gabe in the elevator, *she'd* been the "caveman." She'd thought doing something crazy would shock her system and get her back on track. Had it instead been an example of how she needed to live her life?

She glanced at Gabe talking to Marty, at his forearm resting on the table while he held the stem of his martini glass between thumb and forefinger. The tendons in his arm flexed, and the light caught the fine dark blond hairs, his strong wrists, the sleeves of his sweater pushed up to his forearms. She casually reached for her own glass and took a sip, using the movement to swivel slightly to observe Cort. He laughed uproariously at something Parker said, then tilted his pint glass of beer in salute and took a long swallow. He had strong arms, too, dark blonde hair, but a more solid body, like a football player. Gabe was just as strong, but had more finesse to him. The cowboy and the professor, that was it exactly.

Only, it was the hot cowboy and the sexy professor, and she was the innocent maiden in the middle of their sex sandwich.

A shiver ran through her, tingled across her lower back and shot down to her toes.

She'd never considered a threesome before. Not seriously, anyway. Probably because any previous opportunities hadn't involved two such hot men. She'd seen both of them naked. She knew their capabilities. She could easily imagine their simultaneous orgasm faces.

She set her Bellini down and reached for the water instead, downing the entire thing in an attempt to cool herself off.

But the flames refused to be quenched.

CHAPTER TWENTY-FOUR

Gabe's body still ached all over the next day at elimination judging. Along with two martinis at dinner, he'd also agreed to take a shot or two—or three, God help him—of whiskey when Landry practically challenged his manhood. Since his last bender when Kaily was born, rendering him unavailable for Stephan when Hannah died, he'd promised himself he'd never be stupid enough to indulge that much again. Then last night, his damn ego had shoved that promise aside in a heartbeat so he could prove what a man he was. Well, he'd held his liquor, suppressed most signs of drunkenness as he bid everyone goodnight, saw Teresa in a cab—minus the cowboy—and headed home. Where he'd puked up a perfectly good meal and awoke at one point in bed in a fetal position, one leg of his pants still on, the other pulled off over his shoe, and his sweater half hanging out of the kitchen sink.

And his head throbbing as if a high school marching band played his school song around the inside perimeter.

He'd dosed himself with water, coffee, aspirin and a hot shower, then sweated it out at the gym. It all worked short-term, and he thought he'd survived the worse of it, but the thumping started up again as soon as he reached the studio.

Damn hubris. He never backed down from a challenge, and Cort Landry represented multiple challenges, the main one being a block in Gabe's path to Teresa. He'd tried to play nice, holding back at her request so they could get better acquainted. That had happened, and it seemed they were becoming important to each other. But he saw the shiver shimmy down Teresa's spine when Landry touched her, how her gaze lingered on the cowboy's face, and his hand when he lifted a glass to his lips.

Damn problem was, she'd studied Gabe, too. She'd devoured everything set in front of her, all the way down to licking the chocolate torta off her fork with languorous strokes. Then she'd devoured both Landry and himself with her eyes. It had almost been indecent. And damn arousing.

He shook his head to clear it and focus on the judging round, but stopped quickly when the world swooped sideways at the motion.

So he might not drink like that again, but yeah, he still hadn't learned.

He rubbed his temples, taking breaths as deeply as he could without his head bursting open, then gratefully accepted the cup of coffee PA Katie held out for him. She nodded then passed quietly behind him to take up her usual station behind Camera Three.

Gabe took a few sips and his equilibrium started to recover. At the same time, his blood pressure remained elevated over all that had happened the night before, and he couldn't shake his ire. He'd always respect Teresa's wishes, but the gauntlet had been thrown, and he wouldn't back down until and unless she told him to. No way Landry was going to steal her from him.

He focused in on Darren Michaels chastising Ace for staying in his comfort zone even this far in the competition. He then said something critical about another contestant, and Gabe realized Michaels was also berating Teresa, which meant she was in the bottom two.

"So, Teresa," Lily Wen now said, "your performance this entire season has been hit or miss. We loved your seafood paella from the cruise ship dinner. And your roasted branzino with lemon-thyme-caper Beurre Blanc from the secret supper club was beautifully done, but in between was the gloppy mess of vegan mac-and-cheese, pedestrian canapés that lacked any originality, and your performance hasn't improved overall. It's hard to both forgive and forget those faux pas."

"What?" Gabe said aloud.

Dan gave him the stink eye, and motioned for the cameras to keep rolling.

Lily straightened on her tall stool and said, "Teresa, why are you in this competition?"

"I want my own restaurant," Teresa responded. Her eyes cut to Gabe, and she added, "I want to feed people, and make them happy, but I also want control of my life."

"You realize as an owner, you're fully responsible for everything involved. That takes a lot of grit, and determination, and I'm not sure we've seen that from you in these past few weeks."

"That's bullshit," Gabe spat.

Dan called, "Cut!" and told everyone to shut the hell up, and Lily Wen said in a pleasant voice, "Is there something you want to share with the class, Mr. De Luca?"

"What you said is bullshit, and you know it, you vengeful bitch."

Lily's nostrils flared.

"Off my set," Dan commanded.

Lily stood, brushing down her skirt. "Let him stay. He's just protecting his dalliance. Isn't that right, Teresa?"

The term "expression like a thundercloud" crossed Gabe's mind when he looked at Teresa. She stood tall, no indication she'd had a few herself last night. "I'd call you a vengeful bitch, too," she told Lily, "but I want to win or lose this contest on my own merits."

To Gabe's surprise, Lily laughed. "You will." She turned to the other judges, who looked gobsmacked. "For the sake of our schedule, I'll recuse myself from an actual decision in the elimination judging. We'll discuss everything else after one..." She paused. "Or the other, is eliminated." She flicked a glance at Gabe. "Stay or go as you like, Mr. De Luca. We'll discuss your situation later as well."

"No need," he said. "I quit. But I'm staying through the judging."

They took a small break to regroup, but Teresa avoided Gabe and he didn't have a chance to talk to her before the cameras rolled again.

Teresa and Ace had an hour to create an example of the perfect bite using the surprise ingredient. Joel Klein told them, "It needs to stand out, to be the star, but remember that it can't overwhelm either, because the perfect bite has to be more than one note." He looked from Teresa to Ace, drawing out the moment. "So, your secret ingredient will be...papaya. And your time...starts...*now!*"

Teresa and Ace scrambled toward the supply shelves.

Normally, Gabe would be scribbling notes at this point, standing with PA Katie so they could check the monitors for any sections he'd want to review later. But everything was different today. He barely noted that Ace picked up a mango before he realized his mistake and ran for the papaya instead, that Teresa immediately began scooping out the seeds and setting them aside.

Adding to his shame, Katie stood close during the challenge, patting his arm. He'd fucked up. But how could he stay quiet at that point?

He focused on Teresa as she whipped egg whites into a froth, her strong arms straining against the effort, expression focused on the stainless steel bowl and whisk. She lifted the whisk to check the peaks of the whites, then bent over to continue whipping. She'd pulled her long braids back and secured them with a thick band. She wore no makeup except what looked like rose-petal-colored lip gloss, and its shine made him want to kiss it off.

Damn it all. She aroused him, calmed him, and healed him. He'd been so scarred after his marriage ended, the book tanked, and Hannah died that being around anyone left his head aching. He couldn't imagine starting up another relationship. But then a beautiful woman seduced him in an elevator, and he hadn't looked back. And with one outburst, he'd screwed it all up.

An hour later, Teresa and Ace stood in front of the judges once again. Ace presented his papaya salad on a ceramic Japanese soup spoon and Teresa gave each judge a banana papaya mini muffin, the scent of which had Gabe's mouth watering. He thought papaya salad was uninspired and that Teresa's muffins showed originality, but the two voting judges disagreed. With a sickly sweet smile, Lily Wen declared this to be Teresa's last challenge.

Gabe's heart sunk. Jesus, it all happened so fast.

PA Katie sent Teresa into the back room to be filmed saying goodbye to the other contestants. Gabe waited across the hall for her in the interview room. He no longer needed to do a Q&A, but he had to see her, and Katie agreed to help. It didn't escape him that he stood in the doorway of the same room they'd met in on the first day of filming, and lunged at each other as if they had been stranded in the desert and the other was a big drink of water. He didn't see that happening today, and realized he didn't know what to expect, from Teresa's general mood to whether her feelings for him had changed within the last twenty-four hours. He'd been an ass, but Landry hadn't been a gentleman, either, so if one were being reasonable, neither of them should have an advantage over the other.

But who the hell was being reasonable at this point?

He heard voices and Katie and Teresa came out of the opposite room, heads close together, voices low enough that Gabe couldn't catch any of the words. Katie caught sight of him and patted Teresa on the arm, indicating Gabe as he lounged in the doorway.

"She's all yours," Katie said, and Gabe didn't miss the double meaning.

Teresa and Katie embraced, rocking side to side, and Katie wandered back up the hall and around the corner. Teresa stood where she was, about ten feet from Gabe, watching him in silence. She had no poker face at all, and that was one of the things he loved about her, but he wouldn't make any bets on her current mood.

When she didn't move, and the air around them coalesced into raw energy, as it often did when they got within ten feet of each other, he finally said, "Hi," to break the tension.

Her shoulders lowered a fraction. Her hair was still held back by the thick band, but she brushed at it as if to get it out of her face. "Hi."

"I'm really sorry," he said.

"About which part?" She shifted, widening her stance like they were suddenly gunslingers at the OK Corral.

He sighed, relaxing more against the doorframe in contrast to her own aggressive pose. "Being an ass last night, posturing in front of Landry, drinking way too much and adding to my asshole-ery. And your elimination." He nodded as her neutral expression altered to slightly vulnerable. "Especially that."

She nodded back at him. She looked about to speak, paused and swallowed, collected herself, then tried again. "I can't believe what just happened."

He reached for her, but she shook her head. "I'm sorry," he repeated.

"I stood up for myself," she said, as if she couldn't believe it. "And...and look what happened."

"We'll fight it," he said.

"No. We won't. *I* won't. I don't want to think about it right now. It's all too much." She smiled suddenly, but her eyes were sad."I guess I'll have some time now to go to Kaily's birthday party."

He hadn't been expecting that and blurted, "You want to go?"

"I do. I did even before today. She's a sweet girl. And I..." She

179

looked down at her feet and shifted side to side. When she looked up at him again, the vulnerability remained, with shy added to the mix. "I kind of wanted to meet your family, and see where you grew up. Is that dumb?"

He wanted to touch her in reassurance, but held back. He'd promised himself he wouldn't make any sort of move without a clear signal from her first. "No. Not at all. I wondered if after last night and this afternoon you might not want anything to do with me."

She shrugged. "I didn't at first. When you went after Lily Wen, you were protecting me. But I keep telling you I can take care of myself." She sighed. "I *was* pretty annoyed last night. At both of you," she added, and he appreciated the clarification, despite the jab to his heart. "But that wasn't the main thing." This time, she took a step toward him. "I've never had two men fighting for me like that. I don't...it made me uncomfortable. It's not how I want to live my life or feed my ego." Another step, and one more, until she stood directly in front of him. A tilt of her head, and another of his body, and his lips could be on hers. Her eyes never left his face as she whispered, "It turned me on."

"Jesus Christ," he whispered back, tight all over at the passion in her dark eyes, the intensity behind her words.

"Take me home with you," she said.

"I am a fucking idiot," he said slowly, "but I have to ask if you'd be saying the same thing if Landry were standing in front of you."

She shook her head. "I want to be with you."

She didn't have to ask twice.

CHAPTER TWENTY-FIVE

Gabe stroked a hand up Teresa's back as she lay on her stomach amid the rumpled sheets. They'd taken a taxi to his place, too impatient for the subway, and raced up the stairs, laughing like idiots, only to tug the other's clothes off and collapse on the floor naked together. Gabe had only taken enough time to grab a condom before sliding into Teresa with a moan, thrusting hard and fast until both of them were panting and sliding against each other, slick with sweat. She'd come first, hard, biting his shoulder, and he'd followed, gasping at the intensity of his orgasm.

He'd been unable to move for five minutes, and may have stopped breathing for that time, too. But eventually his breath returned and he insisted they climb into bed together, where they'd made love with more languor, taking time to explore each other's bodies. Then they'd both collapsed into a stupor, and slept for about an hour.

He now moved his hand from the nape of her neck to the gentle slope between her shoulders, trailing his fingers around the curve of her shoulder blade, then back toward her spine to avoid the sensitive spot on her side. No spoiling this moment with a tickle.

He smoothed his hand down to the small of her back, then pressed on the muscles along her spine as he worked his way back up.

"That feels good," she murmured, her eyes half closed.

He thought she felt better, her dark skin smooth under his fingers. "You're like satin." He leaned over to kiss her shoulder.

Teresa's eyelids flickered open and she looked up at him. "Will you read me your work some time?"

"Yeah." He smiled, reduced to a dorky fifteen-year-old by her request. "Not sure I can move right now, though."

She rolled to her side. "Me, either. For now, just say something sexy to me. Poetry or sexy words." She lay back, looking expectant.

He tilted his head, his hair brushing across his cheek. His face near hers, he murmured, "Pulchritude."

She barked out a laugh and covered her mouth with both hands. Lowering them, she squeaked, "What kind of sexy word is that?"

"It describes someone of breathtaking beauty."

"Oh," she breathed. "Say that instead. Pulchritude sounds like something the cat coughs up."

He laughed this time and said, "How about this: asseverate."

"Use it in a sentence."

"I asseverate Teresa Steplowski is indeed recherché."

"Damn straight."

He kissed her shoulder again. "I earnestly declare you elegant and exotic."

"That's recherché?" She rolled closer. "Say more."

"My limerance is ineffable."

"Well, now you're just messing with me."

He shook his head, pressed a long kiss to her temple. "Never. But my state of infatuation for you is indeed too great for words."

"You're infatuated with me?"

"Deeply."

"My limerance is pretty deep, too," she murmured and set a warm hand on his thigh. Her movement shifted the sheet and it slithered down, exposing more skin.

He couldn't resist leaning in to kiss her. Her hand smoothed itself up along his hip and he stretched the length of her body. Arm around her waist, he pulled her close enough for her to feel his intentions. She tilted her head back to look in his eyes, then draped a leg over his thigh, tucking the sole of her foot against his calf.

"Is that an invitation?" he asked.

She pressed closer, tilting her hips. "Best one you'll get all day."

"Best one all year," he breathed, shifting his arm under her neck and around her shoulders. He lowered his head for a taste of her lips. When he slid inside her, they broke the kiss, moaning and sighing, before he pulled back and thrust deep.

She melted against him and he tightened his arms, pulling her hips closer with his palm on the flat of her back even as he pushed into her again. They found a rhythm together and she arched back despite his grip on her.

The blood pounded in his ears and his cock pulsed, thrumming inside her. The heat and sweat built between them as they moved faster together.

Desperate for more of her, he flipped her on her back so he could thrust deeper. Her head thrashed on the pillow and she clutched his wrists as he pulled back and thrust again.

"More," she gasped.

He raised himself up and lifted her ankles over his shoulders, then grasped her hips and plunged deep, gritting his teeth against the pleasure that roared through his body and wanted to break loose.

"Keep...going..." she begged, digging her fingernails into his skin. "Close," she gasped out, and as he continued to pound into her, increasing the friction, she tightened around him, her back arching and her head tilting back.

He watched the passion flood over her body and across her face. "Ohh..." he groaned, *"yes."* He let himself go then, and waves of pleasure so intense to almost be painful burst through and peaked, peaked, peaked, then receded in graduated layers until he was completely spent.

Her legs slid from his shoulders and he collapsed on top of her before sliding to the side, and pulling her up against him.

Her heart pounded out the same rapid beat as his and her breath warmed the cooling skin on his chest. He brushed her hair back from her face and she turned her head to press a kiss on his wrist.

"That," she said, looking up at him with sleepy eyes, "was my kind of poetry."

IN THE HISTORY of the world, Teresa knew she had attained the status of Most Relaxed Person Ever. She couldn't stand the thought of moving, other than tracing the line of Gabe's pecs or the hair from his chest down his belly.

Beyond that, she didn't think she would have to move again. Ever. She ached in places that hadn't seen a lot of action in the past few months, and the pleasure-pain component of those aches led to her thinking about sex again, wanting that delicious friction between her legs to build before it burst forth into excruciatingly beautiful sensation. But then, her thigh muscles were sore, too, and she remembered she wasn't going to move anymore, so maybe another round was out. At least for now. It's not like she had anywhere to be right now, and Gabe seemed perfectly content staying here with her.

With that thought in mind, and lulled by Gabe's steady breathing and warm body, she drifted off to sleep.

The scent of fresh coffee gradually woke her. Her dreams consisted of warm sand beaches, the shush of waves lulling her into slothfulness, but when she woke fully, she realized the warmth was Gabe in bed next to her and the waves were the sound of traffic drifting through the windows from three stories below. And the coffee? Without opening her eyes she murmured, "Please don't let that be part of the dream."

Next to her, Gabe stirred and rumbled, "Dream?"

"The coffee."

The mattress dipped and Teresa rolled toward Gabe, opening her eyes. He lay propped on one elbow, looking down at her, his chest bare, a mug of steaming coffee in one hand very, very close to her nose.

"It's real," she said, "and my dream come true right now." With a sleepy smile, he proffered the mug. "Yes, please." She took the coffee from him with a grateful sigh, and after a few sips said, "Did you know you talk in your sleep?"

He shook his head. "Didn't think so."

"It sounded like Shakespeare or something."

"Writer's habit." His eyes crinkled at the corners when he laughed. He snuck a sip from the mug, then handed it back to her. "I was awake, and thought you were sleeping. I do my best plotting out loud, which has led to some interesting social situations. Even then, I can still get stuck, so I recite Shakespeare. Something about it loosens things in my mind and I can untwist my current plot issues."

"So you're writing a book right now?"

"No. I was turning you into a poem." He moved closer and recited, "'Hear my soul speak. Of the very instant that I saw you, did my heart fly at your service.'"

"That's beautiful."

When she sat up, the sheet slithered down her front, exposing her breasts; she didn't miss Gabe's appreciative review of her body, and felt no need to cover up. With a contented sigh, she allowed herself a scan of her own, from his face propped in one hand down to the pink bite mark on his shoulder that she'd administered the night before and the soft hairs on his chest creating a pathway to his firm abs and other enjoyable pleasures. Those were currently covered by the sheet, but he caught her own glance and shifted.

She tried but failed to hide her smile behind the mug.

"You're a wicked woman, Teresa Steplowski."

"You're not discouraging me much, Gabe De Luca."

He slipped the mug from her hands and set it on a shelf behind him without taking his eyes from hers. "Wouldn't dream of it," he whispered, and kissed her, the taste of his lips combined with coffee enough to make her fall back on the bed in shuddering desire. He trailed kisses along her cheek and down to her shoulder.

"I used to have one favorite morning thing," she told him. "Now I have two." She gasped, arching, and added, "But..."

He gently bit her shoulder, matching the mark she'd given him, then lay next to her. "That sounded like a 'but you need to stop seducing me right now' sort of but."

She curled up on her side to face him. "But I owe you an apology."

"What for?"

"The other night. I'm sorry, too. Both of you fighting over me gave me kind of a rush and I let it take over my good sense. My ego needed a little massaging and you guys did that for me." This was so embarrassing, but she had to say it. He waited patiently for her to finish, no judgment in his expression. "I told you I didn't want Cort back, and I meant it. But I've been really..." She was about to say "vulnerable," but hesitated to expose herself to that degree. What she was saying was hard enough. "I've been so nervous about the show, really scared and alone, and it was...reassuring to have him there, in his certainty in wanting me back."

She let out a long breath and pressed the heels of her palms to her eyes. She was going to have to apologize to Cort, too, and why would he ever believe her own sincerity in being done with him if she fluttered like a moth to his flame the first time she saw him in months?

"He was a known quantity," Gabe said. His voice sounded light, but his face had tightened as she spoke.

She nodded. "And that wasn't fair. To anyone. I'm clear about it now."

"Are you?"

"Yes. No hesitation. I'm sorry I messed with your head."

He nodded. "Thanks for saying that."

She ran her fingertips along the edge of his jaw, his stubble softly scratching her skin. She moved her hand down to his chest, pressing there before placing it against her own heart. "My desire for you scares me, Gabe. I've never felt anything like it before, and if that scares you in turn, I'm sorry. I don't want to push you away, but I also don't..." Her voice had climbed higher as she spoke, and she clutched at the sheet between them as she tried to make her point, terrified it would sound like babbling nonsense to him.

"Hey, hey," he soothed. He held one arm out over her body, a question in his eyes, and when she nodded, he slid both arms around her and pulled her against him. "It's okay," he murmured.

She nodded her head against his chest, at a loss for words.

He pressed a kiss to the top of her head. "You can't scare me away that easy."

He brushed his palm down her back in soothing strokes and she melted into his warmth and reassurance. "I was giving you an out there, you know. Not consciously, but it was there."

"Teresa." He paused long enough that she tilted her head back to look into his eyes. "I don't want out," he finally finished.

"What else were you going to say? It sounded like there was more."

"Do you want to talk about the eliminations?"

"I do not."

He again looked like he was going to say something, but seemed to change his mind. "This hasn't exactly been a straightforward relationship."

"Not even close," she agreed.

"But I like you. And it's more than lust. I _like_ you," he stressed. "I enjoy talking to you, being with you, sharing things with you."

"Me, too."

"Tell me that again after you've met my family."

She pulled back more to really look at his face. "Why? Will they be weird about the racial thing?"

He looked genuinely surprised. "No. That won't be an issue. It's more that after Shatara, they all worried about me. More than usual. With my sisters, it's like I have two more moms, fussing over me like hens, and no one has ever been good enough for me where my mother's concerned."

"So they'll be looking closely at me no matter what." Compared to what she'd been through recently, meeting his family should be a piece of cake.

He nodded. "I guess I'm the one giving you an out now, at least as far as Kaily's party is concerned."

She brushed a hand down his chest, enjoying the feel of the softly curled hair there. "I want to go. For Kaily, since she invited me. But should we figure out what's going on with us before we go and get your moms all a-twitter?"

He snorted, then sobered. "So what is going on with us?"

"We're dating," she said, working hard to keep a straight face.

He grinned. "Is that what they call what we're doing?"

"No, but that's what we'll tell your family."

"Hi Mom, Dad," he intoned, as if introducing her. "This is Teresa. We're dating."

She raised an eyebrow at him, and brushed a hand across his hipbone. "You might want to work on that."

"Why?"

"Your cheeks turned a nice shade of pink when you said it."

He gave her a stern look. "Guys don't blush."

"No?" Her hand strayed a bit farther south.

"No. It's because you're touching me in indecent places."

"Then I would think the blood would be rushing *away* from your face." She grasped him firmly and he let out a groan, dropping his head back.

"Huh," she said. "Look at that. You're going even more pink."

He peered at her through one eye. "Men...do not...," he gasped, "go *pink*."

She leaned over and licked the tender skin at his hipbone and he practically came up off the bed. But he collapsed back down when she tightened her grasp, moving her hand more rapidly.

"Teresa," he groaned, his head back, his breathing ragged.

She nipped the skin at the top of his thigh, keeping her rhythm steady. She moved her tongue in lazy circles up his belly, tracing a line of muscle along his abs. "Just let go," she urged.

His hands tightened into fists around the sheet and he went rigid for half a second before grasping her around the waist, flipping her over and nudging her thighs open with one knee. "Not without you," he growled. He grabbed a condom, rolled it on, and slid into her with a guttural moan.

They both went still. "Christ, you feel good," Gabe told her. He lifted himself up, and moved inside her, watching her eyes. "You look good, too," he rumbled, tilting his hips forward until she hissed in a breath and lifted her legs, bringing him deeper inside. "I want to watch you come, and I want you to come hard."

Lust shot through her, top to toes, and she clung to him while he thrust into her, unable to tear her eyes from his, the pressure building fast until he fulfilled his promise.

CHAPTER TWENTY-SIX

After a huge breakfast at a nearby cafe and at least three frantic messages from PA Katie, Teresa reluctantly pulled herself from Gabe and returned to the real world. Or at least, her current version of it. She only got lost once using the subway to the CuisineTV studios and sat impatiently through Chrissie's spiel about how Teresa would be sequestered with the other eliminated challengers in different lodgings, with strict instructions not to contact the remaining contestants.

Back at the main house, Teresa gathered her belongings, accepting multiple hugs from Cookie. "I got no one to sleep with now," she said. "But fuck the rules, I'll still text you."

"Win the whole thing for me," Teresa told her, before hugging everyone else goodbye. Even MaryBeth joined in the group hug, but Teresa figured that was for the cameras.

At the new place, what Jonas called The Brownstone 2.0, Lynette flung herself at Teresa, and Tony cried. Aanjay, Chance and Karl greeted her warmly, and she appreciated that they didn't weep all over her.

Teresa sat on the couch while the others chatted about how amazing the house was and what they'd done since their losing round, and excused herself as soon as she could. Curled up in bed, missing Cookie's warmth and humor, she clutched her phone to her chest, knowing she could text or call at any time now. But she couldn't think of one thing to say. She didn't want to share Gabe with anyone right now, and her other main topic was forbidden: she couldn't reveal that she had been eliminated until after the show aired.

She dragged herself out of bed the next morning and stared at the contents of her suitcase, wondering what to wear to a five-year-old's birthday party. And to meet Gabe's family. While Lynette chattered about the next cat tattoo she wanted to get, Teresa settled on leopard print flats, dark red capris and a white top with thin red stripes.

To escape her housemates' incessant talk about the show, she grabbed her purse, a dark blazer, and Kaily's present, and sat on the front steps until Gabe drove up in a rental car. She let him run the conversation, pointing out highlights of the drive, but she stayed pretty quiet; her mind had gone flat. She'd enjoyed her time with Gabe the other day, but realized with a pang that it had been another version of running away. An extremely sexy run, but a run nonetheless.

So when they pulled up to his parents' gorgeous two-story Colonial, she had to wonder if agreeing to come here was another bad decision.

Pink, yellow and purple balloons hung from the trees lining the sidewalk, and more had been tied to golf tees set into the lawn next to the front walk, creating a floating pathway. The happy shrieks and shouts of five-year-olds drifted from around the back, but instead of heading in that direction, Gabe guided Teresa to the front door.

"My mom will likely be inside, she's always in the kitchen. She's a good place to start, instead of throwing you in the middle of the pack. Although I should warn you—"

Teresa was so tired of being careful and worrying about different personalities. She was free from the show, from Lily Wen, from her life in California. She stepped onto the porch and took in the columns, flowers and wooden bench; it all looked so benign. "I can handle it."

But Gabe seemed intent on protecting her from his family. They couldn't be that bad, especially not compared to her own family, or what she'd dealt with the last few weeks. Shoot, the last few days. She'd actually called Lily Wen a "vengeful bitch," and survived.

"They'll surround you," Gabe continued, "and before you know it, we'll be separated and they'll be asking you a million questions."

"They who?"

"My sisters and mom and grandma."

She stopped her inspection of the stained glass window in the front door. "Your grandma? You never mentioned her."

"Damn. I'm so comfortable with you, I feel like you know all my family history." He swept an arm around her waist. "My grandma can be formidable."

"So's mine." She stepped away to watch the American flag flapping in the light breeze.

Gabe followed. "You okay?"

She smiled, hefting Kaily's present. "It's a party. And I love grandmothers. I miss mine."

"From what you've told me, mine is nothing like yours." He studied her. "You sure—"

The front door opened and a tall, slim woman charged out and threw her arms around Gabe. Teresa recognized his mom from the picture in his apartment. Mrs. De Luca pressed a kiss to Gabe's cheek, then swiped her fingers across it to remove the lipstick smudge. With one arm around Gabe's shoulders, she slung the other around Teresa and gave her a squeeze before releasing them both. "Look at you two. You," she said, indicating Teresa, "are beautiful. You two will make the most gorgeous children."

Gabe went scarlet. "*Mom.*"

"I'm just being honest." She tucked a stray section of graying blonde hair into her casual updo and smiled at Teresa. "It's always driven Gabe crazy, but I can't help myself." Her arm once again around Teresa's shoulders, she steered Teresa toward the front door, calling behind her, "It's never hurt me, Gabriel, but I daresay it helps a lot."

Nonplussed but also mildly amused, Teresa let herself be led into a large living room furnished with beautiful antiques, and wall-to-wall books. The room's style was equal parts comfortable and refined.

"You have great taste, Mrs. De Luca."

They paused at the edge of the room on the way to the kitchen and Gabe's mom pursed her lips, looking around the room. "Mmm...I do, don't I? And it's Bobbi. Roberta, really, but I've never felt like a Roberta." She leaned closed and whispered loudly, "And Mrs. De Luca sounds like a Kindergarten teacher or something, doesn't it?"

"Mom," Gabe sighed.

"Honey, moms are supposed to be embarrassing. It's my job. You'll see one day," she added with a wink. She charged ahead to a family room connected to the kitchen, and a set of large French doors leading onto a deck. Below that, a huge, sloping lawn led down to a pool. "Seriously. Gorgeous babies. Come on out, everyone's dying to see you both."

She stepped outside in her cork wedge sandals and yellow capris, and Gabe double-stepped to catch up with Teresa. "Sorry," he mouthed, face close to her ear. "I tried to warn you."

Feeling unusually rebellious, Teresa found Bobbi's straightforward manner refreshing and Gabe's apologetic tone grating. Didn't he realize she'd been through hell and come out the other side? She was capable, damn it.

She put a hand on Gabe's forearm. "It's okay. I actually appreciate it."

He reached up and took her hand in his, squeezing. "That's good, because you'll be surrounded by it three- or four-fold in a few minutes. But we'll go in together."

"I could handle it on my own."

He grinned and gave her a quick kiss. "Who said I'm doing it for *you?*"

Hands still linked, he took a step toward the door.

Still in rebellious mode, Teresa said, "She's right about the babies," and laughed as his shoulders tensed up in response.

They stepped onto the deck and into the shade of a trellis with grapevines interlacing the top and sides. Round tables stood to one side, set up with veggie dip, potato salad, chips and guacamole, fruit skewers, lemonade, and a variety of mini foods: pizza, grilled cheese, hot dogs and hamburgers. A few people sat at the tables, but the majority of adults and children gathered on the lawn.

Long lengths of what looked like bubble wrap were spread out and children took turns running across them. Everyone cheered when someone made it to the other side without popping any of the bubbles, so Teresa assumed that was the goal.

Bobbi strode across the lawn to the side of the house as if expecting Teresa and Gabe to follow, which they did. Three men stood around a large barbecue on a concrete slab, each with a beer in hand, staring at the collection of hot dogs, hamburgers and chicken drumsticks. Two looked old enough to be Gabe's dad and the third was closer to Gabe's age.

"Bob," Bobbi called, "come meet Gabe's girlfriend," and Teresa slid Gabe a look. Still holding her hand, he shrugged. *Girlfriend. Bob and Bobbi.* Affection and trepidation joined Teresa's rebellion. She wondered if someone could go crazy from being such a walking contradiction.

One man, in cargo shorts and a madras shirt, handed a spatula to one of the other men, and strolled over. He had thick, wavy blonde hair sparked with gray and shared Gabe's warm brown eyes and welcoming smile. He clapped Gabe on the shoulder, then took Teresa's hand in his warm one. He shared a firm grip and direct gaze with his son, too.

"It's a treat to finally meet you, Teresa."

Teresa cut her eyes to Gabe again. *Finally?* What else had Gabe told them about her? Had he been the one to call her his girlfriend, or had his mother used the term on her own? Had he been moving their relationship forward without making sure she was in the same place?

"Oh, yes, honey," Gabe's dad said, correctly interpreting the look. "Gabe told us he met an amazing woman who could cook his socks off. We're happy to have you here."

"It's nice to meet you both, too." Teresa hadn't actually cooked for Gabe, but she knew what he meant. She gestured at the happily playing children. "And so nice of you to host this party for Kaily."

Bob put his arm around Bobbi and pulled her close. "Stephan and Kaily are family. Kaily's another granddaughter and Stephan's our fourth son."

"Fourth?" Teresa asked.

"Well, sixth, I guess," Bob said. "Stephan, Adam and Nick." He pointed out Gabe's best friends. One nod for the man at the barbecue behind him and another currently being wrapped up as a toilet paper mummy by giggling children. "And our sons-in-law, George and Brian."

Teresa was introduced to George at the barbecue, along with a good family friend named Terence, and then Gabe's sisters strolled up the lawn together. It looked like Stephan and Brian-the-mummy had been elected to stay and entertain the kids.

Both tall and beautiful, Ellen had a wavy brunette bob and curvy figure in a striped sundress, while Nancy took after her mom, with an upswept 'do, navy capris and a sleeveless cream blouse.

"Wow." She hugged Teresa. "Gabe wasn't lying about those

cheekbones. You're gorgeous."

So looks weren't the only thing Nancy had inherited from her mother.

Ellen rolled her eyes. "He also said she's super smart. And a professional chef."

"Caterer," Teresa corrected; she didn't consider herself a chef since she hadn't finished culinary school.

"Are you cooking for us today? Maybe something you've done on that show you're in? I can't wait to watch it," Ellen added. "It sounds so cool. How's it going?"

"El," Gabe began.

"I know we're not supposed to talk about it, but I've never met a celebrity before."

Gabe rubbed a palm along his jaw. "Killin' me here, El."

Teresa eyed Gabe. He looked pained, but she didn't need him to run interference. Maybe she *wanted* to talk about the show. "She's just curious," she told him before turning back to Ellen. "I'm not a celebrity, far from it. And there are certain things I can't talk about, but it's harder than it looks to do a show like this."

"Gabe." Nancy poked her brother with a sharp-looking elbow. "Maybe Teresa would like something to drink?"

"And leave her alone with you two? Not a chance."

Ignoring that just yesterday morning, she'd been murmuring endearments in his ear before crying out his name a few minutes later, Teresa narrowed her eyes at Gabe. "I'd love something to drink, thank you." She held up a hand to Nancy and Ellen. "Actually, could you excuse us a minute?" She pulled Gabe a few feet away. "What are you doing?"

His forehead wrinkled. "Saving you from the swarming alligators."

"I don't need your help. How many times do I need to say it? I'm a big girl, and I've handled worse than your sisters. You're not my dad, you're not my husband, or my keeper. I can stand on my own, and I don't need you. Don't. Help," she repeated.

"Hey, I'm just—"

"Not listening," she broke in. "I'm so tired of people not listening to me, of stomping all over me like I can't do anything for myself. "

Gabe held out his hands in surrender. "Truce," he said, even though the expression on his face indicated he wanted to say more, much more. "You still want something? A beer?"

Once Gabe had stalked off for the drinks, Teresa returned to Ellen and Nancy, and shared an on-set story she thought might be safe to discuss. They all laughed over Darren Michaels complaining about what was written on his cue cards.

After Teresa answered a couple more questions from Ellen, Nancy asked, "So are you going back to San Francisco after the show?" She might look like her mother, and be as straightforward, but she hadn't developed Bobbi's grace. And as Teresa observed her more closely, she saw that Nancy also appeared more brittle, tightly held together. She clutched her drink glass in front of her, as if someone might come along at any moment and wrench it from her.

"That depends on a lot of things," Teresa replied carefully.

"Like if you lose?"

"That would be one factor, yes."

"Is Gabe another?"

And there it was. They could flatter Teresa in front of Gabe, but they still wanted to know her intentions. She wanted to say, "None of your beeswax," but stopped herself in time. Maybe getting a break from Cookie wasn't such a bad thing, because at least she wasn't tempted to tell them to cram it up their poop holes. Yet. "That's really between us."

"Look, he may not have told you, but—"

"God, Nance." Ellen sighed. "Don't be so aggressive right off the bat. Ease her into it at least." Her warm smile seemed genuine, but Teresa wasn't ready to fall for it.

Things were moving too fast all around her, and by coming to this party, she'd stepped onto a speeding escalator. Gabe had warned her, but she figured with all the practice with her own family, surely she could handle his. Once again, she'd jumped too soon and gotten in over her head. She didn't know why she prickled so much at what felt like Gabe's interference, when she actually could have used his help.

Except now Gabe strolled across the field with the necks of two beer bottles hanging from one hand and an older woman on his arm.

"You think *I'm* bad," Nancy said with a laugh, not directing it to anyone in particular. "Just wait for Nana."

Teresa's rebellion withered, and she realized she wasn't ready for Nana. She wasn't ready for any of this.

But Nana was ready for her. It was as if the woman had a check list.

"Hello, dear," she said sweetly, and her warm, soft skin reminded her so much of Mama Step's when they shook hands that Teresa melted. "Where are you from again?"

"San Francisco."

"How old are you?"

"Twenty-eight."

Gabe handed Teresa a beer and took a long chug himself. She moved closer to him to convey an apology, but he looked around the big yard instead of at her.

Nana continued her interrogation."What do you do for a living?"

"I'm a cook."

Nana held a hand to the back of her ear. "A crook?"

Teresa leaned forward and said loudly, "A *cook*. A chef. I...cook things."

Nana stared at her. "Well, you don't need to shout, dear."

Gabe closed his eyes as if he were in great pain. Ellen looked sympathetic, but too nervous to interrupt, and Nancy seemed to be enjoying herself far too much.

"Religion?" Nana snapped.

"I beg your pardon?"

"Why are we standing in this heat," Nana groused. "My makeup's melting." She shuffled to one of the tables with an attached umbrella, managing to snag both Ellen and Nancy's wrists along her way. Clearly expecting Teresa to follow, she asked over her shoulder, "What's your faith?"

Teresa had no faith she'd ever escape this hell.

She gave Gabe sad-bunny eyes, but knew she'd blown that escape route. He took another swallow of beer and said, "I'm going to help my dad with the grilling."

Teresa somehow survived the topics of religion, money and politics before Nick, Stephan and Adam strolled over. Teresa noted all three women, Nana included, preened before the men reached them.

Nick held out his arms and announced, "Nana," before wrapping her in a huge hug and loudly kissing her on the cheek. "How come you've been hiding yourself over here? You've denied me and the boys your company for too long."

"Nana and Teresa have been getting to know each other," Nancy told him, shifting in her chair so her shirt gaped open, and peering up.

Teresa thought she practically batted her eyelashes at him.

"And you're still standing, beautiful?" Nick asked Teresa. "Did she go through her whole list of questions?" He turned to Nana. "Did you cover politics yet, Charlotte?"

Nana grabbed his wrist and shook it. "We're done with the preliminaries, Nick. I was just going to ask Teresa about her family."

"They're nice people," Nick informed her without hesitation. "Regretfully, I need to steal Teresa away. She hasn't met Adam and Stephan yet, and the birthday girl's been asking for her."

"Okay, honey, you can have her for a little while, but I want her back before too long." She winked and smiled at Teresa, and Teresa could swear she caught a hint of canine.

Nancy jumped up, almost spilling her drink, and bumped into Nick. "Do you need any help? I can help. I'm sure my husband's off talking sports and not actually helping out with any of the party, so I can help if you need it."

"And lose important time with your grandmother? She's the only one you've got." Nick took Nancy's shoulders and guided her back to the seat. "Make some precious memories, you guys." His eyes twinkled so hard Teresa thought they might blind her.

He slipped his hand in hers and led her away from the De Luca women, Adam and Stephan trailing until they were out of earshot.

"I'm smart, too, you know," Teresa told Nick. At his look, she added, "You're always referring to me as beautiful. But I'm a lot of other things, too, including smart."

Nick grinned at her. "Agreed. And you're a strong woman to survive that trio. Gabe doesn't deserve you."

He then introduced Stephan, Kaily's dad, who had a sweet smile, but sad eyes, and Adam, the NYU professor. If any of her teachers had looked like him, she wouldn't have been able to concentrate in class. With his sandy blonde hair, and dressed in flip-flops, board shorts and a tight t-shirt stretched over his broad chest, he looked more like a surf bum than a professor.

She shook their hands and thanked them for rescuing her.

"We're the backup rescue squad for when Nana gets on a tear," Adam said.

"But where's Gabe?" Nick asked. "He should've been the first responder."

"I kind of told him to back off," Teresa admitted.

Adam raised an eyebrow, but Nick laughed. "No wonder he's over at the grill with steam coming out his ears."

"I should go apologize."

Nick held up a hand. "Oh, no. He's called me a caveman enough times without realizing he pulls that shit himself with women too often."

"You are a caveman," Stephan said.

"Neanderthal, technically," Adam added helpfully.

Teresa didn't let them sidetrack her. "What do you mean, he pulls that too often?"

Nick sighed. "Mouth got ahead of me again." He glanced at the grill, where Gabe watched them all, his forehead wrinkled. "He's a natural protector. He takes care of everyone else before he takes care of himself, but sometimes he goes too far. And it gets more pronounced the more he likes you."

"The guy brought me coffee every morning when Tina and I split," said Adam.

Nick and Stephan stared at him. "You two split?"

Adam shrugged. "That was my way of telling you."

Nick slapped Adam on the shoulder. "Sorry, man. She was a good one."

Teresa was forcibly reminded of her congratulatory breakfast with Victoria and Kristen; this sounded like the male version of that conversation. She liked Gabe's friends, and hoped she hadn't just pushed away a really good man. She had no objection to being protected, but she needed to stand on her own, too, to know she could take care of herself. She obviously needed to work on her timing.

Why did life have to be so complicated?

"Kaily really was asking about you," Stephan said, interrupting her rollercoaster thoughts.

He led her to the group of children now finished with their game and popping the bubble wrap with gleeful screams and shouts. Stephan called to his daughter, and she dropped the plastic and ran over, the skirt of her little red and white sundress flapping around her knees.

"Teresa!" she shouted, and ran so hard into her that Teresa fell on her butt, laughing.

Kaily threw her warm, sticky arms around Teresa and climbed into her lap. "I'm five!" she said with great cheer.

Bobbi had appeared from nowhere and was snapping pictures of the two of them on her iPhone. Stephan told Kaily to apologize for knocking over Teresa and Kaily immediately burst into tears.

Bobbi handed her phone to Stephan and said, "Oh, sweetheart, too much sugar and excitement." She held her hands out to lift Kaily up, but the little girl grunted, "No!" and pressed her face into Teresa's shoulder.

Teresa automatically wrapped an arm around Kaily's waist, patting her small, sturdy back as she continued to cry. Sitting there on the lawn, Teresa craved a few reassuring back pats herself as a crowd gathered around them while Stephan and Bobbi discussed proper parenting. As Teresa's throat tightened and her chest constricted, she held Kaily tighter.

"Bobbi," Stephan said. "Too much sugar or not, Kaily still needs to apologize for being rude."

"Steph, you're an amazing dad, and you know we love you, but sometimes children just need to be children."

In a quiet but firm voice, Stephan said, "Of all the people here, I know that better than anyone. God willing, my child will grow up, but I'm still going to raise her with manners."

Teresa did cry then, for all that Stephan and Kaily had lost, along with her own unnamed and overflowing emotions, and buried her face in the five-year-old's baby-fine hair to hide it. While Teresa composed herself, someone dispersed the onlookers, and she felt the tension in the air decrease. She and Kaily lifted their heads at the same time and looked at each other. Stephan had sat down close by, swiping through the pictures on Bobbi's phone, and Gabe stood on her other side, spatula still in hand, his expression unreadable.

Kaily patted at the tears on Teresa's face and said, "I'm sorry, Teresa. I didn't mean to push you on your butt."

"I'm sorry, too."

"But why?"

"For not realizing how *strong* you are," Teresa said with a grin, then tickled Kaily until she sprawled in Teresa's lap, holding her sides and giggling.

Still laying sideways, head and feet in the grass, Kaily held out her skirt and said, "Did you see my dress?"

"Yes, very pretty."

"And my beads?" Kaily lifted a strand of purple plastic beads up. "They'd be *divine* with cowboy boots."

"Where'd you hear that word, K?" Stephan asked her. "Divine."

"From Nana. She was looking at Uncle Nick's bottom and said it was *divine*."

Stephan turned crimson and Gabe choked, turning his back so Kaily couldn't see his face. Kaily peered up at Teresa. "Did I use the wrong word?"

"No, honey." She smoothed back Kaily's bangs. "Both you and Nana got it just right."

CHAPTER TWENTY-SEVEN

After the cat-herding equivalent of gathering wired kids and partially plastered adults for lunch, then cleaning up the kids for posed pictures, Gabe was ready to collapse in an easy chair with a beer. But his mother stood on the deck, clapped her hands for attention and announced it was cake and presents time!

"Jesus," he said, swiping at his face with a forearm as the heat from the grill rolled over him. "What they need is more sugar."

"Goes with the territory," Adam said next to him.

"Heard you finally spilled about Tina." Gabe scraped the barbecue clean, then set the wire brush aside and closed the lid, sealing away some of the heat.

"Didn't mean to keep it from the guys. Just needed to lick my wounds a little."

Gabe fished in the cooler and handed Adam a beer.

Nodding his thanks, Adam opened it and took a long swallow. "What about you?" he asked, as they watched the other adults arranging the kids in a semi-circle around Kaily.

Gabe gave Adam some serious side-eye. "What about me?"

"Teresa's way out of your league."

Gabe shoved Adam, but Adam just laughed.

"C'mon, you've been mooning at each other all day, but you've spent the entire party in separate corners."

"She thought I was hovering. She wanted me to back off, I backed off." Gabe shrugged and took a long swallow of beer, thinking, *Conversation closed.*

Adam shook his head. "You're such a dumbass."

"What pretty words you use, professor," he said, then immediately wanted to take it back. Not because Adam might be offended—he wouldn't—but the phrase sounded too much like Cort Landry. Cort Landry, whose attention turned Teresa on as much as Gabe's had. "Shit." He set his beer down. "I am a dumbass," he said, and strode across the lawn and up the deck to where Teresa sat on a blanket on the decking.

Cort Landry hadn't taken no for an answer, but Teresa was still obviously attracted to him. She was also attracted to Gabe; their marathon sex session the other day had to be proof of that. Whereas Cort insisted Teresa didn't know her own mind, Gabe had gone one-eighty and taken her too seriously. In fact, his stupid pride had been stepped on when she told him not to help, so he'd left her completely alone. All of that so close to her elimination round on the show.

He'd witnessed her strength for weeks now as she faced every challenge on *Tasty Dish*. She could also handle his family, but that didn't mean he should have left her completely alone. Let her manage, but be there for her if she needed him. Instead, he'd gone off to lick his wounds, as Adam had suggested.

He picked up a blue and white beaded bracelet with a Sven charm from a basket of party favors and crouched in front of Teresa, holding it out to her. "Truce?" he asked, face close to hers so she could hear him over the cheers of the partygoers as Kaily opened her presents.

She took the bracelet from him and looked at the picture of the goofy reindeer from *Frozen* on its charm. Slipping it over her wrist, one side of her mouth tilting up, she nodded. "Sit with me?"

She patted the spot at her side, but he sat behind her, wrapping his hands around her waist and pulling her close. He sighed into her hair as she relaxed against him, and looked up in time to see Nick pat at his chest, as if his heart were going pitty-pat. Gabe flipped him off and Nick laughed and turned to say something to Nana next to him, her hand tucked in the crook of his arm. She laughed heartily, her cheeks going pink. Gabe shook his head; anyone who took the time to make his Nana happy, even if it might be at his expense, would always be in his good graces. Stephan sat near Kaily, collecting the wrappings she flung behind her as she ripped open each gift, and handed them to Gabe's mom, who saved the bows and smoothed out the paper. She probably had some craft project in mind for Kaily and his nieces next time they were over. Ellen and Nancy both lived around the corner with their families, and the kids spent a lot of time with their grandparents.

When he married Shatara, he'd had a vague idea of having children at some unknown point in the future, but they'd both been partying too hard to even discuss the subject. He'd spent the past five years building his life back up again, and with every interaction with Stephan and Kaily, saw firsthand how tough raising a child could be.

He'd also witnessed the joys and heart-expanding experiences. Watching Kaily, holding Teresa close, he wondered, what would it be like to have his own kids here, celebrating their milestones with his family?

TERESA SANK INTO the car's seat, exhausted. She couldn't recall ever attending any party with so many emotional ups and downs. And none of the people involved had been her relatives. She'd been blind-sided by Gabe's female side of the family, and touched by Stephan's struggles to be a good parent given his situation. He must feel the weight of Hannah's absence every day, but even more so on occasions like this.

Mostly, though, she'd been confused by her reaction to Gabe. The whirling vortex of her feelings for him; her confusion over Cort; rampant homesickness; and unprocessed grief over her elimination from *Tasty Dish* swirled around and within in her, threatening to break her apart. She wanted to take back losing her temper at Gabe, but at the same time, she needed to take a stand. Not just with Gabe, but with everyone. With that came the realization that her conviction could push Gabe away from her.

That thought shoved her already fragile hold over the edge. She crossed her arms over middle, trying to keep herself together.

Gabe drove them through his charming hometown and onto the interstate, glancing her way occasionally, but remained quiet. She wanted to reassure him, but she couldn't even comfort herself. What could she say to him? That she was a whirling vortex and don't come too close or she'd burst apart, with no guarantee the shrapnel wouldn't damage him?

As they crossed bridges surrounded by trees waving in the breeze and beautiful, well-maintained homes on large lots, the picturesque scenery calmed her. They'd been driving for about half an hour before Gabe finally spoke.

"I'm sorry." He glanced from the road and briefly met her eyes. "I shouldn't have left you alone at the party."

"I told you to."

"Yeah, but you didn't mean—"

Her fists clenched against her middle. "Are you telling me I don't know my own mind?"

"You know what I meant."

"No, I don't know what you meant. It sounded to me like you were acting like Caveman Nick and then assuming I didn't mean what I said. And not only that, that I couldn't handle myself with your family. Which, by the way, I could. And did." *So there. Suck it, Mr. Caveman.* She crossed her arms over her chest and stared out the window.

"And they loved you," he said, clearly grasping now.

Well, she was mad, and she wasn't going to save him. "No, they didn't. Your mother thinks I'm only good for making beautiful bi-racial babies, your sisters think I'm a flighty TV personality, and... and I can't even begin to imagine what your grandmother thinks."

When Gabe didn't respond, she looked at him. He clutched the steering wheel, eyes focused on the road, and his jaw worked as if he wanted to say something but was holding back. Or maybe clenching his teeth together hard.

"Gabe," she said to prompt him. Deep down, she knew she was spoiling for a fight, and she should drop it right now, but he was here, he'd been an ass and so had she, and she needed to vent. So screw it. "*Gabe,*" she repeated when he remained silent.

"Don't talk to me right now," he finally said, then pressed his lips together in a thin line again.

"I—"

He looked at her long enough to point and say, "*Don't,*" before turning back to the road.

She shifted in her seat to face him. "Don't what? Don't this, and don't that. I am so damn tired of people telling me what to do and how I should be—when I know perfectly well who I am—and not listening to me. No one ever listens. How loud do I have to shout," she yelled, straining against her seatbelt, "before people actually take me seriously?"

"Are we really doing this right now?" he asked, jaw still tight.

"Maybe we shouldn't do this at all," she said. "Not if—"

And then her phone rang. She fished it out of her purse and stared at the display, her ears ringing from her own shouting in the small space, and her head spinning a little from her outburst. She was already regretting it.

"Julia?"

"You're not at the brownstone."

Her sister's statement confused Teresa's already frazzled mind, so she gave the most straightforward answer. "No, I'm on my way home from a birthday party."

Julia's voice trembled. "Can you get here soon? They won't let me in."

Some of the fog left Teresa's brain and she straightened. "Jules, what are you talking about? Get where?"

"Some bitchy petty functionary named Chrissie won't let me into the brownstone," Julia raged, but Teresa could hear panic behind the words as her pitch increased. "It's against the rules," she added, and it sounded like Julia addressed someone nearby.

"You're in New York," Teresa blurted, and Gabe turned to her, his frown changing to an expression of concern. "What are you doing here?" Even as she said it, the rest of their conversation clicked: Julia didn't know Teresa had been eliminated and now lived in a different house. No outsiders were allowed into the brownstone, although PA Katie probably would have called Teresa to verify Julia's identity and then found a place for her to stay. But Chrissie was a hard-ass rule whore, and she didn't like Teresa. "How did you find the house?"

"Googled it," Julia replied. "You sent me a picture, remember? It had the street name in it."

Teresa couldn't deal with that right now. "Are you alone?"

"I thought you were a star on this show," Julia said with a combination of petulance and bravado. "Victoria calls all the people on her shows *stars*." It sounded like she addressed Chrissie again with her next words. "Stars are supposed to be treated better."

Teresa heard Chrissie grumble something in the background. It sounded like, "Just shove off, kid."

More annoyed by Chrissie's disrespect than Julia's attitude, Teresa demanded, "Hand your phone to Chrissie."

Teresa heard shuffling and mumbling and Julia saying, "God,

don't be such a bitch. Are you bitter about your stupid name or something," before Chrissie muttered, "*What*," into the phone.

If Julia could muster bravado in the midst of fear right now, then Teresa could, too. "Julia is my seventeen-year-old sister. She's in New York alone. I'm on my way there right now." She looked at Gabe. "How far out are we?"

"About forty minutes."

Teresa turned from his distressed expression; she couldn't deal with both situations at the same time.

"We'll be there soon," she told Chrissie. "If no one's in the brownstone, she can stay in the front hall. If Cookie's there, they can hang together. No one else will know she's there."

"I can't," Chrissie said.

"Are you kidding me?" Teresa yelled. "She won't cause trouble, and she's alone right now."

Gabe made a gesture as if requesting Teresa give him the phone so he could handle things. She glared at him, and Chrissie's next words shoved her right over the edge.

"Rules are rules."

"Fuck the rules!" Teresa shouted. "That is my little sister out there, scared and alone in New York. I got kicked off the show and I have zero motivation to behave right now. Let her inside. *Now*."

"Whatever," Chrissie muttered.

"Wow, what did you say?" Julia asked into the phone. "She turned purple, but she's opening the door."

Teresa was shaking, but Julia didn't have to know that. "Is anyone inside, Jules?"

"Yeah, a couple people." Teresa pictured the front hall and imagined Julia peering into the large living room to the left. "Shouldn't there be cameras here?"

"Focus, Julia. Who's there? Describe them to me."

"Um...Hot guy, boring chick, and a lesbian with blue hair."

"She's not a lesbian," Teresa said, "but she is your new best friend. And we need to have a talk about stereotypes."

"We're black," Julia said, as if Teresa had somehow forgotten that fact. "I know all about stereotypes."

"Not even close," Teresa told her with a sigh. "The woman with the blue hair is Cookie."

"*Cookie?* Seriously?"

"What's up, minor Kardashian?" Teresa heard Cookie say, and she laughed with relief. Julia was in good hands.

By the time they got to the house, Teresa had talked to Cookie, heard more of the story from Julia—she couldn't *stand* their uncompromising parents, and had to get away—and talked to her mother, who sounded hysterical in her restrained way. Gabe remained quiet the rest of the drive, although he hadn't exactly had many opportunities to talk. Teresa told him the basics—that Julia had pulled the sullen teenager thing and run away, thinking Teresa could get her on the show and make her famous—and was maybe now regretting that decision. Or maybe not. Teresa couldn't always gauge Julia.

"We'll take care of her," Gabe said on the sidewalk in front of the house. He reached out his hand, and she accepted it gratefully. They needed to talk, but it would have to wait. Spoiled brat or no, her sister needed her right now, and she herself needed to learn to accept support.

CHAPTER TWENTY-EIGHT

Despite everyone's protests, "Rules are Rules Chrissie" kicked them out of the house a few hours later, but Katie got permission from the producers for them all to stay in some extra rooms in Brownstone 2.0. Gabe, Teresa, and Julia took a cab there, and sat in the living room after the other residents had gone to bed. Teresa threw together some food, but none of them ate much. She wanted both to sleep and to talk to Gabe about what had happened between them earlier; neither would happen soon. Julia alternately stared sulkily at her phone and texted her friends.

"Are you a model?" she asked Gabe once. She sat slumped on the couch, her beige toeless boots on the coffee table, while Teresa and Gabe bookended her in club chairs opposite each other.

Gabe shook his head.

Julia sighed down at the text she was composing. "It'd be more exciting if you were a model."

Teresa gasped. "Jesus Christ, Julia."

Julia gave Teresa a bland expression. "You swear a lot more since you came to New York. I bet it's Cookie's influence." She wrapped her sweater duster tighter around her scoop neck top and beige jeggings.

Teresa let her head drop back. "You sound like Mom."

"Ew, don't even." She sent her text and looked up again. "I like Cookie. Have you seen pictures of her husband? *He's* a Navy SEAL," she said pointedly to Gabe. She fanned her face. "Now that's hot."

"Gabe's hot," Teresa said before she could stop herself; she blamed the long day, but it was also true.

"Yeah, but he's a writer. Writing isn't sexy."

"The billion dollar romance industry might disagree with you," Gabe told her amiably.

"He's smart, too," Teresa said. "And smart is very sexy." She and Gabe exchanged a brief smile. She knew it wouldn't be enough to get him to forgive her, but she grasped at it right now anyway.

Julia rolled her eyes. "Whatever."

Teresa rolled her eyes back. "I'm surprised Mom and Dad didn't run away from *you*, instead of the other way around."

"They hate me," Julia said, staring at her phone, which had gone into sleep mode.

"No, they don't."

Gabe stood up. "I'm going to make coffee."

"Jules," Teresa said in a stern voice to get her attention. "They love you. And they only want what's best for you. That's why they're so hard on you."

"Omigod." Julia gaped at her. "You sound *just like them*."

"Yeah, well, despite everything, I love you, too."

Someone knocked on the door, and Julia raced to the front hall. "Mommy!" she cried, and threw her arms around their mother. It softened Teresa toward Julia. A little.

Gabe brought out a tray of steaming coffee cups and set it on the table before standing at Teresa's side. He made no move to touch her or take her hand, and she couldn't blame him. She'd blasted him— and his family—pretty badly in the car, and mostly avoided talking to him ever since. Still, he was here, and that counted for a lot.

Julia, clinging to their mother, led their parents into the living room.

"Hi, Mom, Daddy," Teresa said, unsure what to do next. After that terrible dinner, and her disastrous goodbye to them before leaving for New York, relations with her parents had been strained, to say the least.

Her mom hugged Julia closer, but her dad smiled at her and stepped forward to give her a hug. "Hi baby," he said, and tears filled her eyes as she hugged him back, her face pressed into the scratchy wool of his long coat.

He held a hand out to Gabe. "David Steplowski."

"Gabe De Luca. I'm a friend of your daughter's."

"Which one?" her mom asked.

"Teresa's," Gabe said, at the same time Julia said, "He's her booty call."

"*Julia*," Teresa admonished, even before their mother could.

"What? If you're not doing it with him, you're stupid, because he's hot. And he's a writer," she said, her head tilted up to her mother's. "They make a *ton* of money."

Still looking at Gabe, Teresa's father said, "That's enough, Julia."

"But, Daddy—"

This time, her dad turned around and got in Julia's face. "I said that is enough, Julia," he repeated, in a quiet, stern voice that brooked no argument. It was the first time Teresa had ever seen him do that, or talk to her that way, and it impressed her.

Then David Steplowski turned back to Gabe and said, "Is this true?"

"What's that, sir?"

"Are you involved with my daughter?"

Gabe looked to Teresa. After all that had happened that afternoon, were they? She did not want to share those details with her parents. She and Gabe needed to talk privately, and she needed to apologize—profusely—for her behavior and the terrible things she'd said in the car about his family. But right now? She didn't know where they stood.

"I like your daughter very much, Mr. Steplowski," Gabe finally said, while Teresa stood mute. "She's smart, talented, beautiful." He looked down at her and she found herself mesmerized, as usual, by his eyes. His kind but intense eyes that hid nothing right now; the emotion in them floored her. "I also admire and respect her, sir, but our relationship is still new and I'm letting her decide the next step."

Her dad looked impressed. He should be. Not only was that a great speech, but Teresa knew it was true. It covered everything without revealing too much.

"My children are everything to me, Mr. De Luca," her dad told Gabe. "I appreciate your respectful attitude, but if you'll excuse us, our family has some private matters to discuss."

Teresa thought she couldn't be shocked anymore today, but apparently that wasn't true. Her father rarely spoke so many sentences in a row, usually leaving the talking to her mom, and she'd certainly never heard him say that his children were everything to him.

"That is," her father added with a significant pause, "unless you live here?"

"No, I live in Brooklyn." He shook her dad's hand again and reached around to shake her mom's, too.

"Beverly Steplowski," she said. "It's a pleasure to meet you."

"You, too, Mrs. Steplowski. I'll leave you all to it."

"Wait." Teresa turned to her parents. "The contestants stay in this house. Gabe writes for the show, that's how we met. But the producers opened up a couple bedrooms you can use tonight. There's some coffee in the living room, if you could wait in there? I want to say goodnight to Gabe."

Her father nodded, and Julia led them into the other room while Teresa walked with Gabe to the front door. Despite it being at least three in the morning, and chilly outside, she grabbed a random sweater from the hall tree and stepped onto the front stoop. She did not need any member of her family overhearing her conversation right now.

After everything that had happened, Teresa still didn't know what to say, and struggled for a starting point while pulling on what she thought might be Chance's sweater. That was unfortunate.

Gabe had no hesitation about diving right in. "We need to talk."

"It's late."

"Is that your way of saying no chance in hell of working this out?"

"Gabe."

He held out his hands. "I'm a little raw. Long day."

"I'm really confused right now." She knew how pathetic it sounded, but it was true. "I don't know what to do, but I think…"

She needed time to process all that had happened. And to consider the future. She hadn't given herself any opportunity to grieve losing the competition, and certainly hadn't allowed herself to wonder what to do next. She had to fulfill her commitment to the show, because all of the contestants would appear on the final episode to usher in the winner, but what then? She fully empathized with that sad bunny in the video without its nest mates, very alone and scared, but also determined to find her way.

Somewhere along the line, she'd learned that knowing your own mind didn't mean you weren't scared, or even that your life completely worked. She'd always thought of herself as a walking contradiction, but actually that was *life*.

Gabe would stay by her side, but she was so drawn to him, she didn't know if she could stay away. And she couldn't think when they were together. All the more reason to take a break.

He ran a hand through his hair, and she watched it feather back in place. He turned away, facing down the street, then faced her again. "I meant what I said to your dad. The next step is yours."

Suddenly he was in front of her, his hands on her face, tilting it up to his. "After this," he murmured, and pressed his lips to hers. He didn't move at first, and she absorbed the feel of his warm lips on hers, the press of his fingers against her jaw. Then they were both moving, arms around each other, crushed so tightly together no space remained between them, their breath mingling, and she moaned against his mouth, completely lost in him as always.

Just as quickly, they stumbled apart, breathing heavily. She could tell their effect on each other stunned him, too. And even though it crushed her, because of that effect, she knew she had to take some time away from him. She couldn't think straight otherwise. She had been saying it all along, but had been too cowardly to take action on it.

Her voice hoarse, she whispered, "I need a break."

He nodded, as if expecting her words. "Let me know if you want to mend things," he told her, then jumped down the steps and strode away down the dark street.

With each step he took away from her, she wanted to run after him and bring him back, but she forced herself to stand shivering on the step, Chance's sweater wrapped tight around her. She watched Gabe until he disappeared around the corner, then went inside to face her family.

TERESA'S FATHER SAT in the chair she'd recently vacated, and her mom and Julia snuggled in one corner of the couch, murmuring to each other. Her mom wrapped one edge of her large cardigan around Julia so they resembled a cozy two-headed person. Teresa slumped into Gabe's vacated chair, trying to ignore his scent rushing through her senses, and also trying to figure out what alternate reality she'd fallen into. The one where her father took charge and her sweet, gentle mother doted on her daughters. Well, on her youngest daughter anyway.

"I like your gentleman suitor," her father told her.

And now she'd fallen into an alternate 1850. Her "gentleman suitor"? Where was Julia's patented attitude when she needed it?

"He's not my suitor, Daddy." Teresa rubbed at her head, desperate for sleep.

"Liar," Julia said. "You guys were eye sexing all night."

"There it is," Teresa said aloud, wishing her sister could have directed her attitude at their parents instead of her and Gabe.

"There's what?" Julia asked.

"Never mind." Teresa straightened in the chair. "Gabe's a good guy, I'm glad you like him."

"But you don't?" her mother asked.

Actually, I think I love him, she thought, but kept it to herself. Love and lust could live together quite happily, but she couldn't tell the difference right now. If she and Gabe were going to have a relationship, she needed to find a way to marry the two. But if it was only lust? Then she needed to evaluate for herself if that was enough. And she was *not* going to discuss this with her parents. "Maybe we should talk about Julia running away, and what happened there?"

"Your mother and I..." He cleared his throat, and ran a hand over his short-cropped hair. In the light from the overhead fixture, Teresa noted more gray coming through.

Oh God, they were getting a divorce.

Julia sat up straight and edged away from their mom.

"We've been seeing a counselor," her mother finished. "Both for our marriage, and for our family. I've learned some things about myself that were rather uncomfortable," she added, straightening the pearls at her neck. "They made me angry, both at myself and your father, and Julia was caught in the crossfire."

"So you're blaming yourselves for her running away? You're not making her take any responsibility?" Teresa pushed up from the chair, ready to stomp to bed and put this ridiculousness behind her. She didn't need to be part of their therapy session.

"She will definitely be held accountable," her father said, "and we'll discuss that at home."

Julia glared daggers at Teresa; Teresa ignored her.

"But that will begin with you losing phone privileges," their mother said, and she held out her hand.

"I hate you," Julia told the room in general. "You all suck." But she handed over her phone.

"The second thing will be that you also attend counseling." Her mom slipped Julia's phone into her purse, edged past Julia, and sat on the corner of the coffee table near Teresa's knees. "We'll deal with the rest at home. But I owe you an apology. More than one, actually. The night of that dinner, I got the food from your grandmother's deli because I knew it was your favorite. I had a feeling." She stopped. "I worried you were drifting from us, and I wanted to make you happy. You've always been different." Teresa shifted away, but her mother pressed a hand to her knee to stop her. "Free, independent. I was afraid of losing you." Before Teresa could recover from those bombshells, her mother continued. "Also, I was...embarrassed by your actions. With that cowboy."

"His name is Cort Landry, Mom. And we had sex in front of cameras. And I was just as embarrassed, in case you didn't know."

He mother let out a shaky breath. "I didn't. Nevertheless, I felt your actions reflected on me, like I was a bad mother. A bad person. And I took that out on you. I'm sorry."

Teresa blinked back tears. She didn't think she'd ever heard her mother apologize, to anyone. "Accepted," she whispered. "What you said means more than you know. And you're not a bad person."

Her mom reached out and stroked Teresa's forehead, then ran a hand down her braids, tugging gently at the ends. "And you're not responsible for your sister's actions." She smiled at Teresa, then stood and looked at her other family members. "It's been a long day. You said you have a place for us to sleep?"

Dazed, Teresa showed them the bathroom and bedroom they'd be sharing, then cleaned up the coffee mugs and sat at a stool in the kitchen, looking out the window into the tiny moonlit yard. She clutched her phone to her chest, praying for it to buzz with some sort of communication, but knew it wouldn't. Gabe had been very clear. The next step was hers, and she knew he wouldn't make a move until he heard from her.

She understood this, and agreed with it, because she desperately needed to get her head together before she could do anything in her life, much less be with a man. Her head knew this very clearly. Her heart was another matter.

CHAPTER TWENTY-NINE

The next couple of weeks went by in a blur. Teresa's parents and Julia went home, and the residents of Brownstone 2.0 spent their days exploring New York, filming supplemental segments for *Tasty Dish*, and welcoming the newly eliminated contestants into their new home. Surprisingly, Ace and MaryBeth showed up the next Saturday, although true to her word, Cookie had warned Teresa about the Texas belle. She'd also crowed quite a bit.

"Win the whole thing!" Teresa texted back.

That left Cookie, Rachel and Antonio as the final contestants, and they would have a face-off the following week. When she wasn't with her housemates, Teresa took long walks, and learned that was the best way to enjoy New York. With the weather warming up and MaryBeth now snarling around the house, Teresa's walks grew longer and longer. She also took the time away to think about Gabe and their relationship. She needed to reach a conclusion before the show ended, and that was happening sooner than she could have ever thought.

One day, on her way home, Teresa rounded the corner and strolled up the sidewalk to Brownstone 2.0, her skirt swinging around her thighs. She gripped her phone in one hand, having promised herself by the end of her walk that she'd call Gabe and tell him she wanted to be with him. She was terrified he'd hang up on her or say no or break her heart in some beautifully worded way, which would still be a no.

But she'd faced up to so much in the past few months. She needed to let him know how she felt, all of it, no matter the consequences.

She was in constant contact with Victoria and Kristen, having finally told them everything, even that she had been eliminated from the show. She knew they would keep her secret; Victoria wouldn't even tell Luke. Kristen reassured her she was bringing nutritious vegan food to Cleo, and sent a steady stream of cute Daisy pictures. Teresa also couldn't believe how fiercely she missed everyone, even that little baby. But she missed Gabe more and her friends had encouraged her to talk to him. Thinking about being with him made her heart flutter madly.

About twenty feet from Brownstone 2.0, she looked up from her reflections, and what she saw caused her heart to flutter in a different way.

"Cort?"

He'd been sitting on the steps, and when she said his name, he stood, sweeping his hat off, and held it in front of his heart. "Hey, Tessa," he said, his voice soft.

Before she could react, he strode down the stairs and wrapped his arms around her, pressing her tight to him, enveloping her the way she remembered but no longer loved. His very essence surrounded her, but it was so different from the man she wanted to be with that she started to cry.

She was quiet at first, but with her face pressed to his chest, her tears fell into his shirt, and she eventually let out a gasping sob. He started, then held her closer, murmuring, "Hey, now, darlin', it's all right," and stroking the tears from her face.

She remembered his hands, too, strong and sturdy, callused from playing the guitar, and how she'd loved to feel them along her skin, the shock of the roughness even while he tried to be gentle. It was familiar, but not what she needed. He continued to soothe her, patting awkwardly. They were such a cliché, she realized. He knew her so well, and yet not at all. She was no longer the Teresa he knew.

Making a noise of demur, she pushed against him until he let her go. She bowed her head, swiping at her face, then patted his damp shirt. "Sorry about that," she said, still unable to look him in the eye.

"Not the worst thing in my life," he replied, and she finally glanced at him, catching a glint of humor in those very blue eyes.

He swept up the hat he'd dropped on the sidewalk, and held out an arm, gesturing her to the stoop. She tucked her skirt around her and sat, bracing for the cool cement on her butt.

She knew he'd let her talk about what had made her cry, but there was only one person she wanted to share that with. Cort was a rare man, an alpha male with a sensitive side, but his caveman controlled about 90% of him. And it had taken over *her*, consumed her so thoroughly she no longer knew herself. She was just Cort's girl. And that would never be enough.

"What are you doing here?" she finally asked.

"You," he said simply.

She swiped a forefinger under one eye, wanting to erase all traces of her blubbering the second he took her in his arms. She hadn't cried because she was happy to see him. She'd cried because she was *sad* to see him. No matter what happened between her and Gabe, no matter how familiar and comforting and capable Cort was, their story had ended. She knew that. He didn't. She'd been trying to tell him that for months, albeit poorly. But he didn't want to hear it. She didn't know what it would take.

While she tried to find a way to be perfectly clear, she asked about their friends.

He slapped his hat against his knee and smiled. "That little Daisy has my heart, and she knows it. Luke's got it worse, though. Never seen a man with baby lust like Lucas has. I suspect Victoria's told you all about it?"

Teresa nodded. A lot of it had been conveyed through texts, since they rarely had time to talk, but Victoria had once referred to Luke as "Mr. Diaper Changer formerly known as Mr. Sex on a Stick." Victoria had a strong will, but Teresa wondered if Luke might wear her down sooner rather than later when it came to having babies.

"And Sunshine," Cort continued, using his nickname for Kristen, "is Sunshine. One of the things I love best about her is she is just plain herself. The other day she told me my aura looked a tad blue, and I might need a life adjustment, but in the meantime, drink this nasty tea." He smiled at Teresa and she couldn't help smiling back; they both knew about Kristen's mysterious tea that looked and smelled like asparagus. "It might give me a little course correction, she tells me. I told her I'd rather fly out here and see you for that."

"Cort."

"We fit, Tessa."

They had, like puzzle pieces, quirky around the edges, but snug and creating a whole picture together. But not anymore. She now understood when people who broke up sometimes said they'd always love the other person, because she felt that for Cort. But it had been all about the sex, she realized, and she hadn't wanted anything more. She was also tired of finding different ways to say no to him.

"So how's Kristen's new roommate?" she asked, trying to keep things neutral.

"Anyone named Indica Sativa, well, you know she's going to be nutty," he answered. "But she goes above that. She's maybe the reason Frisco got the reputation it does."

Teresa laughed at this, genuinely delighted.

Cort's face lightened, and he grinned at her. "That's my girl."

"No." Teresa stood up suddenly. Now or never, she realized. "No, Cort. I'm not your girl. Not now. Not again. Ever."

Cort stood too, so tall, but she'd never felt like he loomed over her. He didn't loom now, he actually seemed diminished. He reached a hand out, and it hovered near her cheek, as if he'd stroke it, the way he used to when they said their goodbyes. "Tessa," he said, and tears pricked her eyes again at how his voice broke.

"Cort," she said as gently as she could. She took his hand between both of hers and pressed it tight. "Tessa is gone. It's Teresa now." She squeezed his hand for emphasis. "Just me. No us."

He shook his head.

"Yes." She let go of his hand. "Don't say anything," she told him when he opened his mouth. "I do love you. No," she insisted when he looked ready to speak again. "Not a word. I do love you, and it would be so easy to give in and be with you. You'd be happy, and it would make me happy to do that for you. But you'd consume me. I wouldn't be *me* anymore. We had our moment," she whispered. "You gave me so much. But it's over. Please let me go."

"It's the professor, isn't it?"

Hands on hips, she snapped, "So there has to be another man to make it big enough for me to leave you? It can't just be my own realization that we aren't right for each other?" She pushed against his chest. "You and your arrogant, big-headed..." She spluttered to a stop, not knowing what to add. "*Arrogance*," she finished lamely. "As a matter of fact, Gabe and I aren't together right now. So it's not him, and it's not you. It's me." She pointed to herself. "All me. All my choice. All my *life*, you big-headed, arrogant—"

"Yeah," he said with a grin. "You said that."

"Stop smiling. You don't get to smile during this intensely

emotional moment. This isn't fun. This is terrible," she said, crying again, and brushing the tears away impatiently.

"You're right, darlin'. I'm not smiling at that. I'm smiling because I made the right choice."

"What choice?"

"You. Falling in love with you."

"Don't make me hit you, Cortland Landry."

"No, ma'am, I wouldn't want that." He held his hands out. "I'll back up, give you some space if you need that. But you're cryin' and my mama raised a gentleman. Gentlemen don't let a woman stand there and cry alone." He held his arms farther apart and took a step closer, at the same time making an interrogatory sound in the back of his throat.

And strong women don't fall into a man's arms because of a few tears, she thought. But it was okay, because her newly discovered inner strength reassured her she wouldn't go further. Despite her tears, she pointed an admonitory finger at him. "One friend comforting another. Nothing more."

He nodded and enfolded her in his arms. She wrapped her arms around his waist, holding him loosely, her face once again pressed to his damp shirt. And it was okay. No memories rushed back at her, as they'd done every time she saw him after the breakup. It wasn't that she felt *nothing*, that would be disingenuous, but no passion remained, no romantic interest. It was truly over for her. He might not be convinced of that, but it wasn't her responsibility anymore to convince him. She was done.

Relieved, she pressed a palm to one of his cheeks, and kissed him lightly on the other.

He smiled down at her, and she realized her mistake. She stepped away so quickly, she stumbled, and Cort grabbed her arms to steady her. She grasped his forearms in reflex, but her knees buckled when she looked over Cort's shoulder and saw Gabe on the sidewalk, watching them.

HAVING SEEN ENOUGH, Gabe stalked toward the brownstone. He'd come here with a purpose, he had little time, and he wasn't going to waste it worrying about what might or might not be happening between Teresa and Cort Landry. According to Teresa the night of Kaily's party, it might not even be his business.

But Stephan and Kaily were, and they both loved Teresa. She had a right to know what had happened.

Without releasing Teresa, Landry turned to look at what distracted her, and gave Gabe a casual nod. Gabe wanted to punch him.

Gabe nodded back, but ignored him otherwise; no time for niceties. To Teresa, he said, "It's Kaily."

She immediately stepped away from Landry and over to Gabe, studying his face. "What happened?"

"Coma," he coughed out. The word had circled his brain ever since Stephan's call, so saying it should be easy, but his throat closed up instead. "Coma," he repeated more clearly. "She's in a coma. She fell, hit her head. An accident, a fucking fluke." He gasped after this speech as if someone had sucker-punched him.

"At Disney World?"

He nodded. "Outside the park."

Teresa pointed to the cab waiting behind him. "Let's go."

He held out a hand for her to go ahead of him and she took a step, then stopped on the sidewalk. "Damn." She gave Gabe an indecipherable look, her eyes big and sad, then turned back to Landry. "I have to go to Orlando," she told him. "My friends need me."

"I heard. I'm lettin' you go, darlin'." He nodded in Gabe's direction. "I saw your face when he walked up. You never looked at me like that." He gestured at the cab. "Go on. Don't keep 'em waiting on you."

"I'm sorry you came out here for no reason."

Landry shook his head. "Best decision I've ever made," he said, staring into Teresa's eyes. The intensity of his gaze unsettled Gabe. He'd looked at Teresa that same way himself. Feeling empathy for Cort Landry wasn't high on his list, but he respected him for letting Teresa go.

Gabe couldn't do it himself.

Teresa kissed Landry on the cheek again, pressed a hand to his forearm, then rushed past Gabe and into the cab. When Gabe glanced at Landry to say goodbye, the other man held his hand out.

"Hurt her and I kill you," Landry said mildly.

"Likewise," Gabe agreed.

They shook, firm, both underscoring their intent. They exchanged nods again, and Gabe followed Teresa. She stared out the opposite window, her sweater wrapped tightly around her body. Gabe directed the cabbie to JFK, hoping traffic would be lighter at this time of day, then looked out the front windshield himself. He didn't want to watch Cort Landry, to see how he himself might look if Teresa said goodbye to him.

But she had, hadn't she?

He was still unclear on what had happened between them a couple weeks ago, about the fight, and what Teresa had been trying to say in front of Brownstone 2.0. It had sounded like goodbye on the face of it, but she hadn't specifically said no to him. She'd said she was confused, and needed a break. But that was her way, wasn't it? She didn't like conflict, and she didn't like to hurt people, so she edged around the issue, using terms like "sad-bunny" and "fudgesicles," that touched his heart with their charm.

He stared at the cabbie's ID without seeing it. None of that mattered right now. Getting to Kaily and Stephan was his priority, and he was grateful he wasn't going alone. He had no clue if Teresa would actually talk to him during any part of the trip, but his chest constricted at the thought of walking into that hospital alone, of facing the worst if something happened to Kaily between now and his arrival.

He took a deep, shuddering breath. He would have managed it, because he'd do anything for Stephan and Kaily—anything—but as he let the breath out, he relaxed knowing Teresa was with him on this journey. He looked at her profile, her soft mouth turned down at the corners, her normally sparkling eyes now bright with tears, and the way she clutched her sweater tightly around her middle. He wanted to comfort her, but at the same time, everything in him released its own tight clutch. She did that for him, always had. Before he even knew her name, he'd relaxed in her company, her presence calming, allowing him to do and feel whatever he needed at that moment.

She also roused suppressed feelings in him, and heightened those he believed couldn't get any stronger. Simply sitting beside her, she humbled and strengthened him at the same time.

Touching her, making love to her, was an epic poem all its own.

He finally turned away from watching her expressive face and looked out his own window as they passed Madison Square Park. She didn't seem inclined, but he desperately wanted to talk to her. He'd missed that connection so much the past two weeks that Nick reached a record number of usages for the term "Nellie," and Adam brought him coffee and pastries every morning. He was uncertain what had transpired between Teresa and Landry, but he'd picked up mixed information from what he saw. Teresa had said she was sorry Landry came out for no reason, and he'd said he was letting her go, but that could all be interpreted as an interrupted liaison.

Of course, when Landry shook Gabe's hand, he'd threatened to kill him if Gabe hurt Teresa. A man didn't do that unless the woman was going to someone else.

Gabe realized that he still wanted her to share what had happened with Landry, not because of any prurient interest on his part, or even from jealousy, but because he wanted her to be happy. No matter who she ended up with. Their relationship had begun as a searing sexual encounter, evolved into genuine caring, and continued to burn bright and hot.

He got why Cort Landry would fly all the way out to New York from the opposite coast to see Teresa. Hell if he knew what to do about their own relationship at this point, though. If they even had one. Maybe the flame had gone out, and they were done.

Well, he had another few hours to stew over the whole thing, if he wanted to continue on the masochism ride. Or he could let it all go and be grateful that Teresa was a good enough friend to go with him to see Kaily, and support Stephan during a terrifying time. Or he could accept that she had ended things with him as quietly as she had ended them with Cort Landry.

He nodded to himself. *Okay, De Luca, it's done. Be a man, get over it, be there for Stephan and Kaily, and let these matters of the heart slide into the background where they belong right now.*

As a distraction, he let his thoughts drift to his book. He'd spent the last two weeks incorporating Onnie's suggestions and had one more go-round before he passed it on to his editor. He was mentally considering how best to reveal a particularly tricky piece of information in an early chapter when Teresa shifted, releasing the intense grip she'd kept around herself.

He angled toward her, but she still didn't look at him. With her face turned to the street view as it moved rapidly past them, she slid one hand across the seat and wrapped her fingers around his. The sleeve of her sweater shifted up and he saw she still wore the plastic Sven bracelet he'd offered as an apology at Kaily's party. He closed his eyes in a moment of silent gratitude, then turned his hand over so their palms met and their fingers entwined in a comforting embrace.

CHAPTER THIRTY

At the Orlando Medical Center intensive care unit, Stephan, his eyes red-rimmed and desperate, rushed to Gabe and Teresa. She wanted to hold him tight and make everything better.

"I'm here," Gabe told Stephan.

"We're here," Teresa added.

Gabe looked at her in surprise, and she nodded. He nodded back. "Kaily?" he asked Stephan.

"Okay," Stephan rasped. "Okay for now. God damn it, Gabe." He rested the top of his head on Gabe's chest, his shoulders shaking. Gabe wrapped a strong arm around him, but his expression mirrored Steph's.

Teresa stepped between them and held Stephan, murmuring soothing noises like Kristen did with Daisy, while Gabe went in search of a doctor for an update. Teresa guided Stephan to a set of chairs near the ICU and they sat together, Stephan still clutching her. He'd stopped crying, and rested in boneless warmth against her, the way Daisy did after a big cry.

"How long have you been here, Stephan? How long have you been awake?"

He shook his head, sitting up. "Since it happened. I don't know. Yesterday?" he added, with a question at the end.

"You should try to get some sleep."

He shook his head. "What if something happens?"

His wavy brown hair was smashed flat on one side and his usually warm brown eyes seemed to have sunk into his face. He looked haunted, and remembering Gabe's stories of Hannah's death, Teresa understood why. "Just rest a little, right here. We're here now, we won't..." She was about to say they wouldn't let anything happen, but she couldn't tell that well-meaning lie to a man whose wife had died in childbirth. "We'll wake you up if...if we need to."

"Where's Gabe?"

"He went to find a doctor, to get more information."

Stephan shot up from the chair. "Who's with Kaily?"

Teresa put a hand on his arm; his muscles felt taut as piano wire. She gestured through the glass to Kaily's bed, to the tiny person lying there, and forced herself to remember Kaily's exuberance. That would come back. It had to. Teresa blinked hard. "There's a nurse with her. No one's leaving her alone."

"Not on our watch," said a voice behind her, and she turned in relief to see Adam and Nick, overnight bags in tow.

"The pit crew's here, Steph, no worries," Nick added. "Although it looks like you're in good hands."

While Adam embraced Stephan, Nick put an arm around Teresa's shoulder and kissed her temple. "Nice to see you here, brilliant. We thought the big gorilla might've scared you away for good."

Teresa smiled at him, appreciating that he had listened to her at Kaily's party. "I don't scare so easy."

Nick gave her a knowing look. "I see that."

They exchanged a smile until Gabe showed up with the doctor. Nick kept his arm around Teresa's shoulders, but Teresa slipped away so he had to drop his arm.

"You got here fast," Gabe said to Nick and Adam.

"Got earlier flights." Nick shrugged. "It's only work. Family first."

"Any news?" Adam asked.

Kaily's neurologist told them she was starting to respond. "Her Glasgow scale has shifted from eight to thirteen, and we expect a fully recovery."

Stephan sagged against Adam, and Adam held tight until Stephan collected himself enough to go with the doctor to Kaily's room.

Gabe filled in the gaps from his own discussion with the doctor: the higher the Glasgow number, the better; it reflected a patient's response to various stimuli. Her vitals were all good, but they were keeping her sedated until the swelling decreased more. "It's good," he told his friends with a catch in his voice. "It's good."

The four of them clung to each other in relief, then the "pit crew" went to work. Nick rounded up food and Gabe went in search of a cot for Kaily's room so Stephan could stay with her.

Teresa told Adam she and Gabe had flown over without any notice. "We left as soon as we heard. I need to make a few phone calls." She had to let PA Katie know what happened, at the least. "And I'd like to get some supplies."

His own phone out to call Gabe's family, Adam tossed Teresa a set of keys. "Take my rental. We passed a CVS on the way here." He shifted on one hip, as if about to pull out his wallet. "You need any money?"

She held up a hand. "No, I've got it, thanks. Tell Gabe I'll be back?"

He nodded. "He doesn't deserve you," he said, but his eyes indicated he said it lightly.

"I'm thinking it might be the other way around," she told him and left.

SWEATSHIRT BUNDLED UNDER his head, Gabe stretched out on a row of hard plastic chairs in the waiting area around the corner from Kaily's room. He didn't expect to sleep, but after a day enveloped in fear, he wanted a break. Nick left to get a hotel room in case anyone needed a shower or a longer break, but none of them really wanted to leave the hospital.

Except Teresa, who'd been gone a few hours. Adam said she went to get some supplies, and was Gabe still being a dumbass? Gabe didn't have the energy even to flip him off and Adam seemed to realize his bad timing because he hugged Gabe around the neck, then wandered off to pace the halls, his activity for the past couple hours, claiming an inability to sit and wait. Gabe knew it was dark out, but was too drained to check his phone for the time. Another few minutes, though, and he'd go search for Teresa.

A soft hand brushed his hair back from his forehead, and he smiled, relaxing for the first time in hours. "Hi."

"Hey," Teresa whispered back.

Gabe opened his eyes, blinking against the fluorescents. "You're back," he said inanely.

"I wouldn't be anywhere else."

Without bitterness, he said, "For Kaily."

225

She nodded. "She's the second little girl I've fallen in love with this year. I can't imagine the world without her."

"None of us can." He struggled to sit up, cursing the hard seats. He shoved the sweatshirt away and slid closer to Teresa, so their knees bumped. He looked down and noticed all the bags near her feet.

"Something for Kaily when she wakes up. It took me awhile to find them. Plus, T-shirts, toothbrushes, that sort of thing. We left without any warning."

"Yeah." He rubbed a hand over his face, then took a sip of his cold coffee. "Thanks for that. I know you were...busy."

She shook her head. "I was saying goodbye to Cort when you showed up."

"Were you?" Gabe had gone past the point of exhaustion; his defenses were starting to slip. He crossed his arms and shifted away. "Because you've said it was over before."

"I've said a lot of things before. What was the word you used?" She angled so close he had to face her, to look directly in her eyes. "Oh, yeah. I was a dumbass. So much happened to me so fast, Gabe, I didn't have time to process it. And a lot of that was my fault, like running off with you to your place right after I got eliminated."

"Hell, I'm not sorry about that."

She smiled. "I'm not sorry it happened. Just about the timing." She looked about to say something else, so he waited. "I didn't give myself time to be sad or mad or relieved or feel *anything*." She turned to face him more fully, her fists clenched. "And I *was* mad, I was so mad I didn't know how to express it. I wanted to hiss and spit, and I took it out on you. And your family."

"You did," he agreed. "But I handled things badly, too. I knew you could take care of yourself. I saw it, and you certainly told me enough. But my pride got hurt, and I stomped off like a five-year-old. She wants to be alone, well, I'll leave her alone." He took a risk, and brushed a few braids behind one ear. "Double dumbasses," he said.

She caught his hand and held it between both of hers in her lap. "I'm sorry for what I said about your mom. That was really uncalled for. I was taking things out on my own mom there, too." She traced a nail up the inside of his forearm. "People can be so screwed up."

"I do hear you, you know. And I take you seriously."

She flinched at the reminder of what she'd shouted at him in the car. "I know. And I'm sorry about that, too. I've realized I can make my point about something without shouting. I just need to stand up for myself, and be strong."

"You are strong," he told her. "I saw that from the very beginning."

She nodded. "Thank you for saying that."

"So what happened after I left that night? With your parents and Julia."

She gripped his arm, leaning close again. "You will not believe it," she said, and told him about her parents finally being firm with Julia, how they were all getting counseling, and that her mom had actually apologized to her. "It was...mind-bending."

"Sounds like it was good."

She nodded, stroking his arm again. "It was. I mean, we have a ways to go, but it was a start." She took a deep, shaky breath. "I was just about to call you," she said. "Right before you showed up earlier."

He didn't want to hope, but God damn it, he wanted her so badly. He looked pointedly at her hands on his bare forearm, how she'd pushed up his sleeve without thinking about it.

"I'm touching you," she said.

"You're touching me," he agreed.

"I guess I just took the next step."

The breath caught in his chest, as if he'd been kicked in the solar plexus. Had he understood her right? "Say it again."

"I want to be with you, Gabe. I want to take lots and lots of steps with you. Can you do that with me?"

He smiled for the first time in weeks. "Babe, you had me at the elevator."

EPILOGUE

Three months later...

Hands full with trays of hot dogs, burgers, buns, and fixin's, Teresa bumped open the screen door with her hip and stepped onto the back porch. Despite the heavy load, she stopped for a beat to take in the scene below. The backyard of their rental house rolled down to the still lake, its normal dark blue now a bright cobalt as it reflected the setting sun. Two picnic tables held salads, corn on the cob, plates and utensils, napkins, chips and guacamole, pans of brownies, tins of cookies, makings for s'mores later, and an ancient boombox, currently playing a series of Doo Wop songs. Parker's selection.

Near the tables, the grills were heating up, and closer to the water, the fire pit waited for their marshmallows to toast. And close by, her loved ones manned the barbecues, set out blankets, lit the fire, opened wine. Chatting, laughing, nursing babies, swiping her homemade chocolate chip cookies. That was Cort, and it lightened her heart that he'd agreed to be here today. Parker wandered barefoot at the water's edge with Adam, pointing at the lake, the sky and the trees. Who knew what meditations on nature he shared, but Adam probably explained the Adirondack's geology in his turn. Kristen, Miranda, and PA Katie's girlfriend, Robin, sat three in a row at one of the tables, bent over their babies and swapping motherhood horror stories, smiling the entire time. Urg and Cookie competed over who could do the most pushups. Luke tested the mesquite

228

charcoal at one of the grills, beer in one hand, grill brush in the other, singing "Row, Row, Row Your Boat" in a round with Kaily, making up his own words to keep her giggling and pushing against his leg. "Stoooppp," she commanded, then, "Do it again."

Stephan stood close by, one eye always on Kaily while he talked football with Marty, who also kept an eye on Miranda and their son. Nick flirted shamelessly with Victoria as he lit the fire and she opened a can of Dr. Pepper, instructing him on the proper way to lay out the kindling. She caught Luke's eye and winked at him. He set down his beer, teasingly covered Kaily's eyes with one hand, and mouthed something back that Teresa didn't catch. It must have been good, though, because Victoria blushed as bright as the soda can.

The only one missing was Rachel, who had won the final of *Tasty Dish* and was on her way to her dream: owning a food truck specializing in cupcakes. She'd sent an email saying she missed them all, but she'd be there next year. Teresa herself wasn't sorry she'd been eliminated. It took getting kicked off to realize she'd found what she wanted without winning, and it wasn't her relationship. She'd found her voice, knew she could stand up for herself and follow through. Meeting Gabe was the icing on top of that realization.

Teresa sighed at everyone's unabashed love for each other. She could watch them all forever.

Behind her, Gabe stepped out of the house, also laden with trays of potato salad, coleslaw, french fries, and deviled eggs. He stood next to her and gazed at the sight of their friends enjoying themselves. Hot Henley now wore a tight green T-shirt and cargo shorts that revealed his sexy calves. She could watch him forever, too, except her stomach growled and her arms were starting to ache. She glanced at all of the food Gabe carried, and couldn't help laughing.

"We may have gotten a little carried away."

"Not possible with this group." He leaned around the trays to sneak a kiss. "Not possible with me, either."

The brush of his lips lingered on hers, warming her to her toes. She opened her mouth to speak, but didn't know how to respond. Words couldn't always convey someone's deep feelings.

Gabe tilted his head at the door. "Everyone's busy right now. Let's go inside and ravish each other."

She let out a shocked laugh, but she also mentally reviewed where they could set down the trays without anyone seeing them. They'd spent the rest of the summer in his tiny apartment, and rented the lake house as soon as her commitment for *Tasty Dish* ended. They were still debating whether to stay in New York longer or explore San Francisco together, but in the meantime, had enjoyed whatever private space they could find here.

Maybe a quick something in the pantry now? "Mmm," she began, but Kaily turned from hugging Luke's knees and begging him for another round of song and saw them up on the deck.

"Gabe!" She shrieked with joy and raced up the steps in the pair of little blue cowboy boots Teresa had bought for her in Orlando, and plowed straight into Gabe. He lifted the trays away from her and said, "Whoa, there, miniscule human. We need to get this grub to the starving masses." He lowered one tray and held it out to her. "How'd you like to take the deviled eggs to the table?" Since they were in their own covered container, Teresa thought that might be a safe bet, considering Kaily's enthusiasm.

"Okay!" She grabbed the dish and raced back to the table, plunking the eggs down on one corner before Gabe or Teresa even took one step with their own deliveries.

They exchanged a look. "Later?" Gabe asked.

"Definitely."

"Pantry?"

She laughed again, delighted. "Maybe..."

A pleasant sensation shivered down her spine with the knowledge that he watched her as they went down the steps together and set everything on the tables, wondering how long she'd be able to hold out. But then Cort and Adam took over grilling while Luke put a sleeping baby to his chest, and Parker began singing John Lennon's "Imagine" with Kaily. And when Victoria and Kristen bookended Teresa, their arms all around each other's waists, Teresa let the joy sweep over her in a rush, then cradle her with its warmth. As much as she wanted to be alone with Gabe, she didn't want this night to end, either.

Thankfully, everyone else seemed to have the same idea, and once the dinner dishes had been cleared away and the leftovers stowed, the coals in the fire pit were in the perfect state for marshmallow roasting. Teresa and Gabe sat close, across from Luke and Victoria. Luke had handed back Robin's baby and now cuddled Daisy. He might be satisfying some of his baby lust with so many little ones here, but Teresa wondered if Victoria's decision to hold out on starting a family might shift soon. She'd witnessed for herself how persuasive Luke could be with Victoria.

Nick sat on Victoria's other side, still in flirting mode, but after enough death-ray glances from Luke, he wisely shifted his attentions to Kristen, who sat next to Luke in case Daisy needed anything. Kaily nestled on her dad's lap on the other side of Gabe. The rest of their friends filled in the gaps around the big pit, reaching into huge bags of marshmallows and spearing two or three onto sharpened sticks for roasting. Trays of graham crackers and chocolate bars sat nearby, ready to complete the delicious dessert.

Still full, Teresa decided to wait on her s'mores, instead leaning close to Gabe, the heat of his body warming one side while the fire heated the other. She'd choose Gabe's heat every time. He had an arm around her shoulders and she tucked her knees up and rested her head against his chest, wanting to burrow into him.

Surrounded by so much laughter and love and happiness, relieved that Kaily's doctors had given her the all clear, Teresa relaxed for the first time in months, maybe years. She shifted against Gabe, unfamiliar with the sensation. Tension had ruled her life for too long and when she let out a long, happy sigh, Gabe squeeze her shoulders and said, "What is it?"

She shook her head, unable to find the right words to express her feelings. "Happy," she finally said, and looked up at him. "Happy, happy, happy."

He glanced at Cort, who sat eating a burnt marshmallow, then returned his gaze to her. "No regrets?"

If she had to do it all again, would she change anything? Answering yes to that was her definition of regret. At first she thought she might—having sex in front of cameras was not her best decision—but she realized that every decision had led her here. "None," she said, and meant it.

Kaily bounced up and said she wanted to go to the water. Kristen said she'd take her, but when she bounced up, too, she landed wrong, almost stepping on Cort, and twisted her ankle. She hopped around, her hand on top of his head.

"Easy, now," he said, standing up and leaning into her. "I guess I'll have to escort both of you ladies."

He bent down to get Kaily in one arm, then tucked a shoulder against Kristen's midsection and lumbered down to the water with them both giggling and squeaking.

Teresa caught Luke's eye across the fire. She interpreted his melancholy smile and nod as approval of Gabe, and that Cort would be all right in time. Victoria had told her that Luke hoped she and Cort would end up together. But she knew Luke would be there to watch out for Cort, his best friend.

She mouthed, "Thank you," and turned to Gabe, who had observed the interaction. His own smile radiated warmth and joy, nothing sad about it, and she snuggled close to him as he wrapped his arm tighter around her.

He turned his head to whisper directly in her ear, and his cheek brushed hers, smooth at the top, rough lower down with a five o'clock shadow. She shivered, thinking of all the places that skin could brush against her own, velvet and spark and lust.

He pressed a kiss on her neck, his warm breath heating her instantly. She shifted against him, closer, ready to crawl into his lap right there. When he flicked his tongue against her earlobe, then sucked it into his mouth, she jumped with a gasp, but the sound was covered by the fire's crackle, Kaily's shrieks of delight at the water, and Johnny Cash in the background singing about the Orange Blossom Special.

She reached between them to press a hand to his face, the Sven bracelet he'd given her at Kaily's party tinkling on her wrist. Her fingers traced his cheekbone, the line of his jaw, the smooth skin in front of his ear. He sighed, and his lashes brushed her cheek when his eyes closed.

He whispered in her ear, "I love you."

She jolted in surprise, then relaxed against him. Because she felt the same way; maybe it was the simplest of words that could convey your deepest feelings. "I love you, too," she murmured, and he pulled her close, his arms wrapped so tightly around her she almost couldn't breathe. It was wonderful.

Teresa wanted to grab his hand and run into the house, to take him up on his earlier offer, but as she turned to look in his eyes, saw them soften around the edges as he looked at her, then crinkle at the corners with his smile, she knew they had plenty of time for that.